ISTORIA BOOKS
presents

Kit Austen's Journey

A novel by Libby Sternberg

Get on the Istoria Books mailing list!
Subscribers learn of special limited-time-only discounts. Sign up at the website where you can also view other Istoria Books titles:
www.IstoriaBooks.com

Copyright 2010 Libby Sternberg
ISBN-13: 978-0615656663
ISBN-10: 0615656668

Books written by Libby Sternberg are available through the author's official website:
www.LibbySternberg.com

Other Istoria Books titles are available through the publisher's website where you can sign up to receive news of the sequel to this book:
www.IstoriaBooks.com

To my sister, Mary Ann, who encouraged me to start my own journey as a writer

Chapter One

Independence, Missouri May 1851

EVERYTHING IN HER PLAN had gone well so far—leaving Boston in the dead of night, boarding the train south, securing a room in one of the crowded hotels, assembling gear, even easing into a new identity with no lapses...

But now she was encountering her first obstacle. The obstacle had a name—Daniel Winchester.

"No women alone, ma'am," he said, pushing back the brim of his big hat. "Company rules."

"I'm not traveling alone, sir!" she insisted, stomping her foot for emphasis on the boards that constituted a walkway outside the general store. "I'm with my brother!"

She'd so grown in self-confidence that she stared the handsome wagon train leader directly in the eye, defying him to stop her. But by now, she felt more capable than some of the men she'd seen in town getting ready for the journey. She'd carefully studied the available pamphlets and newspaper advertisements. She had bought supplies and a wagon fitted with an osnaburg cover. With the help of a washer woman recommended by the hotelier, she had coated the cover herself with a boiled mixture of linseed oil and beeswax so that it gleamed a warm, rain-resistant tan. She'd found a good team of oxen, and she'd started collecting the necessary foodstuffs for the long trip.

The only thing she hadn't been able to do until now was find this stubborn Daniel Winchester. For two days she'd searched for him. His reputation as a trail guide was formidable. Everyone recommended him. He had successfully led three California-bound parties through rough weather and testy Indians. But he must have been as restless and busy as she was, for he never seemed to be in one spot long. Almost ready to ask for another recommendation, she finally found him outside the general store, after the kind proprietor had told her, "Daniel? Why, you just passed him coming in, ma'am." She had run back outside, clutching her cloth bag with one hand and her new sunbonnet with the other, and had nearly collided with him.

He was hard to miss.

Nearly six feet tall by Kit's reckoning, he had a long angular face hidden under the shade of his well-worn wide-brimmed hat. He wore strange frontier clothes, a leather-like shirt open at his neck, a dark, canvas duster that touched the top of his scuffed boots. A blue cotton neckerchief, rolled so tight it looked like a thick string, was around his neck. And his guns. They were serious guns, holstered on a belt slung around his hips. His fingers played on the darkened handles as he leaned over her and squinted down at her surprised face.

"What did you say your name was?" His voice was deep and low.

"Kit... Kit Austen." Even now she looked down when she said the name, afraid she'd give away her deception. *No, Lord, it's not really a deception. My mother's name was Austen, and my given name Katherine.*

She felt his eyes sizing her up, evaluating.

"My company has published Articles of Association."

"Yes, I've seen them, read them already in the Gazette," she interrupted, impatient to settle this bit of business and move on to the next. "Where do I sign them?"

Daniel grimaced. "Your brother can sign. What's his name again?"

"Seth." This was an outright lie, and she murmured a prayer asking for forgiveness. *I have to, Lord. You wouldn't ask of me that I...*

"Tell Seth to meet me at Grosvenor's at sunset," he said, mentioning the name of a nearby blacksmith. "I'll talk with him then." He started to leave.

"Mr. Winchester!" Kit called and walked quickly to catch up with him. "Mr. Winchester, I'm afraid... I'm afraid that won't be possible."

He stopped and faced her. "All right, what about first light tomorrow, anywhere he wants to meet," he said, an edge of frustration in his voice.

"No, no... you see, he's not here yet. I'm still waiting on him."

"When you expect he'll arrive?" Sharp quick words.

"I... I don't know. He should have been here. Why not just let me sign on for the time being?" How she hated these falsehoods! They didn't come easily to her. *Please forgive me, Lord. I promise I'll tell him the truth once we're on the trail.*

"No, ma'am," he said softly, as if talking to a child. "No women traveling alone. Company rules. You read them yourself."

Each traveling company had its own rules and regulations, posted in advertisements and in small broadsides handed out to prospective travelers as they disembarked at the train station. Kit knew the rules. She remembered quite specifically the one to which Daniel Winchester referred. Right above the one about how much they all needed to pay into the company treasury by what date was one about the composition of the company. "This company shall be composed of able-bodied men and their families of same constitution...."

"The rules do not specifically say women traveling alone are not allowed," she said, regaining her strength. The company rules had irritated her after she'd seen shoddy preparations on the part of some men in town. She wouldn't let an arrogant cowboy tell her what something said. "They merely state that the company is open to men and their families. I am part of a family." This was true. She had a family—in the past.

Daniel let out an audible sigh of annoyance. "I wrote those rules, Miss..."

"Austen, Kit Austen," she interjected, and he was annoyed again at the interruption.

"I know your name!"

Kit flinched and took a step back at his harsh tone, waiting for a slap across the face that would surely follow. For an instant, she was back in Boston. Her heart raced with apprehension as she thought of what this looming, muscular man would be capable of if he was riled into action. She trembled.

But his demeanor changed as he noticed her reaction. He modulated his voice to a firm but gentler pitch. "I wrote the rules, Miss Austen, so I know not only what they say but what they mean. No single women in the train... "

Kit breathed more easily. He could be reasoned with. He was a disciplined man, but a fair one. This was the company she wanted to join, she decided at that moment, and nothing would deter her. It would take the route to Sacramento in California's great central valley. It would be comprised of families wanting to settle out west, as well as gold rush latecomers. And it would have this man at its head.

"My brother was coming here from Davidson, Missouri," she said, still uncomfortable with these untruths, but equally sure God would forgive her, knowing her dire situation. "I'm sure he'll catch up. If I'm not with you, he'll wonder what happened to me! Please, Mr. Winchester. I know the rules. The rules say a woman can't travel alone. My brother is traveling with me. And I'm sure you'll find that I'm no weakling. I will do my part."

He opened his mouth to say something, stopped and let a smile prick at the corners of his mouth.

"Your brother better catch up quickly, Miss Austen," he said at last. "Men outnumber women on the trail six to one. But I will grant you that the women can be as strong as their men, sometimes stronger. When your brother arrives, I'll make sure you're part of the group."

As DANIEL WALKED AWAY, his brow creased in worry. That woman could be trouble on the trail. First of all, she was pretty, with that hair the color of wheat and those crystal blue eyes and pale skin. She'd need a strong man to look after her, making sure none of those wild gold-seekers didn't take liberties. But there had been something else troubling about her—the way she'd recoiled when he'd raised his voice, as if she'd expected to be thrashed for speaking up. That didn't sit well with him. He'd never in his life hit a woman and had no intention of ever doing so. He didn't think highly of men who did. He hoped her brother showed up soon. He had no doubt she'd get on some train going west, and there were other guides not as scrupulous as he was about taking care of their charges.

He strode off toward the camps, pushing that worry aside. He had a lot left to do, and disease was raging through some of the traveling camps. He didn't want to linger in Independence any longer than was needed. He moved down the street toward the camp of the Josephus Barton family. Old Josephus had been west before. Daniel wanted to ask him to be the lead wagon on the trail as they started out.

Maybe the Barton family could help look after this Kit Austen.

He had to stop thinking about her. She was one among many.

But that look on her face—those eyes like a blue lake...He shook his head and trudged forward.

Chapter Two

BACK IN HER HOTEL ROOM, Kit paced the floor, her arms folded over her chest, her breath coming fast, her face red. Her eyes stung with unshed tears. At last, she dropped to her knees by the side of the bed, bowing her head like a child.

"You've led me here safely, Lord. Help me find the right path now. Forgive me..."

Did she even have the right to ask for guidance? Already she'd committed so many sins.

Forgive me—that was the prayer she'd breathed in Boston nearly a month ago on a cold, spring night. Emptying the last bit of oil onto the dry old divan, she'd tossed a lit candle into the fireplace, onto the kindling and logs she had carefully positioned there. Within seconds, the fire had begun to burn fiercely, casting a hot glow on her cheeks.

She had stared into the flames, thinking of the times when, as a child, she had warmed herself against the chill in early spring, waiting for her father to come in and offer her a treat, a peppermint or a dried apricot perhaps, or even a small piece of sweet bread stolen when the cook wasn't looking.

Those happy memories had been replaced with bitter images almost the moment she had crossed Blue Hill's threshold as Josiah Carlisle's wife. She'd married for love, he for treasure, the Blue Hill estate being but one part of the riches he'd hoped to acquire from her family. That bitter discovery had been followed by others—the worst being his tyrannical ways and his enjoyment of violence to assert his authority of her. She'd lost a babe that way. She'd nearly lost her life more than once. When Josiah himself had gone West to find gold, her life had improved immeasurably. But he'd written earlier in the year that he was boarding the Eustace Marie, sailing down the coast to the isthmus of Panama for the overland crossing and then back up the Atlantic coast to home.

Home—that night it had caught ablaze quickly. Everything had been so dry that spring, and the room, as if full of tinder, all but exploded. She'd stepped back and, with a gruesome curiosity, watched the floor-covering curl up in smoky, fiery tongues, the divan catch the heat, then the table by the wall. Then the walls themselves became painted by flame. Mesmerized by the awful sight, she'd had to force herself away, to move to the next room and to the next, and finally into the night and safety.

She'd watched with growing fascination as the faint glow of the fire appeared in one window, first as a benign radiance but growing quickly into something unstoppable, the pale yellows deepening to a sickening ochre dashed with pinks, and flashes of red overlaid with the transparent wavy blur of heat as an entire room had been consumed.

Blue Hill had been in her family for two generations. Her mother had been raised there. She herself had spent the happiest moments of her childhood in its large and airy rooms, her beloved father and her dear Aunt Sally always nearby to take care of her when she hurt herself, when she fell ill with fever, when she came across the cruelty of the world. They were gone now, her father passing just last year. That was why Josiah had been returning—to fully claim her father's estate. He'd have no need of her any longer.

With the smell of smoke and charred wood in her hair, she had walked through the night into town, to her father's home. She had stayed there that night and all the next day, resting and regaining her strength for the journey ahead.

So far as the world was concerned, Katherine Penwether Carlisle was dead.

It was as Kit Austen she prayed, asking for strength, mercy and clear direction.

When she raised her tear-stained face, her gaze lit on the small desk by the window. A sudden breeze blew a piece of her writing paper to the floor.

With grim determination, she rose to retrieve it.

SHE PULLED HER BAG toward her and ferreted through it for the broadside she had stashed there. It listed supplies travelers should have, recommended John Fremont's book on the expeditions to the western territories, and sketched out a map of the route. From Independence, they would travel to Fort Kearney, and then on to Fort Laramie and beyond. Fort Kearney. Someone at the desk had a letter from Fort Kearney... She put the writing paper on the desk and sat down.

"Dear Sister," she wrote, "By the time you receive this, I will be well on my way to Fort Kearney. My business partner asked me to accompany him there where he will meet up with a cousin on his way to Fort Laramie. I will wait for you in Fort Kearney for two weeks. I am sure you can find a family who would be willing to take you on. You are such a responsible and hardworking girl, any company would be fortunate to have you among them. Otherwise, I would be loathe to leave you alone like this. Looking forward to our reunion, your loving brother, Seth Austen."

She blotted the ink dry, then put the letter on the floor, where she trod on it a few times with her dusty shoes. Deciding it looked sufficiently travel-worn, she took it with her, searching for Mr. Winchester back out on the street.

AT THE BARTON TENT, Daniel tipped his hat to Wilhemina, Josephus's wife. He inwardly frowned as he took in her fragile gaze. Her eyes were shadowed and her face like paste. Just yesterday, Josephus had told him she was expecting a child. A new baby on the trail. He didn't like it. No more than letting a woman travel alone. Josephus soon appeared, a short man in dark clothes. He had a long thin beard and a serious look, but there was something kind about him. Daniel knew him to be a good man, a trustworthy man.

"I hope to leave soon," Daniel said to him. "The company's about rounded up. Got all the stragglers. Don't need any more."

Josephus nodded and Wilhemina discreetly disappeared into the tent so the two men could talk alone.

"How is she?" Daniel asked.

"Fair," Josephus answered. "She'll be all right, though. It's Mary I'm worried about. She's been a little peaked. The sooner we can go... "

Daniel nodded in agreement. The sooner they could go, the sooner they could leave disease-ridden Independence behind. "There's just one person I need to see to after I check on the rest and fetch a new rifle," he told Josephus. "That's all. And we can leave." He heard the girl Mary crying from inside their tent, whimpering. It pained him. She didn't sound good and she was just a small thing, only nine or ten, not too strong. "We won't dawdle," he reassured Josephus. "I promise you."

He moved on through the tents, looking for other company members to talk with. He had met with all of them so far and was as satisfied as he could expect to be with the group. But he knew there was no telling how all of them would sugar out together, what quarrels would erupt, what dissension would occur. That's why the company's rules and regulations were so important, to have everything spelled out ahead of time. Once they hit the trail and encountered the hardships of the journey, the worst and best of a man came out.

Daniel's theory, in fact, was that the trail didn't make men good or bad. It just made them "more so" of whatever they were when they started. So if a fellow was parsimonious at the outset, he was likely to become cruelly stingy on the trail. Conversely, if he was generous to a fault in camp, he was likely to be foolish on the trail. Rare was the traveler with a level head and a kind heart. Josephus was one. Daniel hoped there would be others.

He mentally went down the list of those he wanted to visit, to remind them of the rallying spot just out of town and the hoped-for moment of departure. The Gilmets, a close-knit young couple—they were hard to read because they said so little. That could be a good sign or a bad one. The woman, Lucy, was timid and retiring. Could be good or bad. too. The Crane brothers—always busy, but Daniel wasn't sure their activities were always worthwhile. The younger one had fallen for a wagon repair kit that was worth half the price. He was one to watch; he had a resentful look to him. His brother seemed all right. The

Kesslers—a minister and his wife, Esther. He seemed nice enough, but Daniel wasn't keen on men of the cloth due to an experience with one years ago. The Culpepper boys, good-natured and easy-going—Daniel catalogued them all. It was his job to know them, to predict trouble before it arose. How would a pretty young thing like Miss Kit Austen fit into that bunch? He shook his head. He still couldn't stop thinking about her or worrying about her fate should he not take her on.

HOLDING HER HAT against the dusty wind with one hand and clutching the made-up letter with the other, Kit looked for Mr. Winchester. Independence was bustling with people getting ready to leave for the West. Even though the gold rush was now a year old, the fever to travel to the frontier had hardly abated. Some were going for gold, and others were going to resettle, to start over, to live on the Pacific Coast, being described in letters home as a new paradise. The travelers came from all over the world. Walking past the marshalling camps, Kit heard French and German and musical tongues beyond the scope of her Boston education.

Not seeing his figure among the long rows of tents, she thought perhaps Daniel was at the trading post where she had bought her supplies for the journey. She walked back to that store, but it was filled with strangers, people getting ready to go, townspeople selling items to the store owner. She left and looked up and down the street. Where was that man?

At the end of the street, coming from the tents she had just left, she saw his long, lean figure amongst the camps. He was walking towards the stables at the end of town. She hurried after him, calling his name as she approached, hoping to be heard over the noise of wagons going by, horses neighing and feet stomping across the boarded walks in front of the stores.

"Mr. Winchester! Mr. Winchester!" she called, out of breath by the time he finally heard and turned around. She could only see his mouth and it lifted into an amused smile. His eyes were still hidden by the brim of the hat. He waited for her to catch up, not taking a step in her direction. He looked neither impatient nor restless, just perfectly calm. She could be running to tell him his best friend had died or his supper was ready, and she suspected he would wait for either news with the same look of taciturn ambivalence.

"Mr. Winchester, look!" She fluttered the pages of the letter in his face. "My brother, Seth, is waiting for me... at... at Fort Kearney. I just picked this up. I must be permitted to go with your group now. He'll be waiting for me. You see, I'm not traveling alone. Just to Fort Kearney, that's all."

He took the letter and studied it, and she wondered how well he could read.

"Miss Austen," he said slowly in a funny twang neither southern nor eastern in origin. "Your brother advises you to find a family with which to travel."

She grabbed the letter back and re-read it, irritated at herself for throwing in the line about finding a family.

"But still, he'll be waiting. I will stick close to a family, I assure you. I'll stay near them. I won't be a bother. I can hunt and shoot. My father taught me. Taught both of us," she added quickly. "Taught Seth and me." Yes, her father had taught her. It wasn't completely untrue.

"Fort Kearney?" he asked. "Wonder how he made it there so soon. Didn't say what company he bound to?"

"No, no... I expect... " she trailed off, no more stories coming to mind. She hated lying. Let this be the last one. Why didn't the man just make up his mind?

"All right," he said at last. "Be ready to leave any day now if the weather holds. You'll be behind the Bartons. They're a good family, and they might need some help. I'll talk to them. I'll want to check over your outfit." He looked at the sky as if trying to determine the time. The sun hid behind dark clouds, though. "Let's do it now. If anything's lacking, you'll have the afternoon to gather it together."

Flustered, she mopped her brow in the unseasonable warmth. "All right," she said. "Follow me." A foggy mist covered the city, shrouding it in gloom. A funeral party went by, the fifth she had seen that week. So many in the camps were afflicted with cholera, dying before they even had a chance to take the first step on their journeys west. She looked away and murmured a little prayer under her breath. She had a lot to be thankful for, despite her previous hardship.

In fact, even after taking a large portion of the money she had realized from her lawyer's handling of her father's estate, there would still be enough left to satisfy Josiah when he returned to Boston. Mr. Etienne would undoubtedly tell Josiah of his wife's initial attempts to liquidate the estate before her untimely death. And Josiah would curse and probably even poke through the ashes looking for the melted gold from the coins Mr. Etienne had given her. She had thought of that before she left, and had scattered a few coins in the bedroom and throughout the house.

After a short distance, she led Mr. Winchester around the back of the hotel to the outbuildings. There, without comment, she showed him her wagon. She watched as Daniel touched the rain-resistant cover with his ungloved hand. He said nothing, but she could tell she had passed that portion of his test.

Down the back ways, behind the buildings to the oxen corral, she pointed out her team by their markings and gave him the name of the man who had helped her choose them. He nodded at the mention of the name—a well-known and respected handler in the town. Again, she had acted wisely. Despite his silence, she could tell that things were going well. He was relaxed and agreeable. If he were disapproving, he would let her know. His directness, she decided, was an asset.

"Tell me what supplies you've put together," he said as they stood outside the barn.

She listed them—the spirit lamps and medical kits, flour and water, salt pork and dried fruits, and even a small keg of alcohol. She had blankets and even an extra axle for her wagon.

He smiled when she told him that, and she knew she was making progress.

"I've got a good sidearm," she said. "Plus a rifle and also some money."

"That's a smart choice," he said, nodding again. "Some travelers don't think they'll need it, but there are tolls and travel posts. How much you put aside for the trip?"

She opened her mouth to answer but thought better of it. "I'd rather not say."

He laughed. "Another wise choice," he replied.

She knew he was considering saying yes, but she also knew that pressing him now might result in a change of heart. She suggested they head back to the main road, cognizant of the fact that a single man and woman alone in the backways wasn't a proper thing.

As they walked back, a light rain began to fall, and then thunder cracked the sky.

"Best get under cover, Miss," he said so softly she didn't hear at first. But then he grabbed her arm and pulled her under the eaves of a nearby barn just as lightening ripped through the sky, hitting and splitting a tree a mere ten yards from where they had been walking.

"Oh!" she cried out and dug her fingers into his arm without thinking.

The rain spattered down in a torrent, wild sheets that spit up mud from the road. Even under the barn, they were quickly soaked. He took off his long coat and put it around her shoulders in a gesture that somehow seemed devoid of gallantry. He did it with no affectation, in the matter-of-fact way he did everything, as if it were something anyone would do, not only the most chivalrous of men.

With his coat off, she saw how strong he was under the soft leather shirt. His grasp had been so firm when he pulled her out of the rain that it had startled her. There was something different about it, something gentle and strong at the same time. She looked up at him, but he was gazing into the distance, his eyes narrow slits as he determined whether anyone needed help where the tree had crashed down. Finally, she could really make out his physical qualities up close—dark hair and brown eyes, high cheekbones and full lips, and skin both tan and dry.

"In two days at the most," he said at last. "We'll leave from the rallying ground to the west of town. I'll send word."

Chapter Three

"HEARD ANY MORE from your brother?"

Daniel Winchester sat atop his roan horse looking down at her, the brim of his hat again obscuring his face, leaving it in shadow, leaving Kit to guess what emotions, if any, were revealed there. Was that sincerity in his voice or sarcasm? She couldn't quite tell. She did know they were ready to leave, the wagon train of fifty-four souls in fourteen wagons. She was standing beside her own wagon checking on the lashings of the cover and making one last inventory of her outfit.

"No, nothing more," she said squinting up at him. The sun was bright and the air drier. On his rounds the evening before, he had told her that the lands to the west looked dry and flat and that there would be grass enough for grazing on the way. When she heard from the desk clerk that Daniel Winchester was calling to talk with her that evening, she had quickly fixed her hair bun and sprinkled rosewater on her neck. Silly woman, she had thought to herself, descending the steps to see him. You're acting like he was a suitor, not a trail guide. You have no right to act that way.

He had warned her to be on time, so she had brought her team to the departure point first thing in the morning, struggling a little to control them. Now a nervous knot pulled tighter in her stomach. Had she made plans beyond her capabilities? Would she be able to keep up with the rest of them? Or would she, as Daniel Winchester had feared, be a burden?

As an only child raised by a doting father turned widower too soon, she had been the center of her father's attention. He had lavished on her the care and instruction he would have given to a son. She had loved the time spent with him, learning to shoot and ride and handle animals when she was done with her girlish studies. But her aunt had clucked her tongue in disapproval and her lessons with her father had ended when she was eleven, when she started looking more like a woman than a child. Now she drew on every memory of those earlier years, searching for her father's voice to tell her what to do. Don't ever let the animals know you're afraid, he would say as she had sat atop a nervous horse. They can sense your fear. They can sense if you're in control. Remember, you are *their* master.

She repeated those words to herself as she mounted the wagon and sat behind the backs of the huge, lumbering oxen. They were gentle animals, she recalled her father saying when he had taught her how to drive a team at Blue Hill. Treat them with firmness and kindness and they will do what you want.

She looked up ahead at the Bartons' wagon. Daniel had introduced her to the Bartons that morning, and she had asked if they wanted their little Mary to ride with her. They declined. She was trying hard to get to know them, but they were shy folk. Kit planned to pull out her school books on the trail and work with Mary. She would prove her worth.

Daniel rode past her, making sure everyone was ready. They were a mixed bunch of miners and ministers and settlers like the Bartons. Most of them were men. By

Kit's count, she was one of only four women on the train—five if you counted Mary. It didn't matter, she reminded herself. After Josiah, she could face anything.

After Josiah... she often found herself thinking those words. She wondered if he was now on the ship that would take him up the Eastern coast or if he was traveling by land once he made New Orleans. In any event, he'd be home by midsummer's eve, at least according to his letter telling her of his intentions to return home, after being "unable to find the riches I sought." Her father in the grave by then, she'd known he'd find them when he returned. He'd lusted after the Penwether money when they'd married, and screamed and thrashed at her on their wedding night when he'd discovered her dowry only included Blue Hill and some neighboring lands, but no gold or other coins. How heartbroken she had been! And then broken in body when he whipped the back of his hand across her face.

Even now, on this glorious day, she blinked back tears as she remembered. Surely God forgave her for running from such a monster. She'd not deprived him of money—she'd left enough scattered in the ashes. And she had no intention of marrying again. She just couldn't live with a man who would... hurt her to the point of death. She knew her poor father, who'd been distressed by her unhappiness even if she'd hidden from him the cause, surely would have approved of her escape. But would her Father in heaven? She could only count on His mercy.

Daniel was at the head of the group again. With a nervous thrill, she heard him give the signal to begin. The Bartons' wagon lurched and then started to move forward.

A gentle nudge, she could hear her father say. Just a gentle nudge is all the team needed to get started. Once they saw the movement up ahead, they would know what to do. She listened to the voice and sat proudly, stiffly in the wagon seat, holding the leather reins loosely in her hand. She gave a gentle snap to the reins and murmured, "come on now, come on now..." and sucked in her breath to make a little chirping noise.

The oxen began to move.

As her wagon pulled out, she heard the pops and cracks of whips behind her, the rattling of wagon wheels, the snorting and neighing of the others' animals. It made her feel part of a community, another new and refreshing sensation after so much isolation—first imposed by Josiah and then by herself. She relaxed as the oxen took over, understanding what was required of them. She knew that some folks had described this first part of the journey as tedious, but she was in a heightened sense of awareness as the wagons inched over the land. She wanted to drink in every moment, remember every landscape. This was a new life she was building, with new memories.

The path they followed was well-rutted, causing the wagons to dip and sway. She was glad she had listened to the advice of the outfitters who had recommended bringing along an extra axle and materials for wagon repairs. It was quite apparent she would need them, though she hoped it wouldn't be for a while.

The wagon creaked and moaned, and she heard some of her things moving free in the back. She would have to batten them down more carefully, she thought to herself as she focused on the road ahead. She saw the Bartons' wagon dip down a hill, and she pulled back on the reins to make sure her team didn't move too quickly as the going slowed. But again her father's voice came to calm her. *They know what to do*, it said. *Don't interfere with what they know.*

On and on they traveled, and Kit concentrated on listening to her unseen father's voice. The time passed with little effort and with no strain. As long as they were moving forward, her heart was light. Moving west, away from him, away from Josiah. She wished they could progress faster. She wished she could get down from the wagon and run unfettered into the open land ahead.

After hours of travel, at the bottom of a hill they crossed a small creek, and the smell of damp earth and grass filled the air. She breathed in deeply. It was a brilliantly beautiful day with a cloudless sky of azure blue and a gentle breeze tugging at the rim of her sunbonnet, filling it out like a sail behind her head. She wore a simple rose-patterned cotton dress and her old and worn suede gloves. Beside her was her gray cape, resting on the seat in case she needed it. Her sunbonnet was a stiff gray heavy cotton with a tiny rim of eyelet lace. The constant jostling of the wagon was shaking loose her neat bun, fastened at the nape of her neck. As they pulled the wagons up the other side of the hill, she shook her head to let her long brown-blonde hair fall free and the bonnet fall back to rest on her shoulders. The top of the ridge was almost near and her animals strained to keep a good pace, pulling the heavy wagon with snorts and blows. Finally, they were at the top of the hill, and there to the west was what she had dreamed about—the undulating prairie.

It looked like a blue-green sea. For miles it stretched, blending into the sky at some distant horizon. When the wind blew, it took on a silvery sheen as the blades of grass bent at the same angle and same distance, like some unseen hand brushing over a deep coat of velvet. Without effort, her mind formed a prayer of thanks for this glorious creation. She took in her breath in admiration and smiled broadly just as Daniel rode up next to her. He said nothing but just looked at her transfixed face, surely knowing what she was feeling as she viewed the vastness of the territory. He touched his hat to politely acknowledge her and moved on down the train to check on stragglers at the end.

As they started through the flat prairie, heading toward the west, the going became a little easier. Behind them was the last outpost of the frontier, with timber and trees and houses and stores. Occasionally, they would come across a farm building, and Kit wondered if the Bartons looked longingly at these tidy little homesteads and thought of settling down before they reached the California lands.

It was slow work that first day of the trek. The wagons moved at just three miles per hour, so by the time the sun was right above them in the sky and they broke for a midday meal, they could still see the treetops of the town they had left behind. They were barely nine miles outside of Independence, bound for Fort Kearney, a full month's journey away.

As soon as the wagons stopped, Kit jumped down from her wagon and made her way to the Bartons. She had decided to offer to help Wilhemina with the meal, even sharing provisions with them. When she reached the front of their wagon, she was distressed by what she saw. Mary was cradled in Wilhemina's arms, her face white and waxen.

"She felt poorly this morning," Wilhemina said with fear in her voice. "She's probably just excited." This last statement sounded more like a question. Kit pulled herself up to the woman and felt the girl's forehead. No fever. Just clammy skin. She looked in the woman's eyes and then away. They both knew what it was. They had seen it in the camps before leaving. Cholera.

"We'll be away from it soon," Kit said softly, stroking the young girl's shoulder. Like most who traveled the trail, she shared the belief that they could out-run the disease and leave it behind. "Let me get you something to eat," said Kit. She jumped down again and ran back to her wagon. Her aunt had always made her chamomile tea when she was ill. There was something soothing about the weak, pungent liquid. She hurried to the back of her wagon, rummaging through sack after sack until she found a tin of tea leaves. She looked down the line of wagons. Few were making fires for what promised to be a short stop. Daniel had told them he wanted to make good time while the weather held.

She pulled out a spirit stove. It was for emergency use when timber and buffalo chips were not to be found or too wet to light. So be it, she thought. This was an emergency. She set it up and put on a small kettle to boil. Then she quickly put together a packet of dried biscuit and cheese and a fresh pear that she rubbed on her dress until it shone. When the water boiled, she mixed together some of the tea and some dried mint she had stored in her medicine kit. It was good for stomach upset. She poured the tea into a canteen and took it and the food up to the Bartons.

Josephus Barton was still tending to the animals, but Wilhemina had moved the girl into the back of the wagon, where she was stretched out among their supplies. She was moaning softly and thrashing about in a delirious state. They both knew that was a bad sign. Kit pulled herself into the shade of the wagon and handed the food to Wilhemina.

"Here, you won't have time to fix anything. You have to keep your strength up." Then she sat next to the girl and held her head up, putting the canteen rim to her lips. The tea would be hot, almost scalding, but that was all right. Pressing some liquid down the girl's throat would help burn out the illness. Mary gagged and sputtered but kept the tea down.

"Have her drink all of this," Kit said to Wilhemina, "every single drop. Give it to her in spoonfuls if you have to. And make sure you take care yourself."

Outside, she heard the step of a man's stride coming closer. Daniel was talking with Mr. Barton. Kit got out of the wagon and returned to her own, where she put away her things, lashed down her outfit more securely, and found some fruit and water for lunch. A small line of perspiration appeared on the ridge of her hair as Daniel seemed to tower over her. She became aware of how unkempt she must look, with her hair streaming down her back in wavy coils, the top button of her shirtwaist undone because of the heat, the embroidered lace of her underslip showing immodestly at her collarbone. She reached up impulsively and pulled the shirt closed at her neck.

"You'd best keep your bonnet on, ma'am," he said slowly. "The sun will burn you out here as quick as a fire. You're already showing some of it."

She blushed, knowing he noticed the color of her skin.

"Thank you," she stammered. "I... I'll remember... "

He turned to go, but suddenly feeling lonely out on this wide expansive prairie, she called after him.

"Mr. Winchester!"

He turned back and looked at her, no emotion showing on his lips, his hands resting comfortably on his belt. His hat was tipped too low for her to see his eyes.

"Mr. Winchester, I'm afraid that Mary is ill. I'm afraid that it... "

He strode forward quickly so she wouldn't have to raise her voice.

"I know, ma'am. It looks bad. Josephus is worried."

"I made her some tea... my aunt always made me tea when I was girl... when I was sick... an herbal tea... "

"The Indians use herbs and plants. Sometimes it works... " He stood looking at her, waiting for her to continue.

"Is there a doctor among us?" she asked.

He thought for a moment, then nodded. "Yes. But I don't reckon he could do more than what you've done. He might do worse."

He stared at her as if expecting her to read his thoughts. And she believed she could. The doctor might administer a dreadful foul-smelling poultice or even suggest a bleeding. She had seen these "curatives" in action when her beloved aunt had fallen ill. They hadn't helped. In fact, she believed they had hastened the poor woman's demise.

"Well then, I'll keep an eye on her," said Kit. "I want to do my part."

He nodded again and was gone. She wondered when he would rest, and when he would eat. He seemed like a watchdog prowling the perimeter of the family home, making sure all the inhabitants were safely tucked in. They would be heading into Indian territory soon and she knew the wild stories and rumors that were circulating about how rough things could be.

She was putting away her few things when Daniel returned on his horse this time.

"Movin' out!" he said to no one in particular and to everyone within earshot. Pans clinked and reins whipped. The oxen shuffled back into place and wheels began to roll. In a few minutes, they all were on the trail again.

FROM TIME TO TIME that long first afternoon, she could see within the wagon up ahead the shadow of Mrs. Barton holding her daughter close at hand. She also saw her emptying pans with her daughter's vomit and she knew it was cholera. As long as she saw activity, though, Kit was calmed. If the girl was drinking and her body was expelling the dangerous sickness, she might survive.

Kit had seen a frail woman beat cholera. Right before her marriage to Josiah, a neighbor woman who'd been traveling to visit her daughter came down with the dread disease. She'd been nursed by an old washerwoman who'd forced her to drink and eat nothing but broth. She'd recovered, and Kit hadn't forgotten the lesson—if cholera depleted the body, you had to make up for what you lost and then some.

The ride that afternoon was a journey in splendid monotony. The horizon seemed forever to offer some tantalizing new shape—a tree, a bush, a house. But as they moved closer, those shapes disappeared, replaced by new ones, until she realized they weren't seeing anything at all but the rolling prairies up ahead. Clouds blew in late in the day and were tinged with deep-hued pinks and reds as the sun began to set. Still, Daniel pushed them forward.

Kit's shoulders and arms and legs ached with stiffness from sitting on the hard wood wagon seat and holding the oxen reins. Her eyes were burning from squinting into the sun, and her skin felt tight where it had been exposed earlier. She looked down at her arms, where she had rolled up her sleeves in the midday heat, and was shocked to see them freckled and red. No wonder Daniel kept himself covered from head to toe, she thought.

At last, a real difference in the landscape appeared, a slight incline down toward a lazy river, the perfect place for camp. Daniel rode by shouting instructions for how to bring the wagons into a "corral" so the animals would be safely fenced in that evening. She just followed the Bartons' wagon as it pulled to the bank of the river, staying on the dry patches slightly above the gurgling water.

All of them listened and obeyed. Each of the wagons came to a halt in just the spot Daniel dictated until they had formed a full circle. Then men dismounted from their wagons and mules and horses and led the thirsty beasts to the shore. Kit did the same, first stretching her aching muscles, then undoing the leather straps around the oxen.

"Why, I've not named you yet," she said to them, patting one gently on the rump. "I'll call you Bess and you Bonnie," she said to the lead two, escorting them to the water. As they lapped up their fill, she realized how hard it was to be alone and why Daniel had cautioned her against it. While the others in their parties tended to their animals, the remaining men and women started the evening meal. She would have to wait, however, until this chore was done. As she waited for Bess and Bonnie to finish, she yawned. *At least I won't have to fix anything grand,* she consoled herself.

Back at the wagons, the smell of fires and cooking began to fill the air. It brought pangs of hunger to her stomach. The fruit she had eaten was hours ago. And she was so tired, her muscles crying out for rest. Where would she find the energy to fix her own meal, to visit with and help the Barton girl?

When she returned to her wagon, she was surprised to find a small fire blazing away in a neat circle of stones. Someone had helped her. She looked around and saw no one. The Bartons were busy tending to their own meal and their daughter. Everyone else was consumed with the jobs at hand. Daniel was nowhere to be seen. Too tired to think any more, she began her meal preparations.

As she ate, she found herself straining to see down the wagons. Why wonder where he is, she asked herself. Better to stay out of his way before he decides to ship you back at Fort Kearney.

She focused now on a spindly-looking woman, bending over her husband and ladling something into his pan. He didn't look happy and pushed the ladle away. The woman stood in front of him for a second, then put down her cooking things and went into her wagon. Kit sighed. Just then, another man appeared from behind the couple's wagon, looked with sympathy at the husband, and then glanced up at... Kit. He grinned at her, a devilish smile that made Kit's skin crawl. She quickly looked down and finished her meal.

Most of the others were divided into groups, sharing a "mess" where they divvied up cooking responsibilities. Having resolved to help out with the Bartons as soon as she was finished with her meal, she stopped by their wagon to check on little Mary.

Wilhemina was sitting by the fire, finishing her supper, while Josephus stood a few steps away, staring into the coming night. The sky was turning a dark blue, and the wind that had whipped and refreshed them all day now had a damp chill to it.

"How's Mary?" Kit asked. The sound of her voice surprised her because she had used it so seldom that day.

"Resting. Thank you," Mrs. Barton answered. She was a tired looking woman with an angular face and body. Her brown gingham dress did not fit well. It tugged at her long arms, yet was loose around her bust and waist. She had dull brown hair pulled back in an untidy bun.

"May I check on her?" said Kit.

"Go right ahead."

Kit stepped up into the back of the wagon. It smelled bad inside, the smell of soiled clothes and sweat, but she could hear the girl's steady breathing in the shadows. A good sign. Her hand, which she picked up, felt warm. Another promising sign. The canteen sat nearby and Kit shook it. It was nearly empty. She brushed the girl's forehead, and as she did so, her eyelids fluttered.

"Hush you bye, don't you cry," Kit sang softly, continuing to stroke her head. Kit's aunt had tended her just this way when she was ill as a little girl. The comfort of a loved one nearby helped more than any salve. She let the rhythm of the lullaby carry her away and stayed with the child until the light had completely left the sky. Her legs were stiff when Mr. Barton came to the opening at the back.

"We're grateful for your help," he said softly and simply. "Mrs. Barton is feeling poorly herself. She's with child."

"I want to help, Mr. Barton. I wanted to know if we could share a mess... and some other duties. I would be a help to Wilhemina, and when Mary is better, I could tutor her along the way."

Wilhemina herself appeared from the shadows.

"I would like that, Josephus. Mary needs schooling."

"I see nothing wrong with that. As soon as she's better," Josephus said, obviously happy at the thought of making plans for his daughter's recovery.

Kit was beginning to like them. Their quietness owed not to snobbery but shyness. She left the wagon and breathed in the fresh evening air, rubbing her arms in the cold.

"Keep giving her liquids," Kit reminded Wilhemina. "Don't let up. Even when she looks like she's getting better. Wake her up tonight to give her some more of that tea and some water—fresh water. Lots of it... I'll fix something in the morning for her too."

They wished each other good-night, and she trudged back to her own wagon, which seemed all the lonelier after her brief interaction with other souls. The soft sounds of the other travelers getting ready for the evening watch, or for sleep, carried through the air. She used some water to wash her neck, arms and face, and pulled herself up into her own wagon, where she would sleep, and got ready for bed. She might be making her way in the wilderness, but she would still abide by some of civilization's common rituals. She removed her dress and neatly folded it, then pampered herself with a quick dusting of a lavender powder before donning a white muslin nightshirt with a drawstring neck. As she had since memory began, she said evening prayers, beginning with a plea for forgiveness for her multiplying sins. "Let me atone for these sins, Lord, by helping the Bartons. I promise to be truthful and good."

Plumping up a feather pillow and pulling her gray cape and a blanket over her, she quickly fell into a deep sleep.

KIT WAS SO DEEPLY asleep, in fact, that she didn't hear the studied footsteps of Daniel Winchester as he made his way along the line of wagons, checking to see if everyone was situated for their first night on the prairie. At Kit's wagon, however, he paused. Through the smell of prairie grass and horseflesh, his nose picked up a gentler scent, a woman's scent, something flowery but not too sweet. He breathed it in deeply, reached out to touch her wagon, and then grimaced.

What had he been thinking when he'd allowed her to join up—a woman alone, especially one whose lush hair gleamed in the sun like the gold all these people wanted to mine, a woman whose eager face was filled with spunk and spirit, and whose easy smile melted the hardest heart. She was a dangerous woman, Daniel Winchester thought to himself, the most dangerous kind around.

Chapter Four

DANIEL ROLLED UP a blanket as pillow and laid it on the ground near Kit's wagon. He stretched out on another coarse blanket, still in his clothes and boots. The first night on the trail, he stayed ready. And tonight he was uneasy for any number of reasons. One was the way that Billy Crane fellow had acted during the day, upset with his older brother Pete when Pete hadn't let him drive the team in the morning. Pete had made a wise choice. When Billy had the reins, he whipped and pulled too much, making the animals ornery. If those boys were acting up this early, what lay ahead?

He wished they were more like the Culpepper boys, good brothers who worked everything out with ease. Daniel was already planning on asking the Culpeppers to help with nightly watches. All would have to take a turn, but they looked reliable.

Smiling, he thought of how the younger one, who looked just sixteen, had eagerly taken direction from his older sibling throughout the day, wanting to prove himself.

Those pleasant thoughts were soon replaced by shadow as Daniel remembered another boy with straw-colored hair, a boy much younger than the Culpepper lad but just as eager to learn, even at the tender age of six.

His name had been Martin, after Daniel's father, and he'd been Daniel's son by his beloved and sweet-natured Jane.

Gritting his teeth, he saw their faces, Jane's first as she came out to the field to bring him lunch, and then Martin scrambling after, a smile on his face as bright as the sun. They'd been a hard-working family, ready to put their sweat into the land. But first a crop failed, then Jane caught the fever that fall, lingering on her bed for a month before passing in an early winter storm. Martin caught it, too, and followed his mother into the grave by winter's last moon.

Daniel hadn't been much of a churchgoing man. He'd left that up to Jane. But his heart had hardened against such things at the cemetery when Preacher Simmons had asked God for wisdom in understanding why "we were not worthy to keep this sweet child, why our prayers—voiced and unvoiced—had gone unanswered." It was as if the man had been saying Daniel's unfaithfulness at church was to blame for the tragedy! He'd wanted to scream at old Simmons—*you think I didn't pray enough? I was down on my knees every morning and every night asking for the Angel of Death to pass by my door!*

No, he had little use for preachers and church-going after that. He'd sold the farm and taken to the wilderness, finding work soon enough on the trails, putting as much distance as possible between him and his crushed dreams of happiness.

Those thoughts turned his mind to the trail ahead. He hoped this Kit Austen's brother would wait for her at Fort Kearney. She'd done a tolerable good job today with her team and with helping out the Bartons. But each day would get harder, with the hardest at the end of the journey during the desert crossing and the mountains beyond. If she kept up as she'd done today, she'd be dropping in her tracks by then. You had to pace yourself on the trail, just like the animals, doing only what you needed to do each day and nothing more. Save that for the next day.

Once she reunited with her brother, he wouldn't have to keep such a close eye on her like he'd been doing today, like he was doing now camping by her wagon.

That thought pinched his heart, though, in an unexpected way. He liked looking after her, just as he'd liked looking after his Jane.

JOSIAH FOUND her.

He was chasing her through the dark wood, cackling maliciously as she struggled to keep away. Trees loomed in front of her, one after the other, huge gray pillars, the knots and grains of the bark making contorted faces that leered at her in the night.

Her dress was billowing out in slow silky clouds as she ran, panting, toward the prairie. She could smell it. She could hear the animals as they stomped and bellowed in the night. She knew that safety was just up ahead, just up ahead, if she could only get there fast enough and outrun the monster on her tail. She was breathing fast. A branch brushed against her skin and tore her shirt. Her legs were so slow, like blocks of lead. Something was wrong with them. She couldn't make them move as fast as she wanted. She was crying and screaming as she ran. He was just about on her, taunting her, calling her "a pretty thing" and "a good prize," and finally she was trapped, his arms around her locked in an embrace, his breath the disgusting smell of rank whiskey, his body sweaty and grimy, his face a mask of perverted pleasure as she struggled to break free.

"No! Josiah, Josiah, stop it, stop!" She screamed and screamed as he towered over her.

She heard the sound of metal clicking.

"Get out of here, or I'll shoot you like the dog you are." It was Daniel, his voice as steely and cold as the gun he held.

Kit roused herself from the nightmare she was having. But as she fully awoke, she saw a very real nightmare before her. The man who had ogled her that evening was at the foot of her wagon.

"Everybody knows she's probably headed to no good in 'Frisco," he said, in a whiny nasal drawl.

"Did I hear you apologizing to Miss Austen?" Daniel said, low and insistent. "Is that what you were saying? Say it louder so we both can hear it!" Daniel nudged the man's shoulder with the barrel of the gun.

"Sorry," was all he managed to sputter before slinking away into the night.

Kit blushed in anger and shame and sadness. She pulled the blanket tight around her like a warm cocoon. Daniel holstered his gun and stepped closer to the wagon.

"I heard you cry out. Are you all right? I'll keep an eye on Billy. He struck me as a bad apple from the start."

"I'm... I'm fine," she said, struggling to gain control of her voice. It trembled and so did she. Despite her best efforts, tears were forming in her eyes. She looked away so he would not see her weakness. But inside, her heart was crumbling along with her hopes.

The Josiahs of the world were everywhere, her heart screamed in despair.

"You don't sound fine.

"I'm... just a little shaken, that's all. I can take care of myself," she added quickly. She waited for him to walk away, as he always did, when an exchange was over. But this time he stood there, not moving, with a look in his eyes that made her want to reach out and comfort *him*.

"Who is Josiah?" he said at last.

"My... " No, she couldn't tell him. How she longed to tell him, though, to end this deception. But they were still too close to Independence. He could send her back.

"Someone I used to know," she said, not looking at him. No lie there. "Thank you for your help."

"Try to get some sleep," he said at last. "We'll be starting early."

As he turned and walked away, she found herself wishing once again he wasn't so quick to depart. But then, uncharacteristically, he turned back.

"I'll make sure Billy Cane doesn't bother you no more tonight, ma'am."

"Thank you."

She laid her head back on her pillow after Daniel left, but sleep was elusive now. Every whistle of wind, every animal sound, every creak of the wagon made her think danger was near. And when she closed her eyes, all she could see was Josiah, powerful and evil.

Could she have been a better wife? For the thousandth time, she reviewed her behavior as Mrs. Carlisle. She'd tried her best to be above reproach. She'd never so much as looked at another man. She'd kept the house clean and tidy, even without help, which Josiah refused to pay for. She'd learned to cook, and had spent hours baking his favorite bread and making his favorite stews. Sometimes he would appreciate it. Most times, the smallest flaw—or what he perceived as one—would set him off. Too much salt on a chicken once threw him into a rage as he yelled and screamed about how expensive chickens were to raise. Too little crust on the bread evoked a similar response, this time as he berated her for wasting precious flour on "mealy-mush."

As she looked back now, she realized that almost every tantrum had been sparked by money. Josiah had thought he'd won a bounty of it by marrying her. Her father had been a wealthy man. But he'd not opened his purse to them after she'd wed—she'd not expected him to even if Josiah had. Blue Hill, her beloved home, the home she'd had to destroy in order to be free, had been her father's gift.

A tear escaped her eye, dampening her pillow.

Why couldn't she have met someone like Daniel Winchester?

I made a poor choice with Josiah, she thought. *And I have to accept the consequences. No one forced me to say yes to his proposal. It was my own pride that had fallen prey to his flattery. I'd heard the rumors about his character....*

Even though Josiah would think her dead, she'd stay true to the marriage vows and not give her heart to another. A spinster's life awaited her in California, where she hoped to find a teaching position and live a quiet, peaceful life. Her students would have to substitute for the children she'd never have.

She couldn't sleep. She sat up and grabbed her gray cloak. Wrapping it and a shawl around her, she stepped out of the wagon, walking a short distance to view the bowl of stars as vast as the prairie above her.

She breathed in the cool grass of the prairie, letting its fresh scent cleanse her heart.

Just a little longer, Lord, until we're too far along the trail to send me back. Then I'll reveal my lie. I will make things right.

The sky was clear, and stars dotted it like decorations on a dark blue bowl, flickering like candles seen from a distance. She breathed deeply the bright cool air. Everything was so new. It felt good to be new again. With each breath, she tried to resuscitate hope within her soul, hope that tomorrow would be better, that life in California would provide her with the promise she had thought her marriage would hold. She would find a school that needed her. She knew there would be schools with few teachers to go around. She would settle into a simple life, become part of a church, a community, and live the rest of her days single, yet surrounded by children who loved her.

The constant wind whipped at the fringes of her shawl and tossed her hair to and fro. She wondered how far away dawn was.

As if reading her mind, a voice behind her provided the answer.

"About four hours till daybreak."

It was Daniel. He stood silhouetted against the wagons, his hair blowing in the wind.

"I suppose I should try to sleep," she said, glad to have the company. Then, as an afterthought: "I can't thank you enough. I don't know what would have happened if..."

"Don't think on it. Leave it behind," he said softly. "Lots of things are best left behind."

She wondered what things *he* wanted to leave behind. It felt good to focus on someone else, and not to dwell on her own problems.

"Is that what you do—leave things behind? Is that why you're a trail captain?"

She could tell from the tone of his answer that he was smiling.

"Partly."

"Well, what have you left behind, Mr. Winchester? A string of broken hearts?"

He chuckled softly, a good-natured laugh.

"I left behind a hardscrabble farm in Virginia run by the meanest old cuss you ever did see," he said. "That would be me."

"I can't imagine you mean! You're firm and strong, but not mean, Mr. Winchester."

He turned serious. "Mean in my heart. Disappointment does that to you. It steals hope. And faith."

"I'm sorry." She wanted to know more but didn't think it right to ask such personal questions. She'd already said too much.

"No need for pity. I'm content as I am."

"Did you go to California for gold?" That was an innocent-enough question.

"No. Nobody was talking about gold much when I went. I was going for the same reason Josephus is taking his family. I wanted a new life, something far away from what I'd known, something I thought would be better, different, fresher...but the gold rush started while I was there."

"And you traveled back here, in the opposite direction of everyone else." Now she was smiling. He was a contrarian, swimming against the tide.

"I found I liked the trail more than I liked the idea of settling on the land. Gold rush came along and I had good work."

"You never thought of looking for gold yourself?"

"I saw how the gold possessed men as much as they wanted to possess it. It's better to be free of such entanglement."

Although not directed at her or any other relationship with a woman, this last comment relieved her. "Better to be free of entanglements"—yes, just as she was seeking freedom. She need not worry about him wanting something more from her than she could give.

And why would she worry about that anyway? She shook her head.

"I'm glad you are a trail guide, Mr. Winchester. You're good at it."

"We just started, ma'am. You and your brother can give me a grade once we reach California."

At the mention of her fictional brother, Kit became uneasy.

"I should try to get some rest."

"Yes, you best be doing that."

Chapter Five

THE MORNING STARTED bright and clear, and Daniel had them on the trail shortly after sun-up. To her relief, Kit found Mary Barton to be doing better, but she worried that Josephus and Wilhemina would stop being so vigilant about the intake of fluids because the girl was showing signs of recovery. So Kit took it upon herself to make sure Mary was drinking, sitting with her while she slowly consumed a large mug of tea before breakfast.

The Bartons helped her with her animals that morning while she cooked. They were beginning to come together as one "mess," which lifted the burden off Kit immensely at the same time it helped Mrs. Barton, who was sometimes tired and sickly-looking herself. Kit worried that she would come down with the cholera too. Already, an older man at the end of the wagon train was doing poorly and looked to have contracted it.

After breakfast, she forced one more cup of tea down Mary's throat before pulling herself up onto her seat and taking the reins. Her team was refreshed and so was she. Despite being tired from the night's activities, she felt more optimistic this morning as she looked at the straight and calm figure of Daniel Winchester on his horse gazing ahead into the distance, knowing what lay there for all of them to find. He liked guiding people, he had said. Well, guide me, she thought to herself. I need a guide, a spiritual guide out of the depths of my past.

The wagons started with a jolt. With the same thrill as on the first day, she clicked the reins and felt her team jerk her wagon forward. The movement immediately had a calming effect on her. Each step, each mile, each territory away from Boston was her salvation. She was like a woman laboring under an immense burden that could be removed safely only one crumb at a time.

WHILE OPTIMISM and hope began each day, they were slowly replaced by a determination to stay on pace, to keep one's animals under control, to keep the dust out of one's face, and the aches out of one's shoulders. Kit often moved her arms around and shifted position to keep from getting too sore. It was a futile effort, however. No one was immune from the aches of the trail.

In the evening, she began to drift into a comfortable routine—if anything on this hard trip could be considered comfortable. Mr. Barton would tend her animals with his, and she would prepare the meals for them all. Wilhemina was too weak and tired from her pregnancy and from taking care of Mary to be of much good, so Kit eagerly stepped in, preparing stew and biscuits and coffee and even a steamed cake or pie.

Billy Crane gave her no trouble that night or any soon after. Uneasy with his presence, she often awoke in the middle of the night sweating and scared. Then she would peek outside her wagon to see Daniel nearby. Sometimes he was on guard. Sometimes he was asleep. But always, he watched over her. She was able to sleep soundly once she saw him. She didn't let on that she knew he was keeping an eye on her. With Daniel as her guardian, she didn't think much about Billy, pushing him into the recesses of her mind just as she struggled to keep Josiah there too.

The rules of the company called for stopping on the Sabbath whenever possible, so five days out from Independence, they rested. They were in good grazing country, near a clear spring, and the weather was fine and good. The skies held mere traces of clouds lazily creeping across the huge expanse of blue. It was hard not to feel blessed on such a day, hard not to stop and offer thanks. Even Mary Barton was recovering, gaining more strength every day.

For breakfast that morning, Kit made pancakes and opened a bottle of maple syrup she had brought from back home. She fried crisp bacon strips and apples and brewed strong coffee that she set out with a tiny tin of sugar. With the prairie wind whipping her dress and bonnet, she made a table out of a wooden trunk, covering it with a blue-checked cloth. In a tin cup, she stuck a few violets. All was ready for Sunday morning breakfast, just the kind of meal she had dreamed about preparing for a loving husband before marrying Josiah. Shaking the bad memories from her head, she turned to fetch the Bartons to table and ran square into Daniel.

His hat was pushed back in a lazy way, and his face was clean-shaven. He smelled a little of soap and leather oil. She noticed that he wore a clean pair of breeches and a shirt she hadn't seen before of off-white muslin. His guns, however, hung around his hips as always, a reminder of his captain's role.

"Oh! You startled me," she said, returning his smile with a friendly grin of her own.

"Didn't mean to, ma'am. Just coming round to tell you that Reverend Kessler will be holding a service in about an hour, down by his wagon, if you want to attend."

"Thank you. Thank you," she stammered. "Yes, I'd love to go. It's a perfect day, and I feel so, so..." She searched for words to express the newfound hope she was beginning to feel. "So grateful."

"I know what you mean, ma'am."

"Won't you have some breakfast with us, Mr. Winchester? There's plenty. I've made more than enough." She gestured toward her little table and the nearby cookstove where the food was keeping warm. The Bartons, lured by the smell of the cooking before she had a chance to summon them herself, started gathering too. Seeing Daniel, Josephus too extended an invitation.

"Dan'el," he said, "I'd be obliged if you would join us. Always in your debt."

Kit looked at Daniel, who went over to the table and joined the Bartons now crowding around the nicely-set cloth. Josephus offered a blessing, and Kit jumped into action and pulled out another plate from her mess kit. Then she started serving the food, suddenly nervous that it wouldn't be good enough.

She needn't have worried. From the look on Daniel's face as he ate and his quick agreement to take more when offered, she could see that her cooking pleased him. He looked up at her and smiled as she poured him more coffee.

"You'll be a fine catch for someone when you get to California," he said.

She blushed deeply.

"Thank you, but I don't plan on being anyone's catch," she said firmly. "I'm devoting my life to teaching." As she said it, her cheery attitude left her. When she had set out on this journey and this charade, that had seemed like such an enticing goal. She had imagined herself happy and fulfilled surrounded by school children, maybe even running her own school. Now as she gazed at Daniel's admiring face, these goals seemed empty. For the few moments that she had cooked and served breakfast to the appreciative Bartons and to Daniel, she had felt like a young girl again, a girl who had her life before her, who could reasonably expect a good marriage and family life.

"I didn't mean any offense," Daniel was saying to her as she came out of her reverie.

"What? Oh. None taken. I'm sorry. I was just distracted. Thinking of some things I need to do. Some mending this afternoon."

Wilhemina got up and started to clean up the mess, but Kit stopped her.

"No. I'll do this. You go on to the prayer meeting. I'll be along."

Without protesting, the Bartons walked down the length of the wagon train, Josephus in his broad-brimmed black hat, Wilhemina scrawny and stoop-shouldered, her brown hair blowing out from under her gray bonnet, and young Mary, pale from her illness but eager, as any child, to discover new things.

Daniel stayed behind and began helping her gather and scrape the dishes and ready them for cleaning in the spring water barrel set up for that purpose.

"What did Josephus mean when he said he was in your debt?" she asked to make conversation. He was standing next to her, his shoulder glancing against her, as he put the tin plates and cups to soak. Standing so close to him felt warm and comfortable.

"I just helped him out in Independence. I stood up for him."

"What do you mean 'stood up for him?'"

"Josephus is a... a pure-minded man," Daniel said slowly. He stared into the distance, squinting at the sun as if he were trying to find the best way to put his story. "When he sees an injustice, he feels obliged to step in."

"And he saw one in Independence?"

"He saw a woman who was not receiving a great deal of respect."

"What do you mean?"

"There are men, Miss Austen, who are not what they should be. Josephus became aware of such a case and confronted the man."

"You mean he got angry with someone in the company who wasn't doing their share?" Kit hadn't thought of Josephus as being that interfering.

"No, he saw a man beat his wife in another camp, before we left."

Kit's blood ran cold as she imagined the scene. She was silent while Daniel continued, afraid her reaction would betray her own past.

"He told him to stop or he would deliver the same treatment to the man as he delivered to his wife. Naturally, the fellow was not so happy."

"He fought with Josephus?" she asked, trying to control her trembling voice.

"He was too cowardly for that." His voice became low and sad. "His wife was found dead, and he said Josephus killed her. Said Josephus was seeing her and killed her when she wouldn't see him anymore. Some would have believed him too. He was a respected man. Heading out with another wagon train. I vouched for Josephus, that was all."

Kit was silent again, her stomach a churning knot as she realized that the fate of that unknown wife could just as easily have been hers, that Josiah, too, was capable of murder. She had been right to leave. She was defending herself, not abandoning her duty. Her hands shook as she wiped the last of the dishes dry and put them away. Daniel noticed her consternation.

"I didn't mean to upset you, ma'am. I shouldn't have told you such a story. It wasn't fit for woman's ears."

"No, don't apologize. I'm not some fragile flower ready to tear apart. I can..." She stopped midsentence at the untruth she was about to utter. *I can take care of myself,* she had been about to say. But, of course, she hadn't. "That poor woman," she said, trying to control her emotions.

"A man who treats a woman that way doesn't deserve to live," he said with an edge to his soft voice, the same cold-as-steel edge that was in his voice the night he had told Billy Crane to leave her alone.

"What happened to the husband?" she asked, clearing her throat, pushing back the sorrow.

"He tried to run away," he said, not looking at her. "He tried to leave in the dead of night."

"Tried?"

"He had an accident. His gun went off, shot him clear up the leg through the lung."

Kit looked at him strangely, wondering, but he knew what was in her mind.

He looked her in the eye. "If I was to shoot a man, it wouldn't be an accident," he said. "It would be face-to-face, fair and square. The dead woman had a brother. I expect he had a hand in the husband's fate."

She said nothing, just continued washing, and he turned and stared into the distance again, scanning the horizon, always watching and looking. He was, as her father would have said, a good measure of a man. In the sunlight and in the lighter shirt, his well-formed muscles were even more evident. The set of his jaw showed perseverance, not stubbornness, and his eyes, even squinting as they were now in the light, were pure-looking and kind. Daniel Winchester, she realized with heart-stopping finality, was the kind of man her father would have been proud to call son.

"We should be going to the prayer meeting if we're going to get there at all," she said hastily, trying to blow her disturbing thoughts out of her mind with a focus on the day's activities.

"Yes, ma'am," he said with a smile in his voice.

REVEREND KESSLER stood in the middle of the group of travelers, his right hand holding open the blowing pages of a well-thumbed Bible. He was a white-haired man of about fifty with a long, horsey face now stubbled with whiskers. For this Sabbath gathering, he had put on an old black coat, shiny at the elbows from use and now dusty from the trail. When Kit and Daniel joined the crowd, he was reading from the psalms.

> *"Hear my prayer, O God, do not hide yourself from my petition...*
> *Oh, that I had wings like a dove! I would fly away and be at rest.*
> *I would fly to a far-off place and make my lodging in the wilderness.*
> *I would hasten to escape from the stormy wind and tempest...*
> *For you will bring the bloodthirsty and deceitful down to the pit of destruction, O God.*

They shall not live out half their days, but I will put my trust in you."

His voice was a resonant bass and he was clearly fond of his job. As he spoke of destruction, he emphasized each syllable so that the listeners felt the power of the God he called out to. At the end of the psalm, he slapped the Bible definitively and intoned a prayer on behalf of them all. Then he began to preach after the group arranged itself on makeshift seating set up for the service.

Reverend Kessler was a gifted preacher with complete control over his voice. He used it like an instrument, bringing it to a soft dulcet murmur that caused his little congregation to hang on every word lest they miss any of it, then suddenly shifting to a rousing roar that jolted their senses and rocked their souls.

Kit's ears tuned to the music of his voice and not his words. Instead, she reflected on the psalm. *"Oh that I had the wings of a dove...I would fly away and be at rest....I would make my lodging in the wilderness."* That was exactly what she was trying to do. Fly away like a dove. She bowed her head and murmured silent thanks for the good land and the so-far safe journey. At length, however, her thoughts were drawn back to the Rev. Kessler's preaching.

He preached about their journey, about God's bounty, His mercy, His ability to help them and guide them. He talked about the beauty of creation as evidenced around them, of the lives left behind, just as the Hebrews had left Egypt. He talked about the need for repentance.

Yes, she needed to repent. Would she ever feel completely free of her sin? If she kept to a straight path, perhaps. If she stayed true to her vows, even though the man to whom she'd made them was determined to do her harm. If she stayed true to her plan, helping guide young children through their lessons as skillfully as Daniel was guiding them all west.

Daniel—how hard it was to push him from her thoughts. Here was her first temptation, she realized, the first test of her commitment to her oath to God to be a pure and goodly woman, despite her bad marriage. All right then, she thought. I thank you for this, Lord, for presenting me with a challenge early in the journey when I am strong of heart and mind. I hope I will not disappoint you.

WHILE KIT MURMURED her inner prayers, Daniel struggled to keep his thoughts from drifting into bitter recriminations. As often happened when he spoke to God in his heart since his family had passed, he found himself arguing with the Almighty. Why should I ask You for anything now, he'd inwardly cry, when You sorely disappointed me in the past? Was it because I didn't head out to the church with Jane on Sabbaths? I was tending our fields, Lord, trying to provide for the good woman and son You'd blessed me with! Why was that a sin? Why did You punish me for trying to be a good husband and father?

He usually only attended the wagon train Sabbath services because he thought it set a good example. Today he was there because of the Austen woman. He liked being around her. Maybe some of her godliness could spread to his heart. He wanted to find that place again where he felt a connection to His spirit. He was tired of feeling empty. When he was around Kit, the emptiness went away.

Services ended with some hymn-singing, and the crowd dispersed, glad to have time to rest their pained muscles and bones before the next six days of journey.

As they walked away from the little gathering, he noticed Kit talking to the preacher, her small Bible in his hand. Daniel couldn't help overhearing their conversation.

"My father gave it to me as a girl," she was saying as Rev. Kessler held her Bible. "I cherish it."

He turned it over in his hand, admiring its embellished leatherwork.

"I've not seen so fine a book since I was minister at a church in Worcester, Massachusetts. A bookbinder there made several, and I'd hoped to buy one myself, but the Lord called me elsewhere before I'd had a chance." He stroked the cover with his fingers, then opened the pages.

With a swift movement, Kit snatched the book from his hands before he'd had a chance to scrutinize the inside.

"Yes, that's where it was made. I don't like to let it out of my sight!" She laughed nervously, as if to cover the rudeness of grabbing the book from the minister's hands.

He seemed taken aback, but only murmured more admiration for her treasure, before complimenting her singing voice during the hymns.

"I'm going to set up a church in central California," he said. "A cousin of mine lives there. We'll be starting a school, and I hear you are going to be a teacher."

"Yes, yes. I... would like to talk to you about that."

But instead of talking more, she told him she needed to be on her way, and turned to leave, nearly colliding with Daniel.

He walked with her toward her wagon, the exchange he'd just witnessed troubling him. When she arrived at the wagon, she reached inside to a small case, ready to put the Bible away.

"Would it be all right if I got a look at that fine workmanship? I was admiring it myself at service," he said, eyeing her.

She paused, then placed the Bible in its case and locked it with a small key. Smiling, she turned to Daniel.

"I'm sorry. I'll show it to you next week. I don't like it to be handled too much. It's fragile and it's all I have to remind me of my father."

He nodded his understanding and left. He'd learned two things. There was something in the Bible she didn't want people to see, and she wasn't comfortable talking to the preacher about her future plans. He wondered just who she was and just what she was going to California to find.

SHE DIDN'T SEE Daniel all that afternoon, and when she finally asked Wilhemina where the trail guide had gone, she learned he'd ridden out "probably to scout the trail ahead or to hunt."

Sabbath might have been a day of rest for them, but not for him. Did he never let down his burden?

Try as she might, she could not stop herself from searching the horizon for him throughout the long, peaceful afternoon. He didn't get back until that evening, after brilliant pinks and reds had faded to a majestic royal blue sprinkled with stars and a spring moon. She heard his horse galloping into the wagon train before she even saw him, and with that sound she breathed easier. She felt safe when he was around. Although she stayed away from the Crane wagon, she'd noticed Billy staring at her a few times throughout the day.

That night, she pulled out her father's gun and laid it down next to her bedding. That would protect her, she thought, if Billy Crane or his kind came around. She pulled the blanket up to her chin and blew out the lantern near her head. Amidst the sounds of animals and others making ready for bed, she heard another noise, a man walking toward her wagon. Her breath froze in her as she reached for the cold handle of the gun while every nerve stood on edge.

"Who's there?" she managed to croak out.

"It's all right, Miss Austen," Daniel's soft, sure voice came in return. "I'm here. I won't be leaving any time soon."

She let go of the gun and closed her eyes tightly, murmuring new prayers of gratitude as she drifted off to sleep.

Chapter Six

To Fort Kearney

SHE HAD TO BE more careful. She shouldn't have taken the Bible with her to Sabbath service. It had been inscribed to her from her father and had her maiden and married names written in a family tree on the flyleaf. Flustered when Rev. Kessler had admired it, she'd not handled the situation gracefully. If she'd been thinking more clearly, she could have remained silent on the Bible's origins, perhaps just saying it had belonged to someone in the family. Not a lie strictly-speaking.

She'd also stumbled when the minister mentioned teaching in California. Yes, that was her goal, but she really should have more of a plan to offer people, a sense that she knew where she was going. Perhaps she could say she'd heard of the need for teachers in one of the valleys—oh, what were their names?

At the beginning of the journey, there had been so much to do, so many preparations, that she'd neglected to work out her stories. Oh, she longed to discard them and just tell the truth!

But now that would have to be delayed as well. She'd hoped to "confess" to Daniel once they'd reached Fort Kearney and her brother was nowhere to be seen. But she heard Daniel talking about leaving behind an older couple there who were struggling to keep up. He could just as easily force her to turn back there! As much as she hated the idea, she had to keep the deception going.

So, one early morning, as light had begun to peek through the opening in her wagon, she'd scrawled another letter from "Seth," telling her to keep on the trail, he was right ahead of her and they'd meet up soon. This one she would find "waiting" for her once they reached Fort Kearney.

She was now becoming closer to the Bartons, but also to Rev. Kessler and his wife, Esther. Esther had at first struck her as a rigid woman, but she found her generous of heart and eager to help Kit, a woman alone on the trail. It was her strength—the straightness of her back and her carriage—that had fooled Kit into thinking she was unapproachable. Esther had left an apple cobbler for her the night before, and she now wondered if it had been the Kesslers who'd set up her campfire the first night out.

She also liked two no-nonsense brothers from Missouri named Paul and Ira Culpepper, part of a rag-tag group of "diggers" (as those bound for the gold fields were called), and another family of four cousins, the Carrolls, who were originally from Ohio but most recently from Maryland.

They formed a loose mess together, so Kit no longer did the cooking every night. Instead, she had time to teach Mary, which she gladly did each evening and after each midday meal. She would read her books and go over her figures, and even teach her songs—hymns mostly but occasional ballads that she remembered from her own younger days. In the evening, the others in her group would sometimes request that she sing. She loved those nights when the cool air was scented with wood smoke and prairie grass and her clear soprano cut across the sky, crooning of lost loves and eager youth.

Mary was particularly fond of "The Wild Missourye" and many a night Kit would sing the tale of the man who loved the Indian Chief Shenandoah's daughter, with Mary joining in on the chorus—"*Away, you rolling river...Away, I'm bound to go, 'cross the wild Mizzourye.*" She sang it slowly, not like the sea chanty it had become. Its mournful melody seemed more appropriate for a walking pace.

Daniel, who often joined them for dinner now, would lean against a wagon while she sang, staring into the darkness, a look of peaceful melancholy in his ever-vigilant eyes. The only bad moments came when Billy Crane would shout out to pipe down so he could rest.

Her worries about Billy abated as she noticed Daniel continued to keep his vigil outside her wagon, sleeping by it or staying close by when on guard duty.

She was often so exhausted herself in the evening that promises she made to herself during the day to stay up and thank him for his care were broken as soon as she changed into nightdress and put her head on the pillow. Driving her teams was hard work, and even though she became increasingly confident with the task, she still suffered from sore and tense muscles after a morning's ride. Her pain would only intensify in the afternoon. Sometimes one of the Culpepper boys, who were quiet, respectful men, would take over for her, but even then she had chores to do. Often she would walk with Mary by the side of the wagon, letting Mrs. Barton rest.

Wilhemina continued to look unwell. Her waxen face and tired eyes betrayed her attempts to "not be a burden," as she told Kit whenever Kit wanted to help her.

"Josephus can't know I'm feeling poorly. He's such a good man," she'd say.

Josephus Barton *was* a good man, Kit decided as they made their way west. Deeply religious, he would tell them stories of California, likening it to the "promised land" or "Eden before the fall." He described flat valleys perfect for farming with bright sunshine and mild weather. He told them about rugged parts of the coastline where there was no place for safe harbors, just seas crashing on angry-looking rocks. He constantly referred to it as "God's country," and Kit began to see how he had fallen in love with the land, how it pulled him there more than any lure of gold and riches. He would join with Rev. Kessler in bringing them to sing hymns together, of hope and promise.

On Jordan's stormy banks I stand, and cast a wishful eye
To Canaan's fair and happy land, Where my possessions lie.
I am bound for the promised land, I'm bound for the promised land,
O who will come and go with me, I'm bound for the promised land.

On one such night, Daniel came closer to the group around the fire. Kit noticed how he smiled and nodded his head as Josephus talked after the hymn singing.

"The mountains are higher than any you've seen," Josephus said. "And in the summer, the hills are a dusty brown, bathed in sunshine every afternoon, after the morning mist from the ocean has faded away. If there's no fog in the morning, you know you're in for a hot one. When the heat comes on, you'll find yourself searching the sky for traces of that morning fog. But it's a kind heat, like the hand of the Almighty wrapping you in His embrace. The evenings are cool and the winters are mild. A man who sets up a farm or a ranch has only himself to blame if he doesn't prosper. The land is a gift, a treasure in itself... " Normally a taciturn man, Josephus couldn't say enough when describing California.

"It's like a foreign country," Daniel added.

Kit looked up, surprised to hear him join in the conversation. He rarely did. Now, he stood behind her, so close that she could feel the heat from his body on her back.

"Josephus is right," he continued with a hint of longing in his voice. "The real treasure in California is the land itself, not the shiny flecks of gold men claw from it."

The discussion petered out, and Kit helped Mary get ready for bed. Wilhemina, exhausted from another day on the trail, was already asleep. Although she usually read a short story of princes and princesses to Mary by the light of a lantern, tonight Kit stood by the wagon just patting the little girl's head and talking in a hushed voice.

"Soon you'll be in your own special land, little one. Where the sky is always blue. Where the sun always shines. You'll be the princess there. And some day a fine young prince will come riding in on his grand horse and sweep you off your feet and make you queen of his kingdom... you'll never know anything but happiness then."

Satisfied that the little girl was asleep, Kit walked off to her own wagon where she washed up for the night. She went inside and pulled on a nightshirt, a newly washed white cotton with satin ribbons, a silly-seeming luxury on this rough ride. But she always felt more civilized if she could change into fresh clothes. Dressed for sleep, she poked her head out the back of the wagon to take one more look at the bright canopy of stars that sheltered them.

"It takes your breath away," a man's voice said in a church-like whisper.

It was Daniel, standing by her wagon, ready to take his post on guard duty.

"It makes me sad and happy all at once," she said. "I want it to stay."

"Everything moves on."

"You mean like you, moving on the trails?"

"Somewhat."

"You sounded as if you wouldn't mind staying in California," she said, remembering his words earlier.

"And you sounded as if you wouldn't mind finding a prince to sweep you away."

She flushed. "You were eavesdropping." And he couldn't have been further from the truth.

"I was walking the boundary of the train."

"It was just a story. There are no princes," she said, surprised at the bitterness that crept into her voice.

"Now that's sad to think. Every man's a prince out here. Every man's a king."

"Some are tyrants," she answered, her heart bursting to tell him her true story.

"Some are not," he said and walked away to patrol the wagons one more time.

Her eyes stung with tears. What did it matter if Daniel Winchester was a prince? She wasn't free to be his princess.

THEY MADE IT to Fort Kearney in blazingly hot weather, the last of several spring days when summer seemed to be arriving with a vengeance even before it made its debut on the calendar. They arrived in the evening, so Daniel decided they would rest there the next morning and set off again at midday. Many on the wagon train had letters they wanted to mail and some provisions to buy at the fort's only store. Others needed the time to shift their loads and discard unwanted materials, once thought precious at the outset of the journey.

The fort itself was still very new and not much of an outpost, but there was a blacksmith available and a boarding house and sawmill. Soldiers were housed in wretched-looking sod buildings or tents.

For Kit, the stop at Fort Kearney was worrisome. She would have to pretend to search out her brother "Seth," then produce the note from him saying he had moved on to Fort Laramie without her. It was important that she handle her charade credibly with no possibility of Daniel being able to check on her veracity. Timing, she decided, would be crucial.

Midmorning the travelers scurried to the fort so they could post letters, buy supplies and talk to soldiers about what lay ahead. Those on the train who were headed for gold digging were anxious to know how many in the emigration west had gone before them this year. Soldiers kept track of the numbers and gladly shared the news with those who passed by.

Kit, however, was in no hurry to approach the fort to find information. She took her time helping Josephus with the teams that day even though he told her to be on her way. Daniel rode up as she finished the last of her chores.

"I thought you'd be over at the boarding house," he said, smiling down at her.

"What?"

"Looking for your brother."

"Yes, well... I just need to get these...."

"Josephus can handle it for you. I don't want to be stopping too long."

"Go on, Miss Austen," the older man said.

"Come on, I'll go with you," Daniel said, easily sliding off his horse to walk with her. He gave Josephus some instructions for letting his horse graze and then stared her in the eye, his own eyes kind and soft.

"You *are* eager to see him, aren't you?"

"Yes, of course. I just want to do my share." Her stomach churned with nervousness. She needed to retrieve the letter she had written in which "Seth" instructed her to go on ahead and to meet him on the road. It was stashed under a shirtwaist in the bottom of her trunk. If Daniel went with her to the fort, she would have to distract him long enough to head to the postmaster to "retrieve it."

"Wait," she said, putting her hand on his arm. "I need to fetch something first."

She hurried to her wagon and quickly opened the trunk and pulled out the false note, shoving it in a large side pocket of her yellow sprig cotton dress. She then pulled out a few coins from a hidden money container and jumped back down to the ground to rejoin Daniel, who had caught up with her.

"Oh! You startled me," she said.

"Did you find what you need?" he asked. She couldn't help wonder if he had seen her secreting the note.

"Yes, a little money, that's all. I need to buy some... new blue thread. And a frying pan."

"After you reunite with... what was your brother's name?"

"Seth." She didn't look at him when she said it. Lying was not easy, especially not to a good man like Daniel. *At least I can take comfort in that,* she thought miserably. *Lying* should *be hard.*

They walked quickly in the morning heat to the small group of buildings. Even in that short distance, however, sweat trickled down her neck. They were at the boarding house in a few minutes, a rudimentary dwelling that smelled of rancid oil and sawdust inside. A scraggly-toothed man with wisps of white hair came out of a back room to greet them. Despite his unkempt hair, his clothes were neat and well-mended—a pair of dark brown trousers and a blue cotton shirt that had been ripped on the sleeve but now sported a fine line of tiny stitches holding the cloth together.

"Can I help you?" he asked them both.

"We're looking for Seth Austen," Daniel said for Kit. "Her brother. He was supposed to meet her here."

Without a moment's hesitation, the man replied, "No Seth Austen here. Not ever. I've been here since the house went up."

Daniel turned to her and said, "Kit, describe him. Maybe he's seen him around the fort. He might have camped."

Describe him? She'd never set eyes on Seth Austen herself! And she hadn't bothered to think through what he should look like, in spite of the fact that she had told herself to prepare for such moments many times.

She swallowed hard, thinking of all the young men in Boston at the cotillion dance each spring. Tall, short, medium, blond, brown—they all blurred together.

"Kit?" He looked at her with concern.

Her father. That was it. She would describe what he looked like when he was younger.

"He's a little taller than I am," she began with confidence. "And he has darker hair, brown really. And blue eyes like mine. A no-nonsense way about him and he likes to hum French songs his mother taught him."

"You mean your mother?" Daniel said.

"Yes, yes, that's it." She gulped, thankful she hadn't slipped more.

"No, can't say as I remember anyone like that," the old man said. "But not every traveler stays here, you know. He could have just camped out. Especially if he was planning on moving on. We get a lot of folks who've 'seen the elephant.'"

Daniel nodded. "Seeing the elephant" was a phrase used to describe the decision to turn back. It originated with a story of a man who went to the circus but decided to go home after he had seen the elephant—it was all he had come to see.

"Lots of 'em that go back want a night in a bed before starting out again. I also get some folks associated with the army. Is he with the army?"

"No, he's a fur trader," she volunteered softly.

"Nope. Sorry, ma'am. Try asking some soldiers and checking the tents. If he's looking for you, he would have seen your train come in."

They left the boarding house and went back into the blazing sunshine. Kit squinted in the light, while Daniel put his hat back on his head.

"You needn't go with me," she said. "I'm sure you have lots to do. I'll find him, I'm sure of it."

"No trouble. This is part of my job, after all," he said. "Making sure everyone is safe. Come on, let's talk to the fort commander."

For a miserable hour, they trekked from store to tents to sawmill to encampments. No one had heard of Seth Austen, of course, nor recognized his description. The blacksmith, however, did help Kit's case a little when he nodded vigorously as Kit drew a verbal picture of her fictional brother. He even asked her if Seth was heavyset. When she said "no," he shook his head in the negative. "A man like that came through about a month ago. But he was built like an ox. T'weren't your brother, I'm afraid. And he said he was a digger, come to think of it, from the north woods."

By the time all these interrogations were over, Kit's distress did not have to be acted. She was genuinely at her wit's end. She wanted Daniel to leave her alone so she could "discover" the letter at the postmaster.

"It's not fair to keep you," she said in a quavering voice. "You surely have chores to tend to. This is my problem. I'll keep looking."

"If we don't find him, Kit, you're not going to..."

"I'm not giving up! Please, I think you should leave me alone! Let me go look some more." She spoke with real vehemence and Daniel stepped back, bristling at her irritated manner.

"Yes, ma'am. We'll be moving out in an hour." And he walked off, leaving her among the bustling travelers, shop folk and soldiers.

She felt both relief and regret when he was gone. Finally free to finish her charade, she was nonetheless sad that she had to accomplish it by pushing Daniel

Winchester away. He had just wanted to help her. She watched his figure disappear around a corner of the fort before heading to the postmaster.

They had checked in the postmaster's office already, so Kit would have to have an explanation of why no one there had heard of Seth before, yet here was a letter from him to her that no one had bothered to retrieve. But the office was so busy it would be easy for one letter to be forgotten, she reasoned. Emigrants stood in long lines to post their letters back home, and soldiers dallied in the shade of the makeshift porch, talking and creating a bustle. She waited patiently, now happy to have her mission nearing completion.

She lingered a respectable few minutes, pretending to want to post a letter, then affected an impatient air and left the office again. She had about an hour before the wagon train would be leaving. She didn't want to get back to the camp too soon or Daniel would ask too many questions. She hurried over to the store and made her purchases and then walked all the way around the fort in a leisurely stroll, before returning to the train. She saw them hitching up the wagons as she made her way back to the group. Daniel was near her wagon. When he saw her, he did not approach her, but rather stood, thumbs hooked on his belt, waiting for her to come to him.

"Where is he?" he asked in a hard, tired voice. "We're leaving. He can't be dawdling." He sounded just as irritated as she had been a little while before.

"He's, he's..." It had seemed so easy when she'd plotted it. Now it was hard to muster the courage to spit out the latest lie. She pulled out the letter instead and mutely handed it over to him.

He unfolded it and read. "Dearest sister, When I reached the fort, I was told a wagon train had just gone through to Fort Laramie. After waiting for seven days, I have decided to move on hoping to catch up with you there. If you are not with that group, however, I shall wait for you. Hoping for your safe journey and a swift reunion, your beloved brother, Seth Austen."

"He writes a mighty sweet note for a fur trader," Daniel said.

"He was schooled. Like I was," she countered.

"And it's sweet-smelling too." He put it under his nose as Kit remembered that it had been stored near her lavender powder.

"It was in my pocket!" she said quickly. She turned away from him to get up on her wagon.

"Where do you think you're going?" he asked her, his voice cutting through the air

She was sitting on the wagon seat now and pulling up her reins. "What do you mean? I'm getting ready to..."

"Kit Austen, the road up ahead is like nothing you've seen before. If you think you can ride alone to Fort Laramie to catch up with a brother who's acting like an irresponsible drifter, you're crazier than you are headstrong."

She warmed with a deep blush and didn't look at him. The whole train must have heard him. He wouldn't kick her off now, would he?

She couldn't afford to back down. The same sense of resistance that had filled her in Independence when Daniel had challenged her returned in full force. She would move forward with the train no matter what. This little scene between them was superfluous, not affecting the outcome at all.

"I am going to Fort Laramie to meet my brother," she said through clenched teeth. "Nobody is going to stop me."

With one swift movement, he was up in the seat next to her and whipping the reins. The team began to move, and he guided them to the side, out of the line of the other wagons. Some of the other emigrants were watching. Mary Barton poked her head out of her wagon and stared at the scene, while Reverend Kessler and Esther came forward from their positions to hear what was taking place.

Daniel uttered a soft "Whoa!" and stopped the animals, then looped the reins over the side and got down. Her face was hot from the deep blush that now covered it.

"You'll stay in the boarding house and head back with a group that's leaving in the morning. I'll talk to the captain. There's a family with them that'll take you with them. If I see your brother, I'll tell him what happened. No self-respecting man would let his sister travel alone." He almost spat out the last sentence, and Kit, while touched by his concern, was angered by his refusal to let her go with them.

"No!" With a vigor that matched his, she jumped down from the wagon and stood squarely in front of him, hands on her hips. "You cannot make me go back, Daniel Winchester. Do you hear me? You simply cannot make me! You will have to drag me first!"

From the look in his angry face, it was clear to her that if dragging is what it took to get her off the train, Daniel Winchester would do it without so much as a second thought. His eyes were flinty slits, and his jaw worked hard to keep himself from saying more than the eavesdropping crowd of travelers should be made to hear.

She lowered her voice and spoke so only he could hear her.

"Please, you don't understand." Suddenly tears were coming to her eyes. *Oh, that I had the wings of a dove...* She wanted to explain. Every fiber in her being cried out, pushing her to explain. "I... I... would just die if..." That was the truth. Going back to Josiah would mean certain death. Of that she was sure.

She swallowed hard, unable to continue for fear of breaking down. She couldn't cry in front of him. Not now.

Esther Kessler stepped up and put her arms around her. Her husband walked toward Daniel.

"We'll take her as part of our party," he said.

Josephus came forward, too. "We, as well, Daniel. She's been a blessing for our Mary."

Kit really struggled to hold back tears now, listening to these strangers, now friends, taking up for her. Married to Josiah, she'd had few friends.

Daniel said nothing at first, then sighed heavily. He touched his hat. He grimaced.

Then, he spoke in a low, harsh whisper. "All right, Miss Austen. These good people have decided me. You'll stay on the trail. I don't know what it is you can't go back to. But one thing has to be clear... "

"Yes, Mr. Winchester?"

"I trusted you in Missouri to be straight with me. That's the only reason I agreed to take you on. If your brother's not in Fort Laramie, I want to know the real reason or you're going back for sure."

"Yes, sir."

He turned and again pulled himself up into her wagon's seat, then held out his hand to her. Kit could have cried from joy as she took his strong hand and pulled herself up next to him. She sat in silence as he maneuvered the wagon back into the train. Again, in silence, he got down and mounted his own horse, riding forward to tell the lead wagon it was time to move on.

Chapter Seven

IT BOTHERED DANIEL with a terrible fierceness that Kit was alone on this journey. He'd not been able to protect his Jane from illness, but he'd not knowingly place a vulnerable woman in harm's way. And that's just what he was doing by allowing her to continue.

He shook his head as he squinted into the distance. They were a week out from Fort Kearney and good weather was leaving them. The day had dawned with wisps of clouds blowing in, followed by larger masses and finally huge thunderheads. Daniel was anxious to keep them moving at a good rhythm, averaging eighteen to twenty miles a day, twenty-five if they could handle it. He didn't want them near the Sierra Nevada in the late fall.

Now he pushed at a relentless pace, only letting them stop for a short midday break each day, just long enough to rest the animals and let them water and graze. Sometimes they only managed fifteen miles in a day, the distance measured by the meters attached to several wagons' wheels. This worried him, too. What if Kit held them back at some point? Then he would have endangered not just her but the whole party.

Why had he succumb to such foolishness, letting her stay at Fort Kearney?

Maybe because you know whatever she's running from is a fearsome thing.

Yes, he figured she was running from something. Most of them were on the train—running from poverty at the least, sometimes from lenders, occasionally from wicked men. Was that Kit's story? Several times he'd heard her cry out in the night, and each time, she had uttered the name, "Josiah."

She was hiding something all right. He had a mind to believe there was no brother, but he didn't want to think she'd be that broad a tale-teller, making up a family member from nothing but air.

The wind picked up, making the wagon coverings flap and strain. He looked back at the line of them. The Culpeppers were in the lead today—they alternated the lead position so that everyone had a turn at traveling without the dust of other wagons kicked up in their faces. Wilhemina sat next to her husband at the front of her wagon, and little Mary was with Kit. That girl had taken a liking to Kit, easing Wilhemina's load. That was a good thing, at least.

A strong breeze began to blow, whipping off Kit's bonnet and ballooning up Mary's dress, much to the little girl's delight. It brought a smile to Daniel's lips. He saw Kit notice and look away. He spurred his horse forward to scout up ahead.

"Look, Kit, over there!" Mary said, pointing to the north. Huge black clouds darkened the horizon. And a bright white flash created a jagged line from sky to earth. In a few seconds, the air carried the sound of a low crack, the thunder that accompanied the lightning. Kit heard some of the horses neigh at the sound. Daniel rode back toward the train at a quick clip.

"Keep moving. We might be able to make it to the river before it muddies up the banks!"

Everyone picked up the pace. The animals were in a nervous state with the sound of rolling thunder in the distance and with the change in the atmosphere. The air smelled damp and cool.

"Get in the back, Mary," Kit told the little girl as she twisted the reins tighter around her hands.

They were on a regularly decreasing incline now that they were approaching the Platte River. She could see in the distance a dark thread where the river cut through the land. Daniel was right; if they didn't make it before the storm, they would risk being delayed by muddy shores that sucked wagon wheels into the land.

Her heart beat fast. From her reading, she'd known they would be crossing rivers on the journey, and she feared that any misjudgment on her part during these risky maneuvers would seal her fate and convince Daniel to leave her behind at the next way station. It was important that she handle her team well going across this first major river, that she show confidence and strength, so that when they reached Fort Laramie, Daniel would not force her to stay there awaiting the "brother" who would never show up.

She popped the reins a little to hasten the lumbering oxen's tramp. A flash to her right foreshadowed the crack of thunder that followed a few seconds later. This one was louder than before, like a cannon going off. Horses reared and the oxen snorted and swayed, unhappy and nervous too. Stay calm, she said to herself as she licked the sweat from her upper lip. Even in the breeze, she was warm from effort and worry. *The animals will sense your mood*, her father used to tell her when teaching her to ride. *They know what to do.*

But they're the ones that are scared now, she thought frantically. *Tell me what to do, Papa! Tell me what to do!*

The Culpepper and Barton wagons tipped and swayed dangerously as the animals searched for clear footing on the incline. Daniel rode by again, grim and taut, his back straight as a rod in the saddle, his eyes shadowed by furrowed brows.

"Let Paul take over!" he shouted to her over the rumble of the wagon wheels. "I'll get him back here."

"No!" she cried out with a defiance she didn't know she had. "His brother needs him. I'm fine. I can handle it." The confidence in her voice belied the quivering anxiety in her stomach.

He just stared at her for a second, grimacing, then gently nudged his horse with his heels and rode forward to check on the rest.

When he rode away, Kit wondered if she had made a bad decision. If Paul Culpepper came and drove her team, she could be assured of a safe river crossing. But it would merely add to the impression that this single woman was a burden on the trail.

No, she decided, it was better to risk failing on her own and be done with it. She clicked the reins and talked to the oxen.

"Bonnie, Bess, come on now, come on, it's all right, it's all right," she said in a steady, lilting tone. If they were nervous now, she had to be the one to calm them.

A cracking noise split the air. But this time, there was no lightning or thunder. It was the sound of a wheel axle breaking up ahead. The Bartons' wagon was tilting, the result of the broken shaft. They were slowing and stopping. Kit had to either move her team around them or pull up short. The distance between them narrowed as she struggled. She made clicking noises and stood to get a better sight line. She pulled and tugged on the reins and decided she needed to veer to the left, where the land was smoother. The rest of the train would follow her. Out of the corner of her eye, she saw Daniel galloping by and stopping at the Bartons' wagon.

"Can you rig it 'till we get to the river?" he was shouting to Josephus.

She couldn't stop to hear the reply. Things were moving too quickly now. She passed their stopped wagon and caught up behind the Culpeppers. She saw Paul Culpepper jump down and run back to help Daniel and Josephus. Good thing she had decided not to ask for his help, she thought with satisfaction. She saw them pull out a spare axle from the wagon. Smart travelers had plenty of spare parts.

The wind picked up as they neared the river. Now her heart raced terribly as she thought of crossing the wide, flat, muddy divide. Where was Daniel?

"Kit, Kit! Where's Mama?" Mary poked her head out, hugging to her chest a rag doll Kit had given her. The little girl's face was a mask of fear.

"She's all right. She's with your papa. They're fixing something. Shush now. Go back under cover!"

Kit thought they would stop and wait for Daniel at the river's edge, but Ira Culpepper was forging forward. Daniel had said the river was no more than three feet deep, but what if it had changed? Did Ira know the best place to cross? Were there deep parts they should avoid? The surface was so brown and muddy there was no telling what chasms lay beneath it. She glanced back into the wagon. Maybe she should help Mary jump off and run to her parents? No, she shouldn't be out in the lightning. Better to keep her put.

Just as fear started to clutch at her throat and make her palms sweat, the air crackled with the sound of real thunder, close enough to make her jump. It shook the very earth beneath them. It was a warning of what was to come. The wind blew in mighty gusts, and the skies opened as buckets of water poured down on them. The river became a moving, dancing surface of splashing discs as the huge drops hit it.

Why was Ira moving ahead so quickly? His oxen were stepping into the muddy ribbon now. Should she follow or wait for Daniel? She glanced back at Mary again, whose face was white as she stroked her doll's head.

Ira's oxen were in the river, the water flowing over their hooves as they moved forward, deeper, deeper. Thunder again and more lightning. It was hard to keep track of what sound belonged to what sight. Horses were letting out high-pitched neighs of discomfort. The oxen bellowed as they became more nervous with the torrent of activity. Kit felt her reins slacken as her team started to slow down. They were going to stop and drink if she didn't push them on. That would be disaster. Her wagon would sink in the mud and be stuck for hours.

"No, girls!" she shouted at them. She whipped at the reins and leaned forward. "Come on! Come on! Move along! Move along!"

Her heart pounded so hard it competed with the sound of the thunder. She was soaked through from the drenching rain, which made a terrible racket as it slammed into the water and the wagon covers. Up ahead, Ira's wagon was in the stream now. The surface of the river was just below his wagon frame. They had hitched up all the frames with blocks of wood the night before in preparation for this ride. Daniel had forced them to do it, saying he didn't want to lose time once they hit the water's edge.

Her own oxen tentatively stepped into the churning mud and water. She clicked and yelled again and slapped at the reins, though she was careful not to be cruel. Don't be cruel, her father had told her. Don't treat your animals with meanness or they will return the favor.

"It's all right, it's all right," she heard herself saying to them as she poised for the moment her wagon wheels would sink into the sandy bottom of the river bed. She would have to keep up the pressure to move forward then. Even slowing down would be enough to stall her in the middle of the river.

"Kit! Kit! Are we going to drown?" Mary was crying now.

"Shush, Mary! Shush!" Better to scold the girl than show fear. She had to keep the oxen moving. Ira Culpepper was keeping up a good pace, but she didn't like the fact that the water was getting deeper. It now touched the bottom of his wagon frame. When would it become shallower? What if it seeped into the wagon and weighed her down? What if it picked up little Mary.... She pushed the thought out of her head and snapped the reins again, gently but firmly, coaxing her team to pick up the pace.

"Move along!" she shouted again, standing up for more control on the reins. They were in it now. She felt the wagon shift as it sank into the soft bed of the river. A second river poured over her from above as the dark clouds now rolled over them and let loose their fury. A double crackling noise split the air and she saw a tree on the other side of the river struck by lightening, a branch falling to the ground.

She couldn't look ahead. She couldn't look behind. She could only focus on one thing—the team and keeping it going. With every ounce of strength and determination in her, she pressed her body forward and leaned toward the oxen. She started talking to them in a continuous repetitive chant, telling them to move on, to get along, to go, go, *go!* She willed them to move faster. She looked at their gleaming brown-and-white backs slicked down with rain and their lumbering, bellowing heads and tried to calm them with her thoughts and words.

They were in the middle of the river. To the right and left of the wagon, there was nothing but swiftly-flowing water dancing with raindrops.

Something was wrong. The oxen were turning. They were trying to go with the flow of the river. It was easier to do that than to push against the current. *Oh, no!* She glanced up. Ira was nearly across, but her team was pulling to the side, trying to go downstream. She flipped at the reins again. She pulled on one side. She shouted, she screamed. Nothing worked. They were now almost parallel to the shore. She had to do something!

"Stay put!" she shouted to Mary as she stood up. She jumped into the river on the upstream side of the team. It was icy cold, the fragments of winter still in its currents. The freezing water hit her skin like a stinging slap. Her skirt swirled around her legs, and her booted feet sank into the sand. She leaned back, pulling on the reins with all her might, tugging them towards her, away from the downstream course.

She leaned back so far that water came up to her chin and entered her mouth. She gulped and spit it out.

"Git over here! Come on, come on!"

The water numbed her hands until she could barely feel them holding the leather straps, but she pulled anyway. She looked the ox nearest her in the eyes and coaxed and nudged and harangued until her throat was hoarse.

Come. On.

Please, Lord. Don't let Mary pay for my foolhardiness.

She turned away from the animals, still pulling on the reins, and led the way herself, upstream, upstream and then at right angles to the shore, her legs feeling like blocks of wood, like something separate from her body. She could feel the wagon getting heavier as the wheels got sucked into the mud. They couldn't slow down. It would be disaster. If that happened...

The rain continued its relentless beating—hard-driving drops that hurt when they hit the skin. The water poured over her face into her eyes, but she couldn't take her hands off the reins to wipe it away. Her hands were blue-white with cold. They didn't seem to belong to her either.

At last, they were on a straight course and more river was behind them than in front. She trudged forward, oblivious to the rain and frigid river, keeping her focus on the animals and the strip of land that beckoned to her, her arm muscles screaming in agony as she pulled and pulled.

Just as exhaustion and cold were beginning to overcome her, the water started to recede, and they entered shallower stretches. It got easier now, the moving was faster, the effort less. Her chest was out of the water, then her waist, then her knees, finally her ankles. She was walking on the shore, and she didn't have to pull the animals. They were willing to come onto dry land of their own accord. Her legs felt wobbly from the effort she had just made, weighted down by the soaked skirt that clung to her knees and calves.

She looked up at the wagon.

"Mary? Mary? Are you all right, child?"

The girl came to the wagon opening, wiping her eyes. When she saw Kit and the dry land, a tentative smile answered Kit's own cheering face.

"Everything's fine now. Don't worry," Kit told the girl.

She turned and trudged forward. Ira Culpepper was continuing onward. Across the river, the other wagons were getting ready to cross, but Daniel was leading them through with a steady hand on his horse. The rain was letting up, softer now.

Drained of energy, Kit looked down at herself. Her dress was brown from the muddy water, and she shivered in the cold air. But she had to keep moving. She didn't want to slow down the train. She wiped the water out of her face and put one foot in front of the other, her feet squishing inside her soaked boots.

"What did you think you were doing?"

She jumped with surprise. Daniel was beside her so suddenly she hadn't noticed his horse's approach. He looked down at her in anger and dismay. His face was set in a firm line of indignation, his lips pressed together in controlled rage, his eyes dark slits of fury. Before she could answer, he continued.

"You should never have crossed that river until I scouted it first! You could have lost your team, your wagon, the Barton girl!" He was shouting at her.

"Ira... he was the lead .. I... "

"Ira is a headstrong boy who's lucky he's alive."

She was speechless. Not only was she tired enough to drop, but she now began to tremble from a combination of repressed fear and cold. Her shaking did not go unnoticed.

He jumped down off his horse and pulled off his long coat, draping it over her shoulders. At the touch of his strong hands, she shivered again. Now that he was closer, she could see in his face that it wasn't anger that had darkened his eyes. It was fear. He had been afraid for her, afraid for her safety. How wonderful to feel cared for! She had forgotten just how wonderful that sensation was.

As suddenly as it had begun, the rainstorm now ended. The dark clouds rolled into the distance. Only a soft drizzle and a steamy humidity remained.

"You have to get into dry clothes," he said in a softer tone. "Or you'll be sick for sure. I'll get Paul to come drive your team for awhile."

"But the Bartons... "

"They're fine now. Wheel is mended and they're in the rear of the train. Go change." He said the last phrase with firm authority.

"Mary's in the wagon."

"Have her come out here."

Kit did as he said, scooting little Mary out and pulling the coverings closed for privacy. As she peeled off the wet clothes, she could hear him talking to the child, and then a giggle burbling forth from Mary's lips. Kit smiled despite her weariness. Her arms and legs felt like the water she'd just been through, and her fingers were raw from where the reins had scraped her flesh. She brushed off the sand that had collected on her body and shook her hair free of its bedraggled bun. From her trunk, she pulled out a pale blue gingham dress with a becoming flare, a narrow band of eyelet lace around the neck, and pearly white buttons down the front.

How silly to be concerned about how I look on a wagon train, she thought to herself. Nonetheless, she sprinkled some lavender-scented powder over her bare arms before buttoning up the shirtwaist. She neatened her damp hair as best she could and tied it back with a blue satin ribbon. She'd wash the sand out later. In place of her boots, she tugged on soft suede Indian moccasins she had purchased in Independence.

As she stepped out of the wagon, Daniel was letting Mary pat his horse and telling her he was sure her folks would get some fine ponies in California. He looked up and saw her. His face at once conveyed both surprise and admiration. He swallowed hard and brought his hat off his head as if he had just entered a lady's parlor. Realizing how out of place the gesture was, he quickly replaced the hat and looked away, then put his foot in the stirrup and mounted his horse.

"I've got to get back," he said in a throaty voice and turned to ride away to the other wagons by the river.

Before she could stop herself, she called after him. "Wait!"

He stopped and turned back. She went over to him and stared up at his shadowed face.

"I'm sorry," she said. "I thought I was doing the right thing following Mr. Culpepper. I didn't mean to..."

She saw his mouth open to speak, and a soft but troubled look come over his face.

"Kit," he began. "Miss Austen, I just didn't want... " He looked away, then chuckled softly, as if the joke were played on him. "I uttered many a prayer when I saw you in that river, ma'am. And that's not been my way of things for a long time."

"Thank you. I'm sure it helped."

He looked her in the eyes. "Did it? Or was it your own good sense?"

"I am grateful nonetheless, Mr. Winchester."

A troubled look came over his face.

"Your hands'll be chapped from the water and the reins. Rub some oil on them tonight."

He touched the brim of his hat and rode off to other wagons.

HE COULDN'T THINK straight. He had to lead the rest of the train across the river, and he could barely keep his mind on the task at hand. His mind kept wandering back to the image of her in the water. At first, when he'd glanced at the wagon and not seen her in the seat, he'd thought she'd fallen off, the river carrying her away. And then he'd seen her tugging on the reins, her mouth clamped shut, her arms stretched to the limit, and...

Yes, he'd murmured a prayer then. He'd asked God to keep her safe until he could get his horse and help her. He'd prayed for the first time in many years, a custom he'd stopped when wife and son had been lost to him. At that time, he'd figured he'd make no claims on God as long as God made none on him. With only himself to care for, he'd figured he didn't need to be pleading and asking God for things.

He shook his head as he waved on the next wagon and the river rushed past his horse's legs. He didn't like having someone he wanted to pray for.

Chapter Eight

To Fort Laramie

DANIEL WAS RIGHT. The journey became steadily more difficult after Fort Kearney. It was as if they had passed a dividing line between the civilized and the savage. Those who hadn't made the journey might have thought of Independence or St. Joseph as the gateway to the frontier. But the traveling from there to the fort was relatively easy with grand prairies and good water and even an occasional homestead along the way to remind them that the life they had known was possible even out here in this treeless wilderness. But along with these reminders of civilization were also reminders of the dangers that lay ahead. They passed more and more graves now, some hastily dug and with primitive markings, but all of them casting a pall of gloom over the company.

After the Platte crossing, the mirage of normalcy returned for a while—high plains and good grazing, steady progress, even some good hunting. Although they traveled through Sioux country, they saw no evidence of Indians. The men carried loaded weapons nonetheless, and Kit suspected some of them were anxious to put a bullet in a young brave's heart so they could write home about the adventure. But Daniel told her the Indians were more frightened of the weapons the emigrants didn't flaunt than the ones they did—cholera and smallpox and other hidden threats that the Indians had learned to fear. These diseases had so ravaged the ranks of the tribes that the knowing Sioux left the white men to their journeys, chasing buffalo north as the settlers and gold diggers headed west.

If Indians weren't to be seen, buffalo and antelope were. Several times along the way, hunting parties formed in the mornings and rode off, catching up with the train at midday or early afternoon. Every time Daniel went with such a party, Kit found herself watching the horizon all day, waiting for him to return. She told herself that this was because she valued his protection, that Daniel cared for the company as a whole more than for any individual human being and that it was his duty to protect her, nothing more.

And she prayed for forgiveness—for her continued deception, for the courage to live alone the rest of her days. But it was harder than she'd imagined, and she often found herself on her knees at night asking God to turn her thoughts away from what could have been with a man like Daniel by her side rather than the one she'd chosen back in Boston.

These inner struggles started reflecting her physical struggles as well, making her energy flag. Eager at the outset to prove her worth, she now let others help her with many chores. Esther Kessler stepped in on more than one occasion to help with the heaviest part of meal preparation and planning. In fact, she became like a mother to Kit, watching out for her well-being and coaxing her from brooding moods.

As they were cleaning up after the mess one evening, Esther used this motherly affection to get Kit to open up about what bothered her. She started by mentioning that she noticed Kit had not brought her "beautiful Bible" to Sabbath services since Andrew Kessler had asked to see it.

"I hope he didn't offend, Kit. You should feel free to bring it if it's a precious thing that gives you comfort."

Kit had left it in her case, of course, to avoid having to explain the inscriptions.

"There was no offense, Esther. I'm sorry to have given that impression." She slowly dried the pot in her hand, listening to the night sounds of crickets and tired animals. Her shoulders ached that night from a long day of difficult riding over rutted paths and bumpy territory. No one had been able to help her with her team, so she'd driven them herself the full day long.

Esther looked into her eyes, her own dark eyes sparkling in the firelight. "Then why don't you tell me, child, what's locked up with that Bible that's weighing your heart so?"

Surprised, Kit opened her mouth but said nothing. What could she say—that her heart was broken, along with her body, by a bad marriage? That now that she'd seen what a good man was like her heart was broken anew at the thought of possibilities lost to her forever, that she prayed every night to stay true to her vows?

"Everybody here talks about their places back home, what they're leaving," Esther went on in her soft, firm tone. "There are only two people on this train who don't talk about the past. And yours seems a heavy burden. Do you need to talk to Mr. Kessler, dear? He has helped many a troubled soul."

This raised Kit's lips in a kind smile. Rev. Kessler had probably sent his wife as emissary to this "troubled soul." Kit rubbed the last pot dry and placed it in a neat pile on a bench.

"Thank you for the offer, Esther," she said, intending to turn the conversation away from herself. But Esther stopped her in her tracks.

"What are you doing to do, dear, when we reach Fort Laramie?" She lowered her voice to a whisper. "The Reverend saw you at the postmaster in Fort Kearney. There was no letter waiting for you there. He saw you take the letter from your pocket."

At this revelation, the air went from Kit's lungs. Her knees buckled, and she sat on the bench, hands in her lap. She could protest—she could say that Rev. Kessler must have missed the moment she'd retrieved the letter and put it in her pocket in the first place. Wouldn't that be the wisest course? Another lie?

No, no, she was sick of lying. That was weighing her down, too, as much as her thoughts of what could have been had she not married Josiah. She didn't have the heart to pile lie on lie.

"Has he... has Rev. Kessler said anything to Mr. Winchester?"

Esther came and sat by her in the darkness. "No, child. He has not told him. He's not told a soul except me, and he only did that a day ago. He was hoping you'd come talk to him."

"What does he know?" Kit murmured, twisting the towel in her fingers.

"He surmises that you have no brother. Or at least none who is going to meet you on the trail." Esther wrapped her hand around Kit's. "Why are you heading west, dear? Is it...is it as Billy Crane says? Please let us help you—"

"No!" Kit pulled away, feeling her cheeks warm from humiliation. Was this the price of her deception—to have them believe the filthy lies that a low man like Billy Crane would spread about her? If so, maybe she deserved that fate. Maybe it was punishment for all of her chicanery.

"It isn't that at all, not at all." She shook her head vehemently.

But that was the problem with lying. It begat more lies, even if they weren't told by her. She had to set things right. She'd planned on doing so. Maybe the Kesslers could help her figure out how. She took a deep breath and stared into the night, silently asking for courage.

"Oh, Esther," she said on a sigh at last. "I've done a terrible wrong. But I have to keep on this train. I can't go back." She turned to the woman and collapsed into her arms, sobbing with relief to be able to tell someone the truth. "I've run away from my husband, and if I go back, he will kill me."

HER FACE AND THROAT hurt from so much crying; her chest ached from the sobs she'd poured out onto poor Esther's shoulder. What a cleansing it was to finally tell the truth! She thanked God in her heart that she had the opportunity to share it with another understanding spirit at last, that Esther and her husband were on this train with her.

At the end of her recitation, she hiccupped out her dilemma.

"W-w-w-what am I to do? Mr. Winchester will want to leave me at Fort L-l-l-aramie, I know it. He was angry with me at the river crossing. He won't keep me on if he knows."

Esther kissed Kit's head and stroked her hair. "There, there, child. What a terrible path you've had to walk. But you cannot keep lying. You know that. It's made your burden heavier, don't you think?"

Kit nodded. Already she felt lighter for having told Esther her secret. And Esther had not judged her, had not told her she'd been wrong to abandon her marriage, even if it was to a tyrant. Some ministers—and their wives— would have counseled her to return. Esther had been touched by her story, aghast that her husband had been so cruel, had beaten her near death at least once. She told Kit she couldn't bring herself to judge a woman in those circumstances, that only the Lord could sort out those judgments, that if Kit stayed true to her marriage vow, even far away from Josiah, forsaking all others... then Esther Kessler would not scold.

"I can't go back," Kit murmured again. "And Mr. Winchester will make me go back."

"What makes you so sure, Kit? His responsibility is to keep all travelers safe. Sending you back at this point of the journey would be just as perilous as letting you keep on the train."

Kit shook her head. Despite what Esther said, Kit remembered how Daniel had warned of the worst parts of the journey coming near the end. He'd not hesitate to keep her from those dangers. And there was another issue he'd want to address—her lying to get on the train. He wasn't the kind of man to tolerate that.

Kit sat up, wiping her eyes with the towel. She looked into Esther's kind eyes. If Kit kept lying now, Esther would be part of her conspiracy of untruth. She couldn't ask that of her.

"I can't tell him just yet," she murmured. "But I promise you I will, Esther. I'll tell him once we're beyond Fort Laramie. I think he'd have a harder time sending me back then, no matter how angry he was with me."

"Oh, child."

"I'll understand, though, if you don't believe you can in good conscience keep my secret."

Esther frowned, then looked down at the crackling fire just beyond the bench.

"I cannot keep it from my husband. But I will not say a word to anyone else." She looked back up at Kit, staring at her with grave intensity. "You must keep your promise. Once we get past Fort Laramie, I'll feel compelled to—"

"I know. I accept that. But I won't disappoint you, Esther. I will keep my promise. Once we're past Fort Laramie, I'll tell him. You have been more kind than I deserve."

"All God's children deserve kindness," Esther said, wiping the corner of her own eye. "Don't ever think otherwise, Kit."

Esther stood, getting ready to return to her wagon for the night. She embraced Kit, once again telling she'd done the right thing by sharing the truth with her. Before she left, she held Kit's chin in her hand and said, "If you're going to wait to tell him, be careful, my dear. I think he could be sweet on you. It's best he knows soon you are not free to return those feelings."

Sweet on her? Kit watched Esther's figure fade into the darkness.

Daniel sweet on her? A smile came to her lips, at the same time her brow furrowed. Here was both joy and worry.

OVER THE NEXT FEW days, Kit's energy returned. After her confession to Esther, it was as if a heavy yoke had been lifted from her own shoulders. She now looked forward to the stop at Fort Laramie because it would mean she was closer to the moment she could reveal the truth to Daniel as well. Esther had assured her that she and her husband, the Reverend, would stand up for Kit in that circumstance, urging Daniel to keep her in the company. Esther had even suggested that the Kesslers could tell Daniel, but Kit had declined that kind offer. She'd need to face his wrath on her own. She now felt up to the challenge.

If that problem receded from her worry, another became more prominent. She became more aware of Daniel's presence after Esther's revelation that he was "sweet on her." Now Kit noticed how often he rode near her wagon, how he continued to camp out near her at night when he wasn't on guard duty, how his gaze often fixed on her when he rode back to the train after hunting.

He became more direct in his attention, too, joining her mess for dinner almost every night, complimenting her singing and cooking, and accompanying her to Sabbath services with enthusiasm, not the sense of duty that had marked his first attendance at Rev. Kessler's Sunday meetings.

She now realized, with a pang of sadness, that she enjoyed this attention a great deal. And, as Esther had warned, she should take care and not encourage it. On more than one occasion, Esther had shot her a worried frown when Daniel had shown her a kindness. After Daniel had brought her some wildflowers he'd found in a hunting expedition, Esther had taken her aside and whispered, "My dear, do you want to tell him now before Fort Laramie?" But Kit had shaken her head, no. She couldn't take the chance.

Just a day out from Fort Laramie, the travelers enjoyed a rare treat—a chance to bathe. The weather was warm and sunny, and the river nearby was clear and shallow near the banks. Daniel, Rev. Kessler and Josephus arranged the schedule—women first just before sunset and men after, as twilight fell. While the women bathed, Daniel and other good-minded men would make sure no males in the company went near the water.

The women had a joyful time of it, wading into the stream in their petticoats and camisoles as the sun glinted the water a golden hue, finally washing the dust of the trail from their hair. Laughter echoed from the nearby banks as they shared special soaps and rinsed each other's manes. Kit had opened a rose-scented soap she'd been saving for her new home and used it to scrub herself clean before passing it to little Mary Barton. Wilhemina helped the delighted girl rub her face, hands and arms with the sweetly-scented bar. Then they all washed clothing they'd not been able to launder beyond spot-cleaning throughout the journey. What a pleasure it was to know they'd be able to put on fresh clothes in the next few days.

All too soon it was time to return to the wagon train where Kit and Esther and Wilhemina were happily surprised to find their mess already begun. Fires were crackling and a pot was on the grate filled with onions and rabbit. While the women finished the cooking, the men made ready to wash—those who wanted to anyway.

As Daniel passed Kit on the way to the river, he stopped, closed his eyes and inhaled deeply.

"That's a fine smell, Miss Austen."

At first she thought he was referring to the stew she was adding herbs to. But her face warmed to realize he was talking of the rose soap scent which perfumed her wet clothes set out to dry—all but her personal items, which she'd set about the inside of the wagon.

"It reminds me of—" He opened his eyes and stopped, and Kit remembered what Esther had said to her several evenings ago. There were only two people on the train who didn't talk about their pasts. Kit was one. But Daniel was the other.

"Of what, Mr. Winchester?" Her gaze met his, and his eyes spoke of past pain.

"Of...of..." He looked as if he were weighing whether to say more. She stood still and quiet, not wanting to intrude on that inner struggle.

"Of my Jane," he said at last, staring at her with eyes like the river itself—brown and watery. Then he hurried away as if this small revelation had been too much for him to bear.

His Jane. Maybe Esther had been wrong. Daniel wasn't "sweet" on Kit. He had another girl. His Jane.

This filled her with both relief and regret. If he had a woman to call his own, Kit need not fear him becoming attracted to her. He was an honorable man, after all, not one who'd break a promise or a vow.

But if it were true that he had someone—well, something inside her caved in at that possibility. Despite her best efforts and prayers, she'd not kept herself from enjoying his attention, thinking it was directed at her because of his special feelings for her.

How vain I am, she thought as she continued work on the dinner. She thanked God for the reminder and promised to be more attentive to such temptation.

At least Daniel's revelation made him more comfortable to be around. Before he returned for supper, Kit confided in Esther what she'd learned—that Daniel already had a girl and that there was nothing to worry about there.

Esther had frowned. "He sure doesn't act like a man who has a gal back home," was all she said as she rushed to finish her clothes-hanging before being needed at the campfire.

After dinner that night, Daniel insisted on helping Kit clean up while the Bartons retreated to their wagon to get Mary settled for bed and Esther and the Reverend hurried to finish chores put aside for the washing-up.

The two of them didn't speak at first, as Kit washed each plate and bowl in a basin of river water and Daniel dried them.

"You don't have to help," she said at last. "This is woman's work."

He laughed. "And driving a team is men's," he said.

She smiled. As she handed him a plate to dry, her hand brushed his and he took the opportunity to grab her fingers and hold them.

Her smile left as she gazed into his eyes.

"Miss Austen, I..."

She pulled her hand away. Her heart galloping, she turned back to the basin and plunged both hands in the water, but all the washing was done.

"Tell me about your Jane," she said, forcing a cheerfulness she didn't feel. She hoisted the basin to empty it, but he stopped her, grabbing it instead and walking to the perimeter of the corral where he dumped it.

By the time he returned, she'd finished putting away the mess things and was ready to tamp down the fire for the night. She turned to him, a smile on her face, and repeated her question.

"Don't be bashful, Mr. Winchester. Tell me about your girl. Is she waiting for you in California or back in Missouri?"

He stared into the embers. Not looking at her, he said in a low voice, "She's waiting for me in a grave in western Virginia."

Kit's heart fell into her stomach. "Oh... I'm so sorry. Please forgive me... I thought, when you said the rosewater reminded you of..." She walked over to him and touched his arm, trying to console him. "How long has she been gone?"

"Seven years."

"She was your—"

"My wife. And the mother of my son."

Kit wanted to ask about the boy, but suspected that story held more heartache. Her eyes watered, and she hung her head in shame for so cavalierly opening the door to his sorrow. She had no right.

"I'm sorry," she said again. "You must have loved them very much."

"Yes," he said, still not looking at her. His mind was faraway, probably on his lost loved ones. "It was a fever did them in. Within a year of each other. I took to the trail after that."

He turned to her. "Sometimes you remind me of her," he said, his voice and face lifting. "Not in the way you look, but in how you take on any task with faith and forbearance, sure the Lord will see you through."

"You give me more credit than I deserve," she said, thinking of all the times she'd felt faithless and afraid.

"No, ma'am. I've seen how you've gone after everything with a willing heart."

"Some might say a foolish heart," she said, thinking not of the trail but of her marriage.

To her surprise, he agreed. "Well, the river crossing was a foolish thing to do." His voice was much lighter now, a teasing tone in it. "A foolish thing for any woman alone."

She bristled at the remembrance of that day. She was proud of her work then and wouldn't let him think she hadn't been up to it.

"Didn't I lead my team across the Platte with no help from any man?"

"Just barely, Miss Austen," he said.

"Just barely? I turned them by myself when they were heading downstream!"

"And near killed yourself doing it," he said, the teasing leaving his voice.

"The water was only three feet deep, four at the most!" she hurled back at him. She wouldn't let him win this. He would use it as an excuse to throw her out of the company when it came time to tell her secret. "I saved my team from going downstream. On my own. With no one's help!"

"You barely saved them!"

She could see his face turning red in the fire's glow, and his jaw muscles were working furiously to control his rising temper.

"I got them across. *I* got them across!" Despite herself, Kit stomped her foot for emphasis. "What should it matter how I did it? I did it!"

He reached out and grabbed her by the shoulders, looking her straight in the eye.

"Don't you understand? You could have drowned! You could have *drowned*!" He said it with an urgency that communicated all his fear and all his longing. It was clear what he meant—he wouldn't have been able to bear it should something have happened to her.

"I could have ... I mean I didn't drown, I was able to... " She was drowning now, swimming in the dark pools of his eyes, unable to get enough air.

"Shush, woman!" He swept his hat off his head with one hand and grabbed her to him with the other, pressing on her lips a kiss that silenced her words but drew out of her a longing to be loved by such a good man.

They both pulled apart at the same time, as if realizing the inappropriateness of their action. He immediately apologized, looking down, putting his hat back on. She offered her own regret, now colored by the memory of Esther's caution not to lead Daniel on.

"I...I'm sorry, Mr. Winchester," she said at length. "I might have given you the wrong impression. You see, I'm not free to accept your kind attentions. I'm... spoken for already." There, that wasn't a lie.

His gaze flickered up to her, a look of crushed defeat in his eyes. He swallowed, touched his hat, apologized again in a quick mumble, and wished her good-night before walking off into the dark.

Kit stumbled to her wagon, her vision blinded by fast tears. She'd tell Esther in the morning how she'd set Daniel straight. And then, after Fort Laramie, she'd tell him her whole story.

No, maybe she would take Esther up on her generous offer to tell him the tale. She didn't know if she could bear the look in his eyes when he found out she was not only married, but to a brute.

Chapter Nine

AS THEY NEARED Fort Laramie at the western end of the Platte Valley, Kit consulted with both Kesslers on how to handle the story of her elusive brother. Rev. Kessler urged her to tell Daniel the truth right away, so sure was he of the trail guide's good heart. But Esther, to whom Kit had confided the story of Daniel's kiss and his history, was more circumspect.

"She's made plans to tell him after Fort Laramie, and I trust her to keep to that plan," she told her husband. "I think it's for the best. Mr. Winchester needs to have a clear head now."

Although Esther said this as if she meant Daniel needed to keep his mind on the trail, Kit suspected she meant that his mind might be clouded with his unrequited feelings for her. It wouldn't be the best time to foist a decision on him about her continuing.

She didn't pursue the discussion any further, and wearily thought of how she'd produce yet another letter from the mysterious "Seth," hoping that would satisfy Daniel enough to let her keep going past the Fort. She could barely bring herself to contemplate what to write in the letter. It seemed so dry and cruel, and she was sure God was tired of hearing her pleas for forgiveness.

She had hoped that the farther they traveled, the harder Daniel would find it to send her back. But every few days, they saw some travelers who had "seen the elephant" and were returning East passing with waving hands and smiling faces, glad to be going home. Daniel could easily arrange for her to go with one of them, especially now that there was a cool distance between them.

Since she'd told him she was spoken for, he had barely paid notice of her. In fact, he seemed to stay out longer and longer for his hunting forays and scouting trips, sometimes not hooking up with the company until mid-afternoon. He never joined her group in the evenings now. More often than not he dined alone, or with some other diggers. The one connection to his old sympathy for her was his adherence to guard duty outside her wagon.

Every night he either slept by the back wagon wheels or walked the perimeter of their corrals keeping a close eye on her wagon. She knew this because she was often wakeful. A troubled heart is not conducive to sleep.

The grazing land was irregular now, so if they were fortunate to be around good grasslands, they all had to engage in haying in the evenings. They would store the bales for the "days of famine" as Josephus called the stretches when the land was bare and the animals had nothing to sate their hunger. It made them all a little nervous to realize they were coming up on land where even haying opportunities would be scant. Ahead of them were deserts that would have to be crossed as quickly as possible if they were to survive the heat and drought of that cruel landscape.

To make matters even more worrisome, Wilhemina was beginning to show large with child. Privately, she told Kit that she was worried about the baby. It seemed much too big for this early date, and she was having trouble keeping up with the wagon. Her protruding stomach made walking difficult and any chore twice as tiresome. Kit pitched in as much as she could, taking Mary for long stretches of time, even having her sleep with her so Willa could get a good night's rest. Although Wilhemina's pale face was now burnished from the sun, she was still so frail and thin that her belly looked like an odd attachment to an otherwise slender frame.

Ironically, Wilhemina's condition made Kit feel a bit more secure about staying on the train. With so few women around, surely Daniel would see the wisdom of keeping her with Willa so near her time.

Up ahead, through the clouds of dust kicked up by the animals and the wheels, she could make out a turf-covered building sitting alone in the plains. It was a trading post. Daniel had told them of it and let them know they could use the blacksmith's services and purchase a few supplies before heading on to Laramie, where other re-supply opportunities existed. The plan was for a short visit at the trading post. Those who needed to linger to use the forge could catch up.

But when they pulled up to the old dwelling, Kit was surprised at the greeting they received. Daniel rode ahead of them, tall and confident on his steed. Out of the home came a woman. From Kit's distance, she looked to be her age. She had copper-colored hair and a loud laugh that could be heard throughout the train.

"Daniel, you scoundrel! You've not changed a whit! When are you going to stop this wandering? Come in, come in!"

Kit watched as Daniel dismounted and the woman ran up to him and put her arms around him in a warm embrace. More surprising still was the fact that Daniel did not resist. When the two pulled apart, the woman then linked her arm in his, and they strode together into her little hut.

Soon, the wagons were halting. Out of the hut came a small boy about the same age as Mary—a boy who looked to be of Indian heritage. He offered to help with the animals and direct the travelers to the forge, which was in back of the home. As Kit got off of her wagon seat, she kept waiting for Daniel to come out of the hut, stealing glances in that direction as she unharnessed her team and led them to a nearby pond dug into the hard earth. Even from there, she could hear the woman's raucous laughter.

She saw other travelers headed for the trading post and thought about following, but instead forced herself to do her encampment chores first, not hurrying through a single one. Tend to the animals, check on Mary, see to Wilhemina's needs, pull out the mess kit provisions for the midday meal. Only then, after she had gone through her entire list of tasks, did she walk into the building.

It had the pungent earthy odor of all such dwellings, but the floor at least was made of wooden planks, and the shelves on the walls were also made of wood. They held items such as pans and cooking utensils, tools, mining gear, and even some books and clothing, obviously discarded by earlier travelers. Kit immediately went to look at the books, but as she flipped through the pages of a collection of essays on the uplifting values of country life, she listened intently to the conversation between Daniel and the unknown woman just a few feet away.

Daniel leaned on a high chair-back and the woman stood close by, her arms folded over her ample bosom. Kit glanced her way enough to get a fuller picture of her. She was tall— almost as tall as Daniel—and her red hair was frizzy and unkempt, just barely pulled in a bun that looked ready to explode. Her face and arms were brown from the sun, and she wore a faded green shirtwaist that looked a shade too small. Her sleeves were immodestly rolled up over her elbows and her feet were bare.

Kit knew why she chose green to wear. Even from across the room, Kit could see she had emerald-colored eyes that flashed with good humor. Her face was large, with a firm strong jaw and high forehead. Her lips were large and full. She looked like the kind of women whom Kit had occasionally seen in Boston, the ones who helped run the taverns in town or took washing in. But this was no washerwoman. Her name, it turned out, was Jenny, and when Daniel said it, he was obviously speaking with affection. He had to know her well to call her by her Christian name.

"I'm sorry to hear about Louie," he said. "I heard the news from some traders heading north last spring."

"'Twas quick at least. Mrs. Bordeaux's husband lingered for months after being kicked in the head last winter by one of those wild ponies."

"But cholera... I always thought Louie would die in the saddle, on the trail."

To Kit's surprise, Jenny laughed. "Aye," she said. "And he'd be leaving me with no way of knowin' he was gone. He would have liked that, the old bugger!"

"How are you managing on your own? Aren't you going back home?"

"Home? What's that, Danny?" she asked. Kit bristled at hearing Daniel referred to as "Danny." "My home's here," Jenny continued. "My family's been gone a long time. Only one brother left and he's a ne'er-do-well. And I have the boy here to help."

"You should be careful. With Lou gone... the Sioux might want the boy back."

"He's Lou's son and now mine. They'll have to take him o'er me body if they want him back. I'm a good shot, besides."

"Maybe you should have your brother come out here. I could take him a letter on my way back." Kit didn't like the sound of affection in Daniel's voice.

"I wouldn't know where to send it, Danny. He's hardly in one place long enough." Then, her voice changed. Kit realized, with chagrin, that Jenny was directing her next comments at her. "Miss, if you'd like to buy that book you're reading for free, it'll cost you five cents."

Kit reddened and closed the book, replacing it on the shelf. "No, thank you, ma'am. I'm sorry to be an inconvenience." When she turned and looked at Jenny and Daniel, Daniel had a large grin on his face.

"Kit Austen, this is Jenny McGrath, formerly Jenny Kildaire." Jenny smiled too and held out her hand.

"Sorry to be troubling you, Miss Austen."

Kit shook her hand. The grip was firm and strong. Looking her full in the face, Kit saw that Jenny had an open, natural womanliness despite her large stature and aggressive ways. At the neckline of her green dress was a lacy scarf, secured with a tiny gold shamrock pin, just barely large enough to see in the sudsy lace, hardly larger than a child's fingernail. Her eyes danced with mischief as she looked Kit over, and Kit caught a whiff of a vanilla-scent in the air. Even out here in this rough frontier, Jenny found ways to stay feminine.

"No trouble. I'm afraid I became engrossed and didn't realize I was taking up so much time. Perhaps someone else is interested in the book."

"You're from Boston then!" Jenny said in delighted surprise. "I'd recognize that accent anywhere."

"Why, yes... I... I lived in Boston." She tensed, trying to remember what, if anything, she'd told Daniel about her past with her "brother."

"Did you know any of the Kildaires while you were there? My family were shopkeepers. My brother Francis is still roamin' around there somewhere. He ran the 'Eagle's Crown' for a short time."

Kit recognized the name. It was a tavern on the outskirts of town that had a decent reputation, unlike some of the other taverns where one was likely to meet up with unsavory characters. Her father had told her as much. He had visited the tavern himself on occasion to "hear the political gossip," he had told her. She suspected it was to enjoy the camaraderie of other men.

"I'm afraid I don't know any of your family," Kit said. At least that was the truth. She didn't know the Kildaires. Only their tavern.

"Austen, Austen... " Jenny repeated, her mouth twisted as she thought. "Did you have a sister named Ruth?"

"No," Kit said, offering no more information. But Daniel provided some for her.

"She has a brother named Seth, should have come through here not too long ago. She's supposed to meet him at Fort Laramie." As he went on to describe the fictional Seth, Jenny repeatedly shook her head back and forth.

"No, haven't seen a soul like that," she replied.

Kit wanted to leave the house as soon as possible. She didn't need to be reminded of her lie or have Daniel lie for her.

"But then again, not everyone who takes this trail stops in here to see ol' Jenny and her stepson. Some folks would be wantin' to avoid contact along the trail."

"Her brother's a fur trader," Daniel added. "Might have come in with some goods to sell."

"No, no fur traders. I'd remember that." As she thought, she supported one elbow with one hand and held her chin with the other. Kit just wanted to get out before Jenny expressed any more opinions on who was on the trail and who wasn't.

"Wait a minute," Jenny said. "Does your brother have a little scar just the size of a buttonhole on his right cheekbone?"

Kit had based Seth's description on her father. Her father had had such a scar, acquired in a youthful hunting accident. "Yes," she stammered slowly, not knowing what to say.

"Then, I haven't seen him here, but a man by that description was a visitor to the Eagle back in Boston when I was a young girl. Never forget a face, especially one with character. 'Twas an older man, though, a jolly fellow with a good humor. Widowed with one daughter....he was proud of her. His name was... Perriwinkle... Penwether. That's it! Penwether."

Kit's face flamed and her eyes began to well up as Jenny Kildaire McGrath, hundreds of miles from Boston, described her father to her, her gentle kind-hearted father. This rough woman with her loud ways had seen her father when she was a child and remembered him. He must have been an impressive figure back then, to leave a memory with a feisty young girl who would fight her way through the world on her own. And here was that girl, full grown, telling Kit that her father had been proud of her when she was younger. Would he be proud of her now?

"... but then I left the city and met up with Louis and who knows what happened to the man and his little girl.

But I never forget a face. You're sure 'tweren't your older brother?"

"No," Kit said, clearing her throat. "No. Seth is younger... I'm sorry. I think I need to get back... to Mary. I promised I would... I would read to her...." She muttered more excuses and practically dashed out of the house, feeling as if she were escaping the clutches of her past.

THEY STAYED at the trading post through the midday meal. During that entire time, Daniel remained in the house with Jenny and her stepson. Kit kept looking over at the door, so often that Wilhemina asked her if she was thinking of making a purchase. "You keep staring at the place as if you've left something in there that you wanted," the woman said. But Kit told her no, it was only a book she had looked at, and it wasn't that interesting anyway.

Shortly after that, Daniel reappeared, but he didn't saddle up to lead them out. Instead, he talked with Josephus for a long time, pointing in the distance and nodding his head. The wagon train was getting ready to leave. The teams were being hitched, the cooking items stowed away. Daniel walked past her wagon as she sat, ready to move out.

"You'd better hurry," she called out to him in as lighthearted a tone as she could manage. "Or you'll be the one holding us back!"

"No, I'm not going," he said, looking up at her and squinting in the sun.

Her heart sank, and despite herself, she let out an involuntary sigh.

"I'm staying behind for the evening. Jenny needs some help with putting up a corral. I'll get the boy started on it and meet up with the train in Laramie tomorrow. Josephus will lead the way. You'll be in the best of hands, ma'am." He touched his hat, said nothing more, and moved on.

Kit watched him go. Jenny was standing in the doorway of the trading post waving to some of the travelers. A few diggers were also staying behind to use the forge, and they waved as well. Kit watched as Daniel joined up with Jenny, and they talked with each other, sharing the intimacy of the road, of fellow-wanderers.

The wagon ahead was rolling. Kit clicked and snapped her reins so her team started to move. Just as well, she forced herself to think. Just as well, just as well. *This is a blessing, removing temptation from my path. And I need all the help I can get now.*

DANIEL HAD LOOKED forward to the stop at the trading post as a respite from the torture of being near Kit. Ever since their kiss by the campfire, ever since she had told him she was promised to another, he had felt like a part of himself had been cut out. A hollow ache was left in its place, made worse every time he saw her neat little figure, or smelled her perfumed hair, or heard her pure voice in the night air. Kit Austen haunted him, even appearing in his dreams, just out of reach, or worse still, in his embrace.

The stay at the trading post was like water after a trek across the desert. Jenny was an old friend. He had often stayed with her and her late husband Louis on his journeys west, enjoying a night of storytelling and good company before hitting the hard trail in the morning.

Now he just wanted the comfort of an old friend who knew him well and would help him break free of his thoughts of Kit Austen.

"You know, my friend," Jenny said to him as soon as the last wagon had passed out of view and the other stay-behinds were at the forge. "I am not blind." She led him into the house and went to a cupboard in the back room.

"Don't be bringing me any whiskey, Jenny," he called after her. "My drinking days are over."

Jenny returned empty-handed, raised an eyebrow and set a coffee pot on to boil instead.

"Tell me about her," she said, her back to the room.

"Don't know what you mean, Jenny. I'm just working the trail like I always did. Maybe a little tired. Maybe I need to settle down in one of those valleys near Monterey."

Jenny laughed, a full-throated chortle. "Settle down? Why this must be serious for you to talk about settlin' down, boy. What kind of potion did she use on you? I've never seen you like this."

"You're wrong, Jenny. I'm just... tired. That's all."

"Tired of being alone, that's my guess. Don't think I didn't see the way you looked at her. You've been alone nigh seven years now. It's no surprise you'd be looking at a girl like that as one to settle with."

"There's something about her," he said. "Different from other girls. She's been hurt in some way and I don't know how. She's hiding something. Something deep. She's promised to someone... I can't bear to think of another man...." He broke off and looked down.

"You've got it bad, Danny," Jenny said in consolation. "Worse than I thought. You've got to do something about it."

"What's that?" Daniel looked up, hopeful for an answer.

"Kill her!" At Daniel's shocked look, Jenny laughed again, a hearty cackle that reverberated in the small room. "No, no. But you need to kill that longing in you or you'll just drive yourself crazy. There's only two things to be done. One is you go after her, promised or not. You make her forget the spineless digger she's hooked her wagon to and you don't stop until she's decided she can't have anyone but you."

"What's the other thing?" Daniel asked. "You said there were two things."

"The other is you find another woman," said Jenny, her voice lower and gentler, taking on a serious tone that Daniel had never heard before. "You find a decent woman who is willing to make life grand for you, who will provide for all your needs, who knows how to make a good man happy, who can make even the most committed wanderer want to settle down."

She was talking about herself, of course. She had done the same for old Louie McGrath—a company captain just like Daniel—who'd met Jenny on a trip home to see his mother. He had brought Jenny west with the intention of taking her all the way to California, but they had settled at the trading post and Jenny had helped raise his son from a previous marriage to an Indian squaw who had died in childbirth.

Jenny came over to Daniel and rested her hand on his shoulder. He knew that if he wanted her, she would do anything for him. He took her hand and gently patted it, then let it go. She knew he was turning her down.

"You're a poor lad, Danny. I don't know if I have any medicine for your sickness."

Chapter Ten

THE NEXT MORNING, Kit felt as if a hundred butterflies were swirling around in her stomach. It was hazy and warm when she awoke and she made breakfast with a distracted air, forgetting to put water in the coffee pot and nearly burning the flapjacks. Wilhemina went back to her wagon right after the meal, complaining of a stomach upset. Josephus looked after her, concern coloring his face. He'd slept near Kit's wagon that night after the afternoon's ride to the fort, instructed by Daniel to keep watch.

"She slept poorly," Josephus said of Wilhemina.

"I'll look after her today," promised Kit, pouring maple syrup on Mary's flapjack.

"That's kind of you, Miss Austen, but I know you'll be wanting to get into the Fort."

"No, really. There's nothing for me to do there. I'll stay with Willa."

"But what about your brother? He'll be looking for you," Josephus said.

"Oh. Oh, that's right. Yes, my brother. Well, I'm sure it won't take long... to find him, that is. I can come back and look after Willa then," she said. She was so distracted with thoughts of Daniel that she had forgotten the role she needed to play today, the charade she had to enact.

She cleaned up quickly and helped Mary braid her hair, teaching the girl how to divide the strands evenly and hold them taut while she wove them together. Every few moments, she scanned the horizon behind them. She mentally calculated how long it would take to make the trip from the trading post to the Fort on horseback without a slow wagon train to hold him back. He could be rejoining them as soon as mid-morning, she thought. After fastening a bright ribbon in Mary's hair, Kit got up and dusted herself off.

"Well, I have chores to tend to. You need to look after your mother, little one," she said, bending down to Mary. "She's feeling poorly."

"Oh, Kit, let me braid your hair, please, please! I promise I'll take care of Mama after that!"

Kit smiled. How could she resist? It wasn't as if her brother really was waiting for her at the Fort. She meekly sat down on an overturned crate and let Mary work with her hair. It took her a long time to get it right and she prattled on about all the wonders of the ride west and what she hoped to find there.

"Papa says I'll grow up and find a husband just like Mama did," Mary said in her singsong voice. "He says I'll find someone just like Mister Daniel. I like Mister Daniel, don't you, Kit?"

"Yes, I do," Kit said.

"Mama says she thinks Mister Daniel is a good man. She says she thinks he will find a lady to be sweet on and get married."

"That's nice, Mary."

"Who do you think he'll marry, Kit? Do you think he'll marry me? Or maybe he'll marry you. That would be nice. I could come to your wedding. Would you let me, Kit?"

Kit blushed as the girl's fingers separated and pulled at her hair.

"Oh, I don't think I'll be marrying anyone anytime soon," she managed to say. "I... I need to find my brother and settle into teaching."

"Mama says you'll probably marry somebody and make a fine mother. She says she doesn't think you'll be teaching long."

So Daniel had not spoken of her being promised to another man.

Kit smiled as Mary revealed her mother's thoughts to her. But it was an empty smile, filled as much with pain as with pleasure. No marriage and no children of her own—that was what Kit's future held for her. *But it's the penance I have to do for all these lies, and for abandoning my marriage, even if it had been to a cruel man.*

"Your mother is a fine woman. She's a great mother. She's going to need lots of help when her new one comes along. Do you want a brother or a sister?" Kit deftly changed the subject, and Mary happily chattered on about the value of having a sister over a brother. When she was finished, Kit felt her hair and was pleased. She had taught Mary well. Her hair was in a tight braid down her back. She reached behind her and looped it up and around into a bun that she secured with heavy hair pins.

"Oh, that looks beautiful, Kit! You look just like a princess!"

"Thank you, sweetheart. Now, you run along. I have to go into the Fort. To meet my brother."

The little girl ran off and Kit sighed heavily. No sight of Daniel. It was just as well, she thought. Now she could head into the fort on her own and play out her charade in private. She stepped into her wagon and opened her trunk to retrieve the latest note she had scrawled. This time, she had been careful not to hide it among her scented sachets. This time, she would remember to rub some hay over it to give it an earthy, manly scent.

As she stepped down from the wagon, she was startled to run into Billy Crane.

"Oh!" she said, moving back, her pulse racing. Where was Daniel?

"Good morning, Miss Austen," he said in a gravelly voice, his breath scented with whiskey. "Going into the fort, are you?"

"Yes, I am," she said. He stood so close to her that there was no room to maneuver past him.

"Mind if I escort you? I'm going that way too."

"No. I mean, yes, I do mind. I'd prefer to walk alone... or with Mrs. Kessler. I have to... I'm going to meet my brother Seth. He would be upset if he saw me with a man. He's mighty protective."

Bill Crane laughed. "Oh, he would, would he? Well, I wouldn't want that. Wouldn't want to upset any feller of yours."

"He's not my 'feller,'" she said defiantly.

"Whatever you say, ma'am. What's that you got there, a love note?" He pointed to the folded letter she had in her hand.

"No," she said, gripping it tighter. "It's a letter... a letter to my old school teacher," she said quickly, hating this new lie. "I really must go."

Esther's voice called out to her from down the line of wagons.

"Kit, I'll be walking into the fort with you. Mr. Crane, I suggest you go see to your brother. He looked like he needed help with the wagon."

Kit broke free, pushing past his arm, hurrying toward Esther.

Arm linked through Esther's, Kit made her way to the Fort.

"You don't have to come with me, Esther," Kit said. "I don't want you part of this. It's bad enough that I—"

"Hush now. As far as I'm concerned, this is the first step toward telling the truth. And if you thought I'd leave you to fend for yourself with that Billy Crane, then you have seriously misjudged me!" She patted Kit's hand.

Kit laughed. "I'm so glad I met you, Esther." But then she turned serious. "I really don't want you helping me with this deception. It's not right."

"No, Kit, it isn't right. But you'll make it so. What was your plan today anyway?"

Kit sighed. "The same as before—find a letter from Seth telling me to press on."

Now Esther was the one laughing. "That's such a poor lie, dear. I'm sure Mr. Winchester will see through it!"

"You're not suggesting I come up with another one, are you?" Kit could hardly believe her ears. A minister's wife counseling her on how best to lie?

"No, no, not at all. Just the opposite. I suggest you tell Mr. Winchester you found nothing—no brother, no letter. That is the truth and no lie."

Kit thought about this. Esther was right. No letter was just as good as her made-up one. No letter and no Seth would just mean she hadn't located him. She wouldn't have to lie again, and soon she could tell the whole truth.

She turned to Esther, giving her arm a little squeeze. "Thank you, Esther. You're right."

She stopped, pulled the letter from her pocket and ripped it to shreds.

"There," she said, letting the tiny pieces fall into her woven bag. "From this moment forward, no more lying!"

"And how do you feel?" Esther asked, smiling.

"Wonderful!"

The two women resumed walking, linking arms once again.

FORT LARAMIE HAD MORE to offer than Fort Kearney. It was a wonder, in fact, to come across so many people and such a town-like atmosphere so far into the frontier. A store bustling with clerks and customers sold lemon syrup, cans of preserved quince, bottles of ink, soda powder, candy, even hams and dried fruit. Kit and Esther had a pleasant wander around the fort and its stores, and she could say with honesty that she'd looked all over and her brother was nowhere to be found.

As she and Esther rounded a corner by the postmaster's office, she stopped.

To her dismay, Billy Crane was there. He was leaning against the back wall, a sprig of hay in his mouth, his eyes half closed in the midday heat. Dozens of emigrants were waiting to send news home, and some spilled out onto the walk.

"Find him?" Billy said to her without moving a muscle.

Esther spoke. "Find who, Mr. Crane?"

"Her brother." He pointed to Kit. "And she's got some letter to post. To her old school marm, right?" He didn't remove the straw when he spoke.

Kit looked down. The pieces of that letter were in her bag. "I... I already took care of that, Mr. Crane."

"That's funny. I didn't see you 'round here any time today."

Esther laughed. "You mean to say you've spent all this time just dawdling here? I find that hard to believe, Mr. Crane. And I'm sure your brother will, too, if he's sent you to the fort for supplies."

Billy straightened at the mention of his brother. "I can fetch what I need in no time."

"Then you might want to be on your way," Esther said, gazing at him steadily. "Time's awasting an we'll be..."

She stopped speaking and they both turned their heads as a commotion sounded on the walkway behind them. A woman had fainted—Wilhemina!

"Oh, dear!" Kit said, letting go of Esther's arm and hurrying to help. Esther followed.

Wilhemina Barton lay sprawled on the wooden walkway, her daughter Mary holding her hand and sobbing uncontrollably. "Mama, Mama," she cried, rocking back and forth on her heels. *No wonder she fainted,* thought Kit as she pushed through the crowd. The heat was oppressive.

"Get back!" Kit shouted. She and Esther knelt by Willa's head. Kit felt her skin. It was clammy and cool. "We need to get her some water."

Esther agreed. "I'll go." She raced to a nearby store.

Kit turned to Mary. "Go fetch your father, child. Go ahead and run. Tell him your mama's fainted and needs to be carried back to the wagons."

Esther reappeared carrying a pitcher of water and a cup. Kit poured some and held it to Willa's lips as the woman stirred.

"Here you go, Willa. Drink up. You're dry as a bone. Come on." She braced the woman's head and shoulders against her bosom and helped her drink the water. As soon as she did so, some color started to return to Willa's cheeks.

"Oh dear," she said weakly. "I shouldn't have gone out in the heat. But Mary wanted to... "

"Don't talk now," Esther said, looking worriedly at Kit.

"Josephus is coming," Kit told Willa.

By the time Josephus arrived, Willa was able to sit up by herself, and the crowd had dispersed. His face a mask of worry, he immediately thanked Kit.

"Good thing you were nearby. We owe you our gratitude."

"No, no. Esther was here, too. And I owe you," Kit said, "For taking me on with you. You see, I... I haven't found Seth yet."

"No matter, Miss Austen. Let's get Wilhemina back to the wagon now. I'll help you find your brother later," Josephus said and stood, taking his wife's arm and looping it over his shoulder. Kit went to the other side and did the same, while Esther held Mary's hand. As they straggled out of the Fort, Kit noticed that Billy Crane had disappeared from view.

BECAUSE OF WILLA'S fainting spell, they stayed in camp all day. They had originally intended to leave in the afternoon and get in a good six hours of traveling before settling down for the night. But with Daniel nowhere to be seen and Josephus consumed with concern for his wife, there was little they could do but wait.

This did not sit at all well with other members of the company, especially the Cranes and, to a lesser degree, the Culpeppers and other diggers eager to get at

California's gold. At a meeting in the early afternoon, they complained about the delay and urged the group to move forward.

"I can take the lead," Billy boasted. "I know the trail."

Josephus just stared at him at first, then spoke. "How do you know the trail, Billy?"

"I've read Fremont's book, talked with some folks in the Fort."

"It's not the same thing," Josephus said. "There are treacherous decisions up ahead. Choices that could lead to death if the wrong way is taken. Daniel said he'd be back in time to lead us. He intended us to have a goodly stay at the fort."

"I can follow the markings," Billy argued. "There are plenty of them." He was referring to the many warnings and messages posted by previous emmigres on landmarks and trees.

"No. I vote against it," Josephus said firmly. The Culpepper boys nodded their heads in agreement, a little reluctantly in the case of Ira. "We can leave at first light," Josephus added.

No one spoke for a few moments, then Paul Culpepper chimed in. "Even if Winchester's not here?"

"Yes," Josephus said.

THE SUN WAS at a long, low angle to the earth, cutting across the plains like a brilliant dagger. Kit finished up the last of the mess' cleaning and promised Mary a song after she "tidied up her wagon." She stepped inside and found the old gun that had once belonged to her father. Checking to make sure it was loaded, she set it under her blanket, near her pillow. Then she came out into the blinding light again.

"Too bad your brother's not here," Billy Crane said from around the corner of her wagon. She shivered, glad that she had put the gun where she could reach it at night. "He could probably have led us through. Probably has the right amount of experience on the trails, being a trader and all."

"I suppose," she said.

"Where is he this time, Miss Austen?"

"I... don't know. Probably on to Sweetwater," she said.

Billy laughed.

"Not much of a brother, now, is he? Always leaving you behind? What kind of man treats his flesh and blood that way?"He spat into the ground and walked away.

Kit was glad to see him go and gladder still that she had thought to bring her father's gun.

Even so, she would prefer Daniel's calming presence to any weapon. Maybe he wouldn't come back. Maybe that Jenny woman had enticed him to stay. No—he'd not abandon them. He'd return. Surely he would return.

She waited a long time that night before getting ready to get in her wagon. It was still warm and the sky was lustrous once again. As the campfires died down and the noise of the company lessened, she decided to give up her watch and head for her bedding. She had one foot on the backboard, ready to hoist herself in, when she heard it, the clippety-clop of horses nearing the train. She turned and, in the distance, could make out a dark shadow on the horizon. Relief flooded through her. It was him. Soon other figures appeared, the travelers who'd stayed to use the forge. She waited until he was close by and called his name.

"Mr. Winchester! Welcome back!"

"Good to be back, ma'am," he said, touching his hat.

As his hand reached up to the brown brim, the moonlight caught a shimmer of something gold on the rim. Kit focused on it. With a sinking heart, she recognized it as the tiny golden shamrock that had previously adorned Jenny Kildaire McGrath's lace.

Chapter Eleven

The Black Hills and Beyond

FOR A WHILE, THE TREK was easier. Grazing was good and fresh water was plentiful. The company was at peace as each day passed into the next, the sky more often blue than gray, the air more often warm than sultry.

The landscape changed from high plains to steep inclines as they traveled near the Black Hills, and the double threat of Indians and cholera miraculously disappeared in the cooler air of the higher elevation. Pines and junipers were scattered among the hills, and larkspurs decorated the slopes. Danger seemed remote in this idyllic world, yet Kit was nagged by a sense of loss.

Oddly, Daniel did not ask Kit about her brother's non-appearance. In fact, he continued to keep his distance from her. While she had feared his questions in the past, now she was hurt by his lack of interest. Jenny must be the woman on his mind now, Kit thought. The golden shamrock still gleamed in his hat band, a constant reminder that he had quickly replaced Kit in his heart with another.

Kit's heart was not so easily mended. Inexperienced in love before Josiah, she could not easily shake her affection for the tall, quiet man who always guarded her wagon, despite his new emotional distance from her. She kept reminding herself that when they got to California, she would start a new life and be able to forget him, and that she should focus on atoning for her lies at the first opportunity.

In the weeks after leaving Fort Laramie, the journey eased. Each evening, she gathered with her friends the Bartons, Kesslers and the Culpeppers and some diggers who had joined their group. They would sit around the fire, made from scrub timber, and tell stories or sing songs. Josephus turned out to be quite a good story-teller, more often than not telling tales with morals to them, but gentle stories nonetheless. One of the diggers had a fiddle and was convinced to play it from time to time. After overcoming an initial shyness, he enlivened many an evening with jigs and ballads and reels. Mary would sometimes pull Kit to her feet to dance, and the rest of the group, Wilhemina included, would clap their hands in time as the two girls twirled and stomped.

IT WAS, FOR two weeks, more like a holiday trip than a risky journey across the country.

She'd told Esther she would tell Daniel about her past once they'd crossed the North Platte, a different, more treacherous stretch of water than the fork they had crossed earlier. Once across the Platte, she felt sure he wouldn't send her back. Esther reluctantly agreed.

There would be no blocking up the wagon beds and rolling them through the waters this time. The river was too deep. They would secure the wagons to ferries and let the animals swim across. Because of Daniel's good planning, they arrived at the river the evening before the crossing. This would give them an entire day to get every wagon across, a slow process with only a few ferries to take them.

A group of men had a lucrative ferrying business going and no amount of bargaining would bring their price down from three dollars a wagon and fifty cents a man.

When the ferry boat men refused to lower their fares, some of the men on the train wanted to chop down cottonwoods and string them together making their own crafts. One of them, a lanky digger from Maryland, said he had put together many a makeshift craft to go "oysterin'" on the Chesapeake Bay. Looking at the wide expanse of water before them and remembering how even the relatively-safe crossing of the shallower Platte had been risky, Kit was glad the majority overruled the young man. So, after a fair of amount of grumbling among the travelers, the fees were collected and plans were made to cross.

It would take a good part of the day to ferry all the wagons in the train across, and it would require everyone's energy and concentration. On the other side of the river, the land rose in high bluffs. This would make for slow going once the crossing was achieved, and Daniel advised them on the best route up the bluffs, at an angle, so those who reached the other side first could commence moving forward immediately without waiting for the rest.

Unlike their previous crossing, the weather was fair on the morning they were to make it over the North Platte. Some high clouds blocked out the sun from time to time, but no rain appeared likely. It seemed like a good day, and the river, though wide, appeared calm and flat. Even so, Daniel was firm in giving instructions and warnings about the crossing.

"The animals might want to turn back or head downstream," he said, looking at Kit. "We'll try to keep them turned toward the shore as best we can. When you're on the ferry, be sure to stay in place. Capsizing in these waters is certain death."

From group to group, he repeated his warnings until they were all adequately prepared for the move over the water.

Kit was to board a ferry with Wilhemina, Mary and Josephus. This time they were not the first ones to cross. The Kesslers were in front, due to the rotation of the wagons, followed by the Gilmets, the Carrolls, and then some diggers. She and the Bartons would go right before the Crane brothers.

She watched as the first ferries moved across without incident. The boatmen's muscles strained as they held the ferries in place using huge poles that dug into the river bottom. When the water proved too deep for these, they resorted to large oars set on the side of each ferry. They were breathing hard after each excursion, belying the calm-looking face of the river.

By the time her turn arrived, Kit felt no fear as she set foot on the rocking ferry. She had been through a tough crossing already. On this one she was merely a passenger. But looking down the river, she noticed it was filled with whitecaps farther along, rushing and gurgling with a speed that the other river could not match. Daniel came up to them and checked all the ropes securing their wagons to the ferry.

"She's tethered fine," said one of the lanky, bearded ferryman. "No need to worry."

Daniel looked at Kit. "Keep the girl close to you," he said. "And stay near the wagon, away from the edge."

The ferryman gave a shove off with his pole, pushed again and again, and they were riding into the swirling mass of water. Kit watched the shoreline recede as they plunged ahead, the water starting to make an awful rush the farther they moved into its wide path. She saw Daniel watching her from the shore, a look of concern on his face, but reminded herself he would be just as worried about other members of the company.

As their ferry made its way across, their animals started to enter the stream. Daniel patted the teams on the rear and nudged them to the river. Kit saw her team, then the Bartons', step into the water. She held her breath for an instant as they bellowed, wondering if they'd hold true to the course. To her relief, they did. They started swimming as soon as the water got too deep for a foothold, and they followed her ferry like ducklings after their mother.

Then the Cranes moved up leading their beasts into the water, Billy and his brother Peter pulling and pushing the oxen and mules against their will. Billy pulled out a whip and cruelly lashed the huge oxen across the rump, calling them to get moving. Kit saw his brother Peter say something to him but couldn't make out the words. He looked angry, and Billy put the whip down.

As the animals started to swim, their eyes took on the same glassy, frightened look Kit remembered from her own team. The Cranes then jumped on the next ferry to maneuver across while their animals swam, so they could keep an eye on their progress.

Peter Crane was very tall, with spindly legs and arms and sunken face. He kept to himself most of the time and Kit often wondered if he was different from his brother in other ways as well. At the Kessler prayer services, Peter would often sit in the back, and sometimes not stay for the full sermon. When he boarded the ferry, he kept staring at the animals, as if he was willing them to follow. Kit remembered what that felt like. She had a certain amount of sympathy for the man.

All went well. Kit's ferry moved forward, the animals moved forward, the other ferry followed at a good pace. It looked as if everyone and everything would reach the far shore unscathed. Kit held on to Mary with both arms looped over the young girl's shoulders. But she couldn't keep her from wriggling and straining to look downstream at the turbulent water.

Midstream, Kit's ferry dipped precariously into the water, its forward left corner plunging under with a thud, as if they had struck something. The ferryman shouted out, "A buried root. Been a lot of rain. Trees uprooted." And then he went to work freeing them from the encumbrance.

But Kit noticed Mary shaking and starting to cry. Kit knelt down to comfort her. "It's all right, sweet one. The ferry man has done this many times before. We're almost over... "

Yet another drama began to play out behind them. The animals so cruelly beaten by Billy Crane were not eager to follow their master anywhere, let alone across a raging torrent of water. They started to turn downstream. Billy swore at them, his curses even carrying across the rushing water to the Bartons' ferry. His brother Peter, however, just shook his head, giving Billy a glare of frustration and contempt. Then, he took off his shoes... and jumped into the water.

"Peter, don't!" shouted Daniel from the shore.

Mary, now more frightened than before, let out a shriek that pierced the air. Kit bent to comfort her, but her gaze was distracted by a figure on the shore, getting ready to jump in the river—Daniel!

DANIEL COULDN'T see Peter's head, and didn't know where he was, leaving him no choice but to go after him. He leapt down from his horse and dove in.

The North Platte, fed by melting snow, kept its frigid temperature even in the height of summer. In early summer, such as was the case now, it pierced a man's skin like a thousand needles. Daniel gasped from the sensation but kept swimming forward through the melee of rushing water, swimming animals, and frightened passengers. He could see Peter's head now bobbing in the distance as the man tugged his animals forward and not down river. Daniel could also make out Kit and Mary in an embrace. They were safe. He headed for the Crane boy as fast as his arms would carry him.

As he neared the thrashing scene, he saw Peter go under. He knew from past experience what could happen on these crossings when men jumped in to steer their animals. Overcome by fatigue and numb from the cold, they would lose control of their limbs and soon be lost, their bodies never to be recovered. But Peter was surfacing. Daniel found himself sending a prayer up to help him rescue the man. Daniel swam harder, faster. His blood throbbed through his veins and his lungs screamed for air as he made his way to him.

"Hold on, Peter! I'm coming!" The ferry had pushed ahead, leaving the two men and the distraught animals alone in the swirling river. To Daniel's horror, he noticed that Peter wasn't moving of his own volition. He was floating lazily in the water, an odd sight given all the other movement. It was as if Peter had decided to take a leisurely bath and enjoy the river. Then Daniel noticed Peter's head. Blood was pouring out of a wide gash near his hairline, the red liquid matting the man's hair and mingling with the muddy water. He had been kicked by one of the oxen and now was unconscious in the stream. Daniel fought the current and the cold and made his way to him, catching him by the scruff of the neck.

"Peter! Peter?" he cried, but got no response. While he tread water, he checked the man's senses. He could feel no breath and no heartbeat, but he couldn't be sure in this water, so he hooked his arm around the man's chest and dragged him with him as he swam forward.

It was hard going and he didn't know if he could make it to shore. He heard Kit's voice on the ferry up ahead, urging the ferryman to turn back and help.

"No!" he shouted to them. "Keep moving!"

But he saw her shake her head, and soon Josephus was working with the ferryman to reverse their course.

In a few moments' time, their ferry was beside him. Good thing it was, for his arms were numb and he was near exhaustion.

With Josephus, Kit leaned over the side of the ferry to pull in Peter and Daniel.

"I think he's gone," Daniel sputtered between gasping breaths. No one else spoke as they dragged the icy men onto the raft. Daniel lay panting on the wooden timbers, his lips blue and his skin white from the frozen waters. Peter Crane was motionless. His chest didn't move. Nor did his eyelids. He stared glassily up at the sun until Josephus had the good sense to close his lids.

He was dead. They all knew it even though no one said it.

As they moved toward the other shore again, Kit retrieved a blanket from her wagon and wrapped it over Daniel's shaking body.

"Now you're the one freezing. Here, let me help you," she said. As her hands tended to him, they started to shake too, and he realized it was because she had experienced what he had felt when he'd seen her in the river weeks ago—she'd been afraid for his life. His hand, like a block of ice, reached up and grabbed her arm.

"Thank you," he said, "ma'am."

"Don't talk," she said. "We'll be ashore soon."

Their ferry took on the air of a funeral procession. All were silent as they neared the shore. Before they could even say a word, their somber faces gave away the truth. Billy Crane, whose ferry had arrived, stood with arms crossed over his chest, his face a mask of grief and rage, didn't need to be told. One look at his brother's icy body told the tale. He and the Rev. Kessler came to pull Peter Crane's body off the boat. Gloom descended on them all.

Billy knelt by his brother's body and pulled at his shirt as if it would revive him. He listened to his chest as an afterthought, wondering if the others could be wrong. No one stopped him. The animals that had made it to shore then caught his attention and he grabbed his whip to go after them, striking them with such fierceness that Daniel stepped in to remove the whip from his hand.

"The Lord giveth and the Lord taketh away," Rev. Kessler intoned. "Blessed be the Lord." Someone in the gathering crowd murmured "Amen."

Billy was unwilling to let it be.

"No!" He shouted, turning on Daniel. "The Lord didn't take Peter. *You* took him!" He pointed an angry finger of accusation at Daniel. "You could have saved him!" he said through gritted teeth. "But you were too moon-eyed over your whore there to pay no notice!"

Despite his weakened state, Daniel pulled away to go after Billy.

"Watch your words, boy," Daniel said, tired and low. He took a step forward.

Josephus stopped him. "He's crazy with grief. Pay him no mind. You neither, Miss Austen."

Reverend Kessler played the same role with Billy, stepping up to him and leading him away, talking to him softly under his breath. Whatever he said seemed to calm Billy, but Kit wasn't sure the young man's anger was completely gone. As the crowd dispersed, she looked over her shoulder at the bereaved man. He was shaking his head back and forth as Rev. Kessler comforted him. Kit shivered.

After all the wagons were up the bluff, they buried Peter Crane. They chose a spot near the banks of the river, under a lone tree whose branches spread out like a huge canopy. It was a peaceful place, a stark contrast to the tumult that had surrounded Peter's death.

All the men joined in to dig the grave. When it was finished, the entire company gathered and Rev. Kessler conducted the service. He read the Twenty-third psalm and a passage from the Book of Revelations, then preached a short sermon about a just and merciful God. They then sang a hymn—My Shepherd Will Supply My Need. When the service was over, they all went back to their wagons in silence, their spirits low.

As they walked back to their own encampments, Josephus talked to Daniel.

"You did all you could," Josephus said to him. "I saw a dozen men drown the last time I came west. It's a treacherous crossing."

Daniel said nothing. He pulled his hat a little lower to shade his eyes. Just as they were nearing their wagons, Billy Crane came up from behind. He pulled on Daniel's shoulder, twirling him around to face him.

"I meant what I said," he growled at Daniel. "My brother would be alive right now if you had been doing your duty."

Josephus stepped forward. "Son, we know you're hurtin'. But all eyes could see that it was Daniel who jumped in the water the second he saw your brother needed help."

"That ain't the way I seen it. And it ain't the way some others seen it neither. They saw Daniel making eyes at that...." He pointed to Kit, but before he could spit out the word he wanted to use, Josephus stopped him.

"Halt it right there, boy. Miss Austen's a good woman. No use in insulting her."

"Whatever she is, he was more interested in seeing her safely across than he was in lookin' out for the rest of the party," Billy said. "He should have stopped Peter from trying to take on those animals. He should have done it himself."

"I'm sorry about your brother, Billy," Daniel said in a sad, slow voice.

"You should be more than sorry. You should pay for what happened!"

Chapter Twelve

AFTER PETER'S BURIAL, the company paused for a day of rest. Rev. Kessler held another special prayer service in the morning, and there was no laughing or singing that night. Esther didn't say much to Kit as they worked on the mess that night, and it wasn't just because of Peter Crane's death.

"You have to tell him, dear," Esther said, drying a plate. "We're past the point he could send you back."

"He hasn't paid much mind to me since Fort Laramie," Kit said.

Esther turned to her. "God pays mind," she said. "You know you have to tell Mr. Winchester the truth—not for his sake, but for your own."

They went back to cleaning, and after she dried the last plate, Esther embraced Kit and kissed her on the cheek. Holding both her hands in front of her, she said, "Be of good faith. The Lord will lead you to the right words. Call on me and the Reverend should you find yourself faltering."

Kit smiled and said thank-you, then watched Esther walk back to her own wagon.

Esther was right. It didn't matter if Daniel cared enough to keep her on the train or send her back. She had to tell him she'd been lying. She'd thought about it a long time in those days since they'd left Fort Laramie. She'd gone over and over how to tell him the truth. And she kept putting it off until the next day. There was no point in prolonging the agony.

Kit took a deep breath and looked around. Daniel had not lingered after dinner, which he'd spent with them that night, wandering off to check on some traveler's wagon. She listened carefully and heard his voice.

She followed it along the wagons until she came to the Culpeppers' outfit. Daniel was bent low over the rear wheel, looking over some spokes that appeared damaged. After exchanging some words with the Culpeppers about possible fixes, he turned to go, surprised to see her standing there.

"May I have a word with you, Mr. Winchester?" she asked, her voice already trembling.

He looked at her, then at the Culpeppers. Nodding his farewell to them, he said, "Of course," and walked with her toward her wagon.

The campfire was still lit, and no one was about, so she pointed to the bench still left out from supper.

"I need to talk to you about... about a woman I once knew," she began, not looking at him. Her breath came fast, making speech difficult. This was harder than she'd imagined—not because she feared him sending her back any longer, but because she was afraid of what he'd think of her once he knew she'd been deceiving him.

She had decided that the best way to calmly tell the story was to treat it as if it really were a story, one she told to Mary in the evenings about someone else, not herself. Someone far away.

He said nothing, so she continued.

"This woman was dearly loved by her father. She had no experience of the world and thought that all men would be like him—kind and generous and, above all, loving."

She inhaled deeply.

"And she... she made a bad choice. When a man asked her for her hand in marriage, she assumed that this man loved her as much as her father had. She thought he would take care of her as her father had, and cherish her and... and..." She blinked fast to fight off tears.

Daniel looked at her, worry creasing his brow. "And he didn't?"

She shook her head. "No, he didn't. He had married her, you see, thinking that a great part of her father's fortune would be bestowed on them after the wedding. But that didn't happen, so the husband became very angry and he...he..."

Daniel's jaw tightened. His fingers clenched into fists on his legs.

"He treated her very badly," she said at last. "No matter how hard she tried to be a good wife, he found fault with her and..."

"How badly?" he asked, his voice thin and filled with fury. "How badly did he treat her?"

"He... I shouldn't talk of such things..."

"How badly, Kit? Did he kill her—or try to?"

She just nodded. "Tried to."

"Because of the money?"

"Yes, the inheritance."

He let out a snort of disgust and threw a piece of bark into the fire.

"And what did she do?"

"She tried harder to please him, to be a good wife. She kept thinking she'd done something wrong, and she tried to fix it." It was no use. She was crying now. She wiped tears from the corners of her eyes. "But he... he kept beating her and..."

He looked at her again, his own eyes wide with horror and anger. He put his arm around her.

"What did you do then, Kit?" he asked.

The deception was over. He knew. Some wall inside her came tumbling down. Suppressed grief poured out of her, tears streaming down her cheeks, sobs choking her.

"I... left. He was away, and he wrote that he was coming back. And my father was gone then, so I knew..."

"You were scared he'd kill you?"

"Yes. I was... I didn't have the strength to face him. I didn't have the faith..."

He let her cry in his arms. Like Esther, he stroked her hair and cooed to her to calm her. From then on, she didn't need to say any more. He figured out the rest.

"So you decided to head west yourself and lied about a brother to get on this train."

"Yes. I'm so sorry. It caused me much grief to tell such lies, especially to you. You didn't deserve anything but the truth."

"You were afraid I'd send you back if I found out Seth wasn't real."

"That's right." It felt so good to tell him, so good to have him hold her and comfort her.

"And that's why you're spoken for," he added.

"Yes."

He sighed. He kissed the top of her head.

He held her closer, patting her shoulders, stroking her hair while she sobbed away the unhappiness of her past married life and the prospect of her lonely future.

"Sh... sh," he whispered. "It's all right. He can't get you." He swayed back and forth as if she were a child he had to rock to sleep.

"Josiah—that's his name, isn't it? The name you call out at night. Josiah can't find you here, Kit. Not here."

It was as if a huge weight had been lifted from her shoulders. The relief was so overwhelming that she wept from both joy and sadness. The secret she had carried with her had burdened her almost as much as the truth that she ran away from. Now Daniel knew and understood. She twisted her face completely into his shirt, holding onto it and to him as the flood gates of her long sorrow opened.

He continued to comfort her until eventually she calmed down. When the tears no longer came, and she was silent, he still held her in the quiet, dark night. She hugged his side, clinging to him like a child. She felt protected and safe in his arms.

"I didn't want to hurt you," she whimpered.

He touched her chin and moved her glistening face up to his.

"How did you hurt me?"

"I lied to you. I've sinned against you and God."

"No!" His voice rang with harshness. "You are not a sinful woman, Kit Austen. Don't let anyone make you think that. Ever!" He kissed her on her matted hair. "You're a strong and righteous woman."

She wasn't sure how long they sat there, but she felt as if she could have stayed in his warm embrace forever. With her burden lifted, she could look him in the eyes. Finally, she did so, pulling away and sitting up straight.

"My name is not Kit Austen," she whispered. "It is Katherine Penwether Carlisle. Your Jenny must have met my father in a tavern in Boston."

"My Jenny?"

She pointed to his hat beside him with the tiny gold pin Jenny had placed there. He laughed as he looked at it.

"I hadn't realized she'd done that. She and Louie were good friends of mine." He turned back to her. "What shall I call you?"

"Austen was my mother's maiden name, and my father used to call me Kit as a girl."

"Then your name is true."

She nodded. "True enough."

He stood and she followed suit, wiping her eyes with the backs of her hands.

"Thank you for forgiving me. And letting me stay on the trail."

"What will you do in California?"

"I was going to find a school that needed a teacher."

"That shouldn't be hard. I might be able to recommend you to some people."

"The Kesslers have talked of keeping me with them."

"They're good people."

A look of dry pain had entered his eyes. She knew what it signified. It mirrored her own. She loved him. She suspected he loved her. But they weren't free to be together, not as long as Josiah Carlisle was her husband.

PETER CRANE'S DEATH seemed to mark a dividing line in their journey. Blessed with good travels and good health up until then, they sustained several losses in the next week.

The landscape changed yet again to barren hills and occasional pools of water. But the water was poisonously alkaline, and if animals drank it, they collapsed. Despite their best efforts, several animals succumbed. One digger lost a mule. The Gilmets lost two oxen. And the Culpeppers nearly lost their horse.

As they neared the Sweetwater River where they would find safe drinking water at last, an older digger dropped from a seizure. In a few seconds he was dead, and the company stopped for a second burial, another sad service over which Rev. Kessler presided.

Now that Kit's deception was over with Daniel, she set about making amends to all she'd deceived. She told the Bartons she had no brother and was sorry to have told them otherwise. She didn't explain about Josiah, only that she was leaving a bad past and setting out to start afresh in California. Billy Crane, too, had to be told the truth, but for this she relied on the Kesslers' good aid. The Reverend took him aside and explained that Kit Austen had, in fact, lied to get on the train, had confessed her sin and was now a respected member of the company, in good standing. He told him in such a way so as to communicate Billy should not be thinking mischief was a suitable response.

Kit kept her distance from Billy Crane, but also from Daniel. The truth had opened a painful chasm between them. They both knew that they could stray from a righteous path if they weren't careful.

Daniel did not go out hunting during this lonesome part of the trip, nor did he gallop too far ahead to scout out the trail for the group. Every day he stayed close to the wagon train. Kit wondered if he felt it necessary to show everyone that he was looking after them.

Their feelings of isolation and gloom were aggravated by a wind storm that kicked up sand and dust and chapped their lips and irritated their eyes in the next few days. They all wore bandanas around their mouths to keep the grit from their teeth. The women tied their sun bonnets on tight and the men pulled down their hats likewise. Wilhemina stayed in her wagon with Mary. But no one could avoid the dust. It was everywhere.

When the company finally reached Sweetwater, things seemed different. Silent and brooding from the days of mourning—and sore and dry from the wind storm—they all sensed that their adventure had turned deadly serious, and they were always a hair's breadth away from disaster now. Still, the stop at Sweetwater proved a treat for the company. The water was safe, the fishing was good, and a few men struck lines. The animals could graze, and Daniel made plans to go hunting again while they paused for a Sabbath. Even Rev. Kessler agreed that hunting had to be allowed on the Sabbath with desperate times behind and ahead.

Wilhemina was again feeling ill, now beset by stomach pains. Josephus decided the way to help her was to find some rabbit or deer so she could have a fresh meat stew instead of the salt pork, bacon and ham they were eating regularly. After a brief prayer meeting, he pulled out his rifle and joined up with Daniel, the Culpeppers, Bart Gilmet, and a few diggers.

To Kit's chagrin, she noticed the hunting party also included Billy Crane. He sat atop his late brother's horse, his rifle across his lap and his hands resting on the saddle. While the other men fretted with last-minute details or talked of where to head for the best shooting, Billy stayed silent, staring at Daniel's back. Before the party galloped away, she ran up to Daniel's horse.

Talking low enough so only he could hear, she issued an urgent plea. "Don't go out today, Daniel. I... I think it best for you to stay in camp. The others might need... " She trailed off, no ready excuse coming to mind as he leaned forward to hear her.

"I have to go," he said. "I can't spend the rest of the journey running away from Billy Crane."

SHE HEARD THEM before she saw them. The dull pounding of horses' hooves on the earth carried far in the quiet evening. Mary, too, caught the sound.

"Papa's back," she cried and stood up. Kit got up too and peered into the darkness. As the figures neared, she counted the horses and the men. They were traveling fast and one of the horses—her breath came sharply at the realization—one of the horses was without a rider. Someone was injured! *Daniel,* she thought. She told Mary to stay put as she walked out into the dusk to greet them, searching, searching, squinting to try and make out the figures. Esther and Rev. Kessler, who'd stayed in camp, joined her, Esther holding her hand. She must have felt it too—the crackle of danger in the air.

There he was. Sitting tall in his saddle, riding as naturally as if he was part of the horse himself. Daniel was all right. She nearly wept with relief. But her joy was quickly replaced by concern as she saw that Josephus was the injured one, being carried low on his horse—he was nearly prone against the animal's broad neck. His arm was wrapped in a makeshift bandage.

"What happened?" she called out as she went forward to greet them. Daniel dismounted first and gently helped Josephus down with Rev. Kessler's aid.

"A stray shot grazed him. It's nothing serious," Daniel said. "But it pains him and he lost a bit of blood." He turned back to the rest of the party. "Let's help him to bed. Ira, you take over his wagon in the morning."

"It will be all right," Josephus said, but his face was ghostly pale and his voice was weak. Daniel and Ira helped him to the campfire, while Esther put on a pot to boil.

Kit thought of Willa. There wouldn't be enough room for both of them in the small wagon. "Willa can lie in mine. I'll bed down outside."

Daniel threw her a quick look. He knew she didn't like to be out in the open with Billy Crane on the wagon train.

Now Mary ran forward, calling for her father. When she saw his injured arm, she started crying. Kit comforted her as best she could and told her to look after her father.

"Esther and I will wash out the wound," Kit said to Daniel. He nodded in agreement and went with the rest of the men to take care of the horses. "Mary," said Kit, "fetch my medicinal bag from my wagon—the brown one with the leather drawstring."

Willa came out of the wagon to be with her husband.

"Oh my, Josephus!" She choked up with tears as Kit placed her hand on Willa's shoulder.

"Don't fret, Willa. I'll take care of it. Just sit here with him. Tell us what happened, Josephus, while I bandage the arm." Mary returned and dutifully handed her the bag, glad to be of assistance. Kit began to work quickly, unwrapping the makeshift bandage and removing Josephus's coat and shirt.

"Thank goodness," Esther said when she saw it. "It truly is a graze." Then to Josephus and Willa, she said, "He'll be right as rain within a day or two."

Although the wound site was bloody, it had stopped now and didn't look unhealthy or festering. Kit gave him a swig of brandy from her kit, and then poured some of the burning liquid on the sore. He gasped at the searing sensation but uttered no swear.

"We had spotted an antelope," Josephus said, his voice gaining strength now. "Ira, Daniel, and I were in one group. Billy and some others had gone off. They were supposed to be way east of us, beyond a ridge, so we wouldn't run into one another on the hunt. I shot the animal, a good clean shot too. We brought his carcass home. Good stew meat."

"Then what happened?" Kit asked as she wrapped a clean bandage around the arm with Esther's help.

"I was going to fetch the game. I was walking out in the open and all of a sudden—I was shot."

"But didn't you say you had just shot an animal. I mean, surely whoever it was... "

"Billy. It was Billy. He admits as much," Josephus said with no rancor.

Esther inhaled sharply.

"Surely Billy knew you were there if he heard the shot that brought down the antelope," Esther said.

"He says he didn't hear it. He says he got separated from his group." Josephus's voice indicated his skepticism at this claim.

Kit made no comment, just tied off the strips of cloth. Why would Billy shoot Josephus, she wondered. Simply because he had taken up for Daniel?

"I'll check on it again in the morning," Kit said, finishing up. "Willa, you're sleeping in my wagon tonight... with Mary. Your husband will bed down in yours and rest most of tomorrow."

"And you'll sleep with us," Esther added, giving Kit a knowing look.

Kit stood and, into her cloth bag, put away the bandage material, scissors and small bottle of brandy she had brought along for medicinal purposes.

She let them say their good-nights and speak alone together while she retrieved her own bedding from her wagon.

In a few moments, Willa and Mary and Josephus were all getting ready to sleep in their assigned wagons, and Esther was on her way to make room for Kit in the Kessler encampment. With her charges safely abed, Kit tamped down the fire and walked down the train toward the Kesslers. Along the way, she encountered Daniel, back from watering and feeding his horse.

"Are they all right?" he asked.

"I think he'll be just fine. You were right. Just a surface wound."

"That's good."

"What happened out there, Mr. Winchester?"

"Stray shot. An accident."

"I don't believe it. And I don't think Josephus does either," she said vehemently.

Daniel said nothing.

"What I can't figure," she continued, "is why he would go after Josephus. Josephus hasn't hurt him. He's only taken up for you... and no more than Rev. Kessler did that day... the day Peter... "

"We both had put our hats down while we were sighting the animal. Josephus picked up the wrong one when he went to fetch the carcass."

"Billy thought it was you." She brought her hand to her mouth, as her heart galloped.

"There's no proving that."

"Daniel!"

His head shot up at the use of his Christian name, and he smiled at her

"There's been varmints on the trail before. I can deal with him." He looked serious again. "There's no point fretting. I can take care of myself. And you too for that matter. I'll be nearby tonight."

And he was. After she'd bedded down with Esther in the Kessler wagon, she heard Daniel camping nearby, talking softly with Rev. Kessler before they all went to sleep.

Chapter Thirteen

The Desert Crossings

DEVIL'S GATE, THE ICE SPRING, Willow Springs—the names passed in a blur as each day rolled into the next. Days of feast and days of famine, Kit thought to herself as they cut hay in grassy hills and prayed for good water through alkaline sinks.

The sinks were a dying ground for oxen. Putrescent corpses were strewn throughout their path, their offensive odors turning stomachs while their decaying flesh reminded them all of their own mortality. They watered their animals from their casks when crossing the salt flats, hoping that the next day would find them in a more hospitable environment.

In mid August, they reached the Little Sandy, a mountain stream that allowed them to forgo the casks and lead their animals to the running water. But if there was water, the grazing was bad. With no natural feed, they had to fuel their animals using baled hay stretched by a meal mixture of flour and water.

At the Big Sandy, Daniel stopped them, raising his hand as the signal for the slow-down just as the sun reached its zenith. Everyone dutifully pulled on their reins to arrest their forward movement. Kit gratefully used the opportunity to get down from her wagon and stretch. She looked at the stream and thought longingly about washing herself and some clothes. Daniel rode up.

"We're stopping for the day," he told her before moving on down the line. She didn't care why they were stopping. She was glad to be able to catch up on chores and looked forward to bathing. But her views were not shared by everyone on the train. As Daniel made his way to the other travelers, Kit heard angry voices raised. She turned and saw Daniel sitting on his horse, his hands crossed on the saddle, staring at Bart Gilmet with a grimace turning down his lips.

Bart was shaking his head. His hands were still on his team's reins, as if he wasn't sure he wanted to stop.

"Another day lost," Bart said. "We can't afford that. It's high summer. We have to be at the mountains soon."

"It's late summer!" Billy Crane said, walking up to Bart's wagon. His speech seemed slurred, and he looked even more disheveled than usual. Kit had noticed how he seemed to be drinking regularly now. She'd heard that his brother had packed several cases of whiskey to sell once they'd reached California. It was to have been their capital, for use in building their stake. She wondered how long his cache of liquor would hold out and what would happen when it was gone. "We've already lost good time because we didn't take that cut-off."

"Every immigrant from here to Charleston has their own special 'cut-off,'" Daniel said with disgust. "I know, I know—they're all the shortest, easiest routes. I've heard about them all. None's quicker than this. We'll be there soon enough."

"That's easy for you to say," Bart chimed in. "You're not going out for a stake. Some of us have our families to think of. We planned to be in the diggings by September." He looked over at his wife Lucy, who sat uncomfortably next to him, staring straight ahead. She nodded almost imperceptibly when her husband looked her way—an automatic reaction, thought Kit. Agree with him and he won't get angry. Lucy was a quiet woman who rarely strayed from her own wagon. Kit frowned.

Daniel grimaced, too. "Then you planned unwisely," he said. "End of September maybe. Not beginning. That was made clear at the outset."

"What do we gain by resting here a day?" Bart continued.

"Teams that'll be able to make it across the deserts."

"If they can't make it, they'll rot in the sun," Billy said, and then burped. "Everybody 'pects to lose an animal or two."

Daniel said nothing at first. He clenched his teeth as he tried to control his anger.

"Not everybody, Billy," he continued, looking back at Bart. "Some families hope to keep their teams together as long as they can. They can't afford to sacrifice an ox or mule. Better to rest a day and prepare. Fill everything you can with water."

Bart was putting down the reins. But Billy was unwilling to give in just yet.

"Maybe some of us can go on ahead," Billy said. "Those of us willing to travel fast and light."

Daniel picked up his reins, a signal he was going to move on. "You could. Up to you. But it's a mean crossing. If you get wandering, it won't just be the animals that die. And it's not an easy death, Billy."

He leaned forward towards Billy. "You know what happens when you don't have water? You get so desperate you start drinking anything liquid. And when that dries up, your tongue gets swollen and black and your head starts to ache like it was split with an ax. By that time, you're hallucinatin', seeing ghosts and monsters and all manner of unearthly creatures—but it's not enough to dull the pain. I've heard of parents that kill their children rather than see them suffer through that. Death would be a mercy when you're sufferin' so." He straightened up. "But if you want to try it on your own, Billy, I can't stop you."

With that, he rode away to tell the others, leaving Billy staring into space at the horrible image Daniel had just conjured up.

Daniel came back along the line and told them how to prepare. It wasn't just for the animals' sake that they had stopped. They all needed to rest because Daniel was going to lead them through the deserts at night. It would be cooler then, he said, and easier on them and the animals.

They spent the day filling every available jar and jug and canteen with water and trying to sleep. Daniel would lead them out in the evening, to start the journey to the Green River about fifty miles away.

Most of them tried to rest that afternoon. Kit gave up her idea of bathing and focused on merely washing out some clothes before retreating to her wagon to nap. As tired as she was, it was difficult to sleep in the day. From the noise of the camp, she suspected others were having the same problem.

When the sun began to set, Daniel warned them that they would be leaving soon. People hurried to finish suppers and pack up. The atmosphere was bristling with fear and excitement. Kit quickly put her few items back into her wagon and doused her small fire. She had been alone most of the day because the Bartons were staying to themselves, and Esther had had so much mending to do she had barely been able to smile a good-day.

"Willhemina's not well," Daniel told Kit, riding up to her wagon. "Josephus won't be much help to you or anyone else for the trip. I can get Ira to ride with you."

"No need," she said, picking up the reins. "I can do it. I've done it before," she said.

"It's a hard journey, the first of several," he said lowly. She could see his brows come together in worry. "Don't feel you need to prove anything to me. You've done that already."

She thanked him, but insisted on driving her team alone. If the journey were to be so hard, she wouldn't ask another to sacrifice for her when she'd deceived them to come on the train by herself.

As they began their nocturnal trip, it became clear that some of the travelers seemed to enjoy the night crossings. She heard men singing what sounded like military songs. The Culpepper boys joined in too. It *was* like an Army march, she thought, soldiers stealthily finding their way through the night to surprise the enemy. But she found no pleasure in it. And she mused over what "enemy" they would overtake in the morning. Their enemies were internal ones—boredom, sickness, and, worst of all, hopelessness.

Even in the face of physical discomfort, Kit was serene. In fact, the physical obstacles, the pain, the struggle, all gave her strength to deal with her harder conflict—remaining friends with Daniel, staying close to him and companionable, while reminding herself that she couldn't ultimately be with him, that a departure date was inevitable.

Perhaps it was the thought of departure that made the rough journey so much more acceptable to her than to the others. Dry lands, dying animals, bad food, heat, wind, dust—all these seemed inconsequential when placed next to the rending pain of leaving him. Even when he rode off ahead, gone just for a short while, she felt it. When he was around the wagon train, out of sight, she knew he was there.

At Green River, they ferried across with no incident, just some mean murmurings from Billy warning others to "look out for yourself. Nobody else'll do it." Daniel let it pass.

Josephus's arm healed quickly, but, with Kit's help, he spent much of his time tending to his wife. Willa was growing larger and feeling worse. Neither of them liked what this could portend.

Willa managed to hold on, however, and they crossed Bear River and Raft River without incident. Each day they moved closer to their destination one step at a time, sometimes eighteen miles a day, sometimes twenty. Now on the Pacific side of the Continental Divide—a milestone hardly anyone noticed—everyone's tempers were on edge, and rumors floated about the wagon train like spirits. One held that Indians had burned the Humboldt Valley. Another had the gold diggings closed to newcomers. And a particularly wild one claimed they were really doubling back on themselves and traveling in circles. The changing landscape belied this last, farfetched tale. And as it did, even the hardiest of them began to fold to fear. The worst desert crossings were soon upon them—forty miles of absolute desert where the Humboldt River expired in desolate countryside barren of life. With so much land to cross, some day travel was inevitable.

THEY HAD FILLED their water barrels to overflowing. They had commandeered every available implement for water storage. For days, they had bundled hay for the animals in preparation for the drive through the Humboldt Valley, where hot sands, blistering heat and little water would be their lot. If all went well, they could make a crossing to barely passable water in one dreadful, bone-rending day of travel, relentlessly pushing forward in the face of heat and dryness, dust and fatigue.

That was the case with the first crossing that they made in the day. Trapped in a glowering heat with no end in sight, even their midday stop for food and rest was no respite. It made them all feel like caged animals. Even the shadows of the wagons provided no cooling shade. It was all heat, heat, heat. Parched heat and dusty trails. No escape. So dry and hard that the animals' hooves were splitting and bleeding, and their own feet were sore from the travel. And their throats—they were so dry from sun-drenched days and brittle heat that they cried out for moisture.

Yet they could take little, being careful to ration what they had to make the journey safe. All eyes looked on the man who ladled himself a cooling draught. They were like vultures ready to pounce. The water had to be preserved. When evening came and they were safely across their first such crossing, Kit felt as if she would weep for joy. The cool night enveloped them with its soothing balm.

But it was a thin veneer of calm. Tensions were high from the crossing and spirits were low from the deaths they had experienced on the trail.

When they faced another desert crossing, Daniel again decided the company would best make the journey at night. He was sure this crossing would take more than one day. They would travel a little over half of it in the cool of night, stop at dawn, and rest until nightfall.

This presented its own form of torture. While traveling under the brilliant stars was an eerie and wondrous experience, few could adjust to the change in sleep patterns. Kit, who worked with her team that night, found her head nodding to her chest, awakened suddenly by the movement of her chin hitting her breast bone. Over and over again, this action repeated itself. The rhythmic movement, the cooler air, the darkness—all conspired as no lullaby could to put them to sleep.

Daniel rode back and forth constantly urging them on, calling on them to keep moving, and keep awake. Kit fell into a half-dream state where she had trouble discerning reality from haze. Daniel was riding by. *Daniel. Beloved Daniel*, she thought. Or did she utter the words out loud? She didn't know. She didn't care. No one spoke. No one made any noise. There was only the clip clop of the animals' hooves, the slow monotonous thud of their feet on the dry earth, the muted grinding noise of wheels sinking into baked mud, the occasional snort or bellow from the oxen's mouths, the whining and creaking of the wagon, and Daniel's lone voice urging them forward.

When dawn came, Kit thought she had never seen such a glorious sight. At first, the light streaked across the sky in narrow bands, then it became brighter and brighter. When would Daniel let them stop? Finally, he raised his hand and called out the "Whoa!" they were all waiting for. Again, Kit felt like crying with joy. She stepped down from her seat, aching and tired, feeling every bone in her body. But she forced herself to make a meal—was it dinner? Breakfast? No one knew. No one cared. They were so tired that exhaustion won out over hunger. Slipshod meals were quickly eaten before they bedded down for rest.

But what a rest it turned out to be. As the sun blazed high in the sky, the wagon train was caught in a bell jar of heat. Even in the shade, it was hot enough to make a resting man sweat. No one was comfortable. No one slept well. Nothing living stirred. Not even lizards and ants, the companionable nuisances along this part of the trail. Kit herself tossed and turned in the oven-like confines of her wagon. She had stripped down to her slip, allowing the blanket to fall off of her. A film of sweat covered every limb, and she felt like she was suffocating. Outside, she occasionally heard the foreboding call of the vulture, circling overhead, looking down at the dead-looking wagon train, just waiting, waiting...

For the first time since the journey began, Kit thought longingly of home.

Chapter Fourteen

KIT WAS DREAMING. Josiah had hit her and she lay unconscious on the floor. Someone was trying to rouse her. *Kit, Kit,* the person called. *Wake up, wake up, we need you...*

But it wasn't a dream. She slowly came to, the heat reminding her of where she was—not in cool Boston but in the deserts east of California. Josephus was standing at the back of her wagon, not looking directly at her but down at the ground as she lay there in her thin slip.

"Kit, Kit," he whispered urgently. "Wilhemina needs you. Her time has come. Please, get up."

As sleep gave way to consciousness, she observed that Josephus's voice held a tender anxiety she had never heard before. In those simple words, in that call for help, was embedded all his love for his wife.

"I... I'm awake, " she said, sitting up, drawing the blanket up to her chin.

"Kit, Willa's bad. The baby's coming. She's tried to keep it back. But it's no use. This is the time."

"Don't worry, Josephus. I'll be right there. Where's Mary?"

"She's asleep in the shade of the wagon. She doesn't know anything yet."

"Let me pull on some clothes... Go fetch Esther. I'll be right there."

She pulled her dress to her. She could hardly bear the thought of putting it on in this heat. She rolled up her sleeves. She tied her hair back with a ribbon and got out of the wagon, running in the sun's glare to the Barton wagon.

Josephus was inside, holding Willa's hand. She was sweating profusely, and her eyes were closed. But her face was a mask of pain—contorted muscles stiff with effort. When Josephus saw Kit, he warmly told his wife. "Kit's here. She's going to help you, dear."

Kit had never presided over a birthing before, but Esther soon arrived, filled with purpose.

"Get some water," Esther directed Josephus. When Josephus left the wagon, Kit and Esther entered it. Kit picked up the woman's hand. It was clammy and hot.

"How are you, Willa?" she asked softly.

"It's not... going well," Wilhemina answered through gritted teeth. "It's too early. Oh, Kit..." She started to cry softly.

"Willa, it's going to be all right," Esther said, wiping sweat already gathering on her brow. "We'll make sure it will be. Don't you worry. Please, don't you worry." She kissed the woman's hand and searched around for a cloth. She found a cotton sheet and used it to wipe Willa's face. "I'll make you as comfortable as possible. Let us pray." Holding each other's hands, they listened to Esther's short, heartfelt plea for the Lord's help.

"But we can't stay here," Willa choked out after the Amen. Kit knew exactly what she meant. They couldn't linger in the middle of this desert for a childbirth. It would mean death for all of them.

"Then we won't," Kit said, continuing to wipe Willa's forehead. "We'll be across before you know it. Don't fret."

Josephus returned with water and with Daniel. As Willa sipped at the water, Daniel and Josephus stood outside the wagon talking in low voices.

"How is she doing?" he asked Josephus. "How long will it be?"

"There's no telling," Josephus answered. "Mary was a hard birth. Two days..." His voice trailed off, and he obviously was pained by the memory.

Daniel stood thinking. Kit noticed a sigh. And his shoulders looked tired, as did his face. Lines of fatigue and worry crinkled near his eyes, and the eyes themselves seemed dull with tiredness. They were all dulled, like instruments left out in the blazing sun and sand.

"We can't linger," he said quietly and definitively. "It's probably best if we move out now instead of waiting. If we wait it out and then she can't be moved... I'll rustle up the rest of the company."

Kit looked up at the sky. The sun was just above them. It must have been noon, the hottest, most brutal time to travel. She knew that Daniel's decision would not be received kindly by the rest of the group.

"Maybe we can get moving and the rest can wait..." she offered.

"No," Daniel said. "We all move together. Too risky to separate here." He walked off, immediately starting to rouse the rest of the company. Kit heard their groans as he awakened them. Little Mary, who'd been sleeping in the shade of the wagon, woke up as well and ran to be with her mother.

"All is as the Lord intended," Esther said to the worried little girl. "You're just going to have a little brother or sister soon, that's all." Mary's face lit up with joy and she started to hop up into the wagon, but Kit stopped her. "It's hard work having a baby, so you're going to have to go to my wagon. Mister Winchester will take care of you."

With the company awake and ready to go, arrangements were made for Ira Culpepper to drive Kit's team with Mary in her wagon.

With the first turn of the wagon wheel, Kit knew it was going to be tough. Willa grabbed her hand and squeezed it so hard that Kit felt her bones would surely shatter.

"The pains are regular and close," Willa said in a strangled whisper.

Already drenched in sweat, Esther turned to the wagon cover on the side. "We need to have these lifted just a bit to get some air in here," she said. Kit nodded. She called out to Josephus on the wagon bench, asking him to help. In a few moments, he had rallied Daniel and they both had secured the oil-soaked cover up a few inches even as the wagons rolled forward. Air could reach them, but it was still nothing but the blast of a fireplace on a wintry night.

"I've got my medicinals," Kit said to Esther.

"Give her a sip of brandy to cut the pain," Esther suggested, and Kit poured a thimbleful of the strong liquid, then held it to Willa's mouth.

She sipped at it and sputtered after it made its way down her throat. Willa started to relax. Her head lolled back on the sweat-stained pillow. Kit pulled off the timepiece pinned to her shirtwaist and brushed some hair from her face. Willa started to moan again and Kit looked at her watch, noting the time.

"Think of winter, Willa. Think of cold, snowy days when the flakes kiss your cheeks with ice." Willa grabbed for Kit's hands again and squeezed. When the latest contraction was over, Kit checked her watch. It had lasted a full minute, which she mouthed to Esther, who nodded. Esther soaked a rag in some water, using it to brush the hair from Willa's face.

"Wouldn't it feel good to be so warm on a wintry day?" Esther cooed. "With the wind whirling around your house and the snow and ice driving against the window panes?"

"I can't let Josephus down," Willa murmured.

"You're letting no one down," Kit and Esther said almost together.

Daniel appeared at the back of the wagon. "How's she doing?" he called in to Kit.

"She's about the same," Kit said, looking at him with frantic eyes.

He himself was so tired looking that she found her heart burdened with another worry. The strain of leading them through the desert and having to be on guard against the likes of Billy Crane was starting to show.

"If you need me to stop, call out to Ira," Daniel continued. "He'll signal me. Otherwise, we'll push on through." He turned and rode away.

Kit went back to Willa and Esther and talked in a low and soothing voice. She thought of any story she could find—of her childhood in Boston, of her father, of Blue Hill and the Charles River, of her dances when she was a young lady coming out into society. The pains were now regular. Willa was like a limp rag doll. Her cotton sheath was drenched with sweat, her face waxy, and her hair matted from perspiration. Esther, too, looked bad. The heat had been hard on her and now her face was pale as the cabin cover, and she swallowed often, trying to settle a stomach jostled by wagon and heat.

Kit looked over at Esther. "We should spell each other," she said. "Here, take this." She handed Esther the damp rag. "Wipe yourself and rest. I'll take the first watch."

Esther started to protest but had no energy. She did as Kit had said, leaning back against the wagon wall, closing her eyes and dampening her face and arms with the rag.

Kit wet another rag from their small supply of water and washed Willa's face. She hummed to her and let her grab her hand when pains came. The rocking motion of the wagon, the heat, Kit's empty stomach, the pain in her hands from where Willa squeezed them tight—all combined to make her feel nauseous. But she pushed aside discomfort, focusing all her energy on Wilhemina.

The afternoon passed like this, with Kit talking so much to soothe Willa that her own throat became dry and rasping. Esther drowsed, awakening once during a particularly violent labor pain, but Kit shushed her back to sleep, knowing Willa was comfortable with her tending now. With the sun still blazing in the sky and no relief from the heat in sight, Daniel halted the train.

"The animals have to feed," he explained to Esther, riding by as she poked her head out. Kit heard the rest of the company dismounting, grumbling from the fatigue of interrupted sleep. This stop would certainly not endear them to the rest of the group, she thought. She looked behind them and saw the reason Daniel had stopped. An ox had fallen and lay thrashing as it died. He rode up to the poor creature, drew his gun, and with a swift motion, shot it in the head. Josephus came around to check on his wife and Kit stepped out of the wagon into the merciless sun to stretch her cramped muscles, Esther following shortly, looking dazed and unwell herself. Mary came running up to her.

"Mama, how's Mama?" the child cried. "I want to see her!"

"No, little one, you can't. It's hard work having babies and she's tired right now," Kit said, taking the girl's hand in hers. Mary started to cry, but Kit knelt down next to her and touched her under the chin.

Daniel returned, walking this time, his horse resting with the others and slurping thirstily at improvised troughs. "We won't rest long," he said, looking up at the sun. "If we hurry, we can make it across just after sunset. There should be some water and grazing land there, just a little beyond," he said, leaning on the frame of the wagon.

"You're exhausted," she said, staring him in the eyes. "You have to rest. You've been on guard duty too much. Why don't you stay in the wagon?"

He smiled at her just a little, as if raising the edges of his mouth was an effort beyond his willpower. "I appreciate that, Miss Austen."

"Call me Kit," she whispered, her parched lips barely forming the words. She was too tired for formality.

He kept his smile and looked as if his burden had eased. "And me, Daniel."

Just then, Willa let out a moan so loud it carried the length of the train. Esther jumped back in the wagon first, followed by Kit as Daniel told Mary to get back to Kit's wagon with Josephus.

Inside the Barton wagon, Willa looked deathly, her skin shiny and her lips dry and chapped, foam at the corners. Her eyes were half closed and her hand rested limply by her side.

"It's c-c-coming," Willa said in low pants.

"Give her another swig of brandy," Esther suggested.

"No!" Willa cried. "Have to be... strong...."

But strength was far from her at that moment and both Kit and Esther exchanged worried looks.

"Pray for us, Esther," Kit suggested. Esther nodded and began the Lord's prayer while Willa moaned and Kit mouthed the words.

Esther then moved on to the Twenty-Third Psalm.

"Yea, though I walk through the valley of the shadow of death... "

With a jolt, the wagon started, their rest stop over. Never had the psalm meant more, or resonated more— even more than when they'd said them at the memorial services along the trail. Here they were, walking through that valley, the sun and heat taking their strength, killing their animals, pulling their very breath from them.

But the words had a soothing effect, even Willa moving her lips along with Esther.

Now it was as if another force had taken over, a stubborn desire to live through this valley, to prove themselves worthy of the challenge. Color returned to Esther's face, and she handed the rag to Kit while she saw to the birthing herself. She continued to pray while Kit kept Willa cool, and Willa herself thrashed when the pains came fast. There was only this moment to get through, and the next and the next and the next.

Esther instructed Kit to roll some sheets together for a little pillow to slip under Willa's back, easing some of her discomfort.

"Have her squeeze the water rag over her chest when she has a pain," Esther said, noting how red Kit's own hands had become.

When Willa squeezed at it, droplets of water splashed on her nightshirt.

Through bumpy miles of searing desert they traveled. Esther took charge, telling Kit to sing a hymn or say a prayer, or just asking her to join in encouraging Willa to be strong and of good faith as her delivery was at hand.

Each jolt of the wagon elicited another moan from Willa. To Kit's dismay, however, she noticed that Willa's groans were becoming softer. The woman was losing her strength and she needed it to push the baby out. This time, Kit remembered something from her own past and reached over to a provision barrel where she scooped a little sugar into the water mug. She gave the sweetened water to Willa and told her to drink it. With slow sips, Willa managed to drain the cup and her eyes brightened.

Esther nodded her approval.

How long had it been? Kit looked at her watch. Hours... hours had passed since their stop. How had that happened? Were they really alive? Perhaps they had all perished during their sleep. Perhaps Kit was in some pre-death state where she had to account for her sins before meeting her Maker.

Kit's sins... what were they? She counted them— one, squandering her love on a heartless man; two, deceiving a good one and others around him.

Willa groaned again. Another pain. When the next pain came, Kit look at Esther.

"Is it near?"

"Yes."

"That's it, Willa, go ahead and use the pain to push out the baby. You can do it!"

The wagon jolted over a rock, pitching forward. Kit had to reach out to the frame to keep from toppling onto Willa.

Willa cried as she groaned again, a huge wracking pain sweeping through the woman's body and making her shudder. "Let me... rest... "

Kit sat upright and shook Willa gently.

"No! No rest now. The baby's almost here."

The words were barely out of her mouth when another pain convulsed the woman.

"Keep her awake," Esther told Kit as sweat poured down her face.

Willa was lying limp on the sheets, breathing shallowly, her eyes glazed and half open. "Tell Josephus... Mary... I loved... "

Kit took the jug of water nearby and started to pour some into a mug. But she didn't offer it to Willa's mouth as she had planned. Instead, she rudely splashed it on Willa's face, causing her to sputter and spit.

But color started to return to her lips. Kit grabbed her shoulders and stared in her eyes, her face just a few inches from Willa's own.

"Don't you give up, do you hear me? God's blessed you with a beautiful daughter and a loving husband. And now a new baby. Don't you give up! There's many that would want what you have."

"Kit!" Esther called, breaking her rant. "Let her be. The baby's almost here."

THE SQUALL OF AN infant floated on the air. Willa fell back and sighed, a smile coming to her lips at last. Esther murmured a prayer of thanks and Kit laughed until she cried. By the time the birthing was finally over, they were all crying tears of fatigue and joy.

A boy, a sweet, little baby boy lay nestled in Willa's limp arms.

"Oh, Willa, he's beautiful!" Kit said.

"A little troublemaker," Esther said. "You'll have to watch him, Willa."

Kit noticed, for the first time, that the air was slightly cooler. She poked her head out the back of the wagon. It was after sunset. They had been traveling all afternoon and early evening and none of them had paid heed. The ground was different too. They were leaving the desert. She thought she could even smell water in the air.

While Willa tended to her child, Kit and Esther tidied up the wagon, Willa and themselves as best they could. Kit brushed Willa's hair and gave her a new night shirt to wear. Then Kit wiped off her own neck and arms and reached up to undo her hair, which was a frazzled mess. Esther did the same. The wagons slowed and eventually stopped. In a few seconds, Josephus was with them, his eyes welling with pride as he beheld his new son.

Stiff and worn, Kit and Esther stepped out of the wagon. Mary came running up.

"You have a little brother, Mary," Kit told her.

"Can I see him? Can I see him?"

"I don't see why not," Kit said, helping her up to be with her mother and father.

Esther looked at Kit, tears welling in her eyes. She held out her arms, and both women embraced, Esther stroking Kit's hair.

"You knew what to do," Esther said.

"And you."

After pulling away, Esther rubbed her eyes and said, "I had two boys. One was lost to typhoid. The other made his way west."

"That's why you're headed there," Kit said in wonder.

"Only partly. Rev. Kessler has always felt a calling to lands bare of churches." Esther stared at Kit. "And you? How did you know what to do—giving her the sugar water?"

Kit looked down. Esther knew so much already, but she hated to burden her with more.

"I had a stillbirth. The midwife did it for me."

"Oh, you poor dear."

What Kit didn't tell her was the reason for the stillbirth—Josiah, bringing on early labor with his cruel blows.

But it was as if Esther guessed it. "No woman deserves to have life ripped from her like that," she whispered, wiping her brow.

"Let's not speak on it." Kit didn't even like to think about it. The midwife who'd tended her had told her she'd be unlikely to have more children. Yet one more sorrow to heap upon the others. Even if she were free to be with Daniel, they'd never have been able to have a family together now.

DANIEL MADE SURE she was well cared for that evening. After he did his own chores, he joined her for a light supper of hard biscuits, pork stew and dried apples put together by the Culpeppers. She revived quickly after drinking mugs of cool water, brought from a nearby stream. But her body and soul ached from the day's events, and the soft cry of the newborn baby in the next wagon reminded her of the dry emptiness in her own life. There was no water that could quench that thirst.

Daniel was going to let everyone rest the next morning. They wouldn't be taking to the trail until midday at the earliest. She was glad, not just for her sake, but for his as well. He seemed so tired and preoccupied, his eyes dull from fatigue and his movements slower and more deliberate.

The stars began to pierce the night sky, and few travelers lingered around campfires after such an exhausting day. But Daniel sat near hers. They were two silent friends staring into the flickering flames, comfortable in each other's presence. Kit's mind was empty of thoughts, filled only with the beauty of the evening and the safety of being near Daniel. After a long time, he spoke, not looking at her but continuing to gaze into the fire.

"You seem like a good woman," he said softly. "You do your share. You did much more than that today."

She looked at him, her heart full.

"Once we get to San Francisco, I think you should keep on with the Kesslers," he said, looking at her with sad eyes. "They can watch out for you."

"And where will you go?" she asked, her heart beating so loudly she was sure he could hear it.

"I'm heading down to Monterey, and after that, even I don't know." He looked into the fire. "I'm not the kind of man, Kit, who would take up with a married woman."

She hung her head. "Nor I the type to break my marriage vows."

Chapter Fifteen

Into the mountains

FOR WEEKS, they had looked longingly at the horizon, waiting to see the mountains that would signify the last major obstacle to their destination. During the swelter of one desert crossing, some swore they saw the rugged tops of the Sierra Nevada in the distance. But these were merely heat-induced mirages. Nothing grew on the arid deserts, no salt bush, and no cactus, and they were littered with animal carcasses and worse. Death had seemed all around them.

Their work was rewarded when they came at last to the edge of the Black Rock Mountains, where hot springs and timbered hills began to appear. Soon it was on to the Sierra Nevada and its passes, with Daniel telling them they would come into California from the north, then head southwest to Sacramento and beyond. The trip was almost over. The end was within reach.

While everyone else sighed with relief, Kit's and Daniel's feelings were less sanguine. They looked at the mountains and saw only loneliness. Kit knew, from their brief talk after Willa's birthing, that Daniel would be lost to her forever once they reached their destination. She prayed nightly for the strength to accept this.

California seemed to offer little promise now and much heartbreak.

THE SIERRA NEVADA loomed in the distance, majestic mountains that stirred both awe and fear. It was now the beginning of September and the company disunity that had begun miles back had festered and exploded along the way. A few diggers had taken off on their own, buying out their portion of the mess or whatever supplies they had in common and paying off their company fees. Daniel took it in stride, telling Kit that this wasn't unusual. People were restless to get moving and some could make it faster alone. Choices were in front of them now—which pass to take, which cut-off, which short cut. They were important choices that some men preferred to make for themselves.

The weather was cooler, and the shadow of the Donner party—those poor souls who had been trapped in the autumn snows of 1846, resorting to cannabalism when their food gave out—hung over everyone who walked the trail. Would they make it before the snow came? Sudden weather changes in the heights were the stuff of many wild rumors.

One thing they could be thankful for—water was plentiful and the animals were always able to satisfy their thirst. Feed was a problem, though, and they often had to stop a day when the grazing was good to bundle hay for the more barren stretches ahead, where only pine needles were to be found on the hard forest floor.

Willa's health returned, and the Barton family became a cheerful group no longer darkened by worry. Esther and her husband tried valiantly to tend to the company's spiritual needs, but some folks regularly skipped the Sabbath to work on gear.

And Kit—she entered a strange mood where she forcefully pushed the future aside, enjoying each day's individual blessings. She allowed herself friendly talks with Daniel in the evenings, but both of them knew now that there was no hope for them as a couple. After Kit had reassured Esther that Daniel was well aware of her situation and respected it, the older woman ceased to worry about Kit leading Daniel on.

Kit found joy in her duties as surrogate mother to the little boy Wilhemina had borne on the trail. The Bartons had called him Robert, after Wilhemina's dead father, and he was a pleasure to watch when Willa rested. Despite his smallness at birth, he grew rapidly. He had a head of dark, fine, curly hair, a healthy wail and an equally satisfying gurgle. Now Kit's songs in the evening were lullabies for the infant, whom she reluctantly gave up to Wilhemina when it was time to put him down for the night.

What clouds could drift across this little circle? The weather was good, the road was fair, the troubles of sickness and desert were behind them. And, the fractionalizing of the train even played to their benefit.

Their only problem now was being on the lookout for Indians, who were known to make nighttime raids to steal animals. Daniel posted extra guards after receiving word that some previous campers had suffered losses when they had failed to be watchful.

Word had also come to them from reinforcement troops sent into the mountains by the army that the trail up ahead was clear of early snow. After the Donner fiasco, California's military kept a steady stream of supplies going into the mountains at the end of summer. They brought beef on the hoof, water and news.

Even though their party was hardly suffering the deprivations faced by the Donners, Kit and the rest of the company were grateful for the new supplies. It was good to have fresh food after such a long journey, when dried apples, pilot bread and sourdough biscuits were all the palate had tasted in a long time. Just as delightful were the stories and newspapers left behind. For days, men in the camp read over the papers again and again, even though most of them were months old. It didn't matter. It was a lifeline to the settled world of California.

Kit's life was full and busy and it was easy to pretend that she was happy. On a day when they settled for a stretch of haying and grazing, she spent the morning washing clothes in a cold stream, giving herself a gentle bath in the same clear, icy water with Esther and other women, watching Robert while his mother slept, reading to Mary, starting a beef stew and mending some of Daniel's shirts, which she had offered to do on many occasions. Only recently had he taken her up on it. By late afternoon, when the sun was glinting in orange and red shafts across the sky, she was happily tired. Her stew smelled delicious, evidenced by many passing comments, and she had managed to set a table for the Bartons, Kesslers and Daniel and herself using an upturned crate. It was one of the few times lately when they dined together because one of them was usually involved in some chore.

"Ira's watching the animals," Daniel commented as she ladled him his third bowl. "Until nightfall. Then I take over."

"It's my turn," Josephus said.

"No, Josephus. You'll be doing your stretch tomorrow night—every fourth night."

Josephus nodded, remembering the schedule. It was easy for days to run together out on the trail.

"Can we sing songs tonight and dance?" Mary asked hopefully. "I want to dance with Robert!"

"Oh, he's too young for that. We'll rock him to sleep instead," Kit said gently.

"No! We do that every night!" Mary's lips spread out into a full blown pout. As much as she loved her new brother, she was beginning to resent the restrictions he placed on her own pleasures.

"Well, we'll read then," Kit offered.

"No! We've read every book a hundred times!" Mary folded her arms over her chest in protest. Her mother leaned forward to chide her.

"Now, young lady, you will end up doing nothing but going to bed if you don't apologize right now for that disrespectful tone."

Mary looked stubbornly down at her lap. "I'm sorry," she murmured at last, and Kit breathed a sigh of relief that the little girl wouldn't have to be punished.

"Here's a compromise," Kit offered. "We'll read some of the papers the soldiers left behind. That will be something new."

Mary's face brightened at the prospect.

After dinner, Wilhemina insisted on cleaning up the dishes with Esther while Kit took Mary and the baby to the fireside. She retrieved a few of the papers and slid the storybooks under them to have ready for when Mary inevitably discovered how boring real news could be. Daniel sat down beside her with a last cup of coffee, looking up to where the trees were now cut-out silhouettes against the blue sky of evening.

"I'll keep you company for a little while," he said.

They were like a family, she thought wistfully. Yet the thought had heartbreak in it. She pushed it aside. The baby nestled in her arms asleep. Mary snuggled nearby. Daniel leaned back ready to listen.

"Here, spread one out in front of me and I'll begin," she instructed Mary. The little girl dutifully followed instructions, pulling out one of the old broadsides and opening it very carefully for Kit to read. Kit noticed that it was dated months ago, when their journey began, and that Mary had positioned it to an inside page where some stories were continued from the front. She scanned it quickly and found a few that started on that page. In a clear voice, she read of a miner striking a gold vein near Sacramento, of a dispute between three brothers and a cousin over a claim, of a flood along the Sacramento River, of the death of an early settler, of the opening of a new road...

As she droned on about these everyday events, she could see Mary's eyelids begin to droop. After her fourth story, Kit stopped and smiled at the girl.

"Well, you seem to be tired. Maybe it's time for sleep."

"No, not yet! Please, one more, one more!"

"Maybe one from a storybook instead," Kit said.

But Mary wasn't going to let on that she was bored. Instead, she defiantly turned back to the paper and scanned its blocks of print, finally resting her finger on the ending of a story from the front page. "Here, this one. Just read this one. Then I'll go to bed."

"That's not a whole story," Kit began, but then decided it wasn't the story itself that was important. It was doing what Mary wanted. She started to read the disjointed tale.

"This was the first loss since last April, when the Golden Eagle was run ashore in a lee wind," Kit read without really paying attention. She was busy half-looking at the baby, whose lips occasionally turned up into the most delightful smile. "All souls aboard were lost and the ship owner has incurred a financial loss as well... " She could see that Mary's attention was already drifting, so she stood up and declared the story at an end. "Get ready for bed now. It's time for your brother to go too."

"Let me carry him, please, please?" Mary insisted.

Kit looked down at her with stern eyes. Mary was allowed to hold Robert on occasion, and it was only a few steps to the wagon.

"All right, but be extra careful." She handed the peaceful baby to Mary's open arms and walked just behind her as she went to the wagon. Wilhemina thanked Kit and took the baby and her daughter. Everyone was settling in for the night. It was the quietest, most peaceful time on the trail. Esther kissed her on the cheek before heading back to her own wagon.

Kit breathed in deeply—cool, refreshing air. It reminded her of the beginning of the journey. With that remembrance, she smiled. At last, new memories were replacing the old ones with Josiah.

She sighed and began to pick up her books at the side of the fire. Daniel sat quietly, staring into the distance. She smiled at him and continued her chores. Such comfort, she thought. When would she ever again feel so at peace? *Prepare yourself,* an inner voice responded. *You must leave him eventually. Get ready for it. Don't think on what you've lost but what you've gained—love, respect, self-confidence. These are gifts. Treasure them.*

Daniel picked up the newspaper and closed it. Kit's gaze caught the headline of the story whose fragment she had read to Mary.

"Eustace Marie Sinks. All Lost," was the headline.

Eustace Marie...

That name. She'd heard it before.

The letter from Josiah.

"Oh, my!" Her hand flew to her mouth. She felt like the air had been knocked out of her.

"What is it?" Daniel asked. He stood up and came to her, but she brushed past him to pick up the newspaper.

The Eustace Marie had sunk off the coast of San Francisco, as it had begun its journey south toward Panama. It had been carrying cargo and passengers returning from California to the east.

Her heart racing, she remembered Josiah's letter. He had been boarding the Eustace Marie.

He had been on that boat!

But all those other lost souls—she put her fist to her mouth, sinking to the ground as Daniel rushed to support her.

"Kit?" he asked, sitting next to her. "Tell me."

"This," she pointed to the newspaper. Words wouldn't come. Those poor, lost souls—Lord, have mercy on them. Guilt washed over her as she thought of how free she was now—but at what cost? She'd not wanted it at the cost of so many others' lives!

Daniel picked up the paper and read where she pointed, but still didn't understand.

"Josiah... he wrote me before I left... he was on that ship!"

She was free.

She collapsed into Daniel's arms, crying, ashamed to be so happy when so many others had perished with

Josiah, sad that she had wasted years of misery on such a miserable husband, glad to have her life back, fearful that it wasn't true....

She pulled away and picked up the paper again, kneeling by the fire in the growing darkness in order to read it, suddenly afraid she had imagined it all. He knelt beside her. There it was, in black and white. She hadn't imagined it. His ship was gone. He wouldn't be returning home.

Home. Blue Hill. She need not have destroyed it. She could have stayed. She could have led a normal life, reentered Boston society. Blue Hill. Tears again came to her eyes, different ones this time, tears of piercing regret and longing for a life that could have been. But then Daniel reached out for her, pulling her out of her muddle, calling to her, softly, gently.

"God forgive me," he said in a low voice. "I'm glad he's dead."

She reached her arm out to him, and in a moment she was held fast in his embrace. She felt him breathing in the scent of her hair, stroking it, murmuring her name.

"Kit, Kit," he said in a rush. "You're not promised to anyone anymore. Not anyone."

"Daniel, I'm sorry I was... "

"Don't speak." He found her chin with his hand and tilted her head up to his, kissing her.

"It's not right to ask you at this time," he said, after pulling away. "But know this—I will be pleading my case with you soon, Kit Austen. I'll be courting you proper."

She smiled at his honorable intentions, glad he wanted to wait a suitable period of time after the sad news of those who'd perished along with Josiah.

"In the fullness of time, Daniel," she said, "know this—I intend to agree."

He laughed and stood. "I need to be on the watch."

"Good night, Daniel," she said. For once those words held no regrets, not thoughts of what might have been.

Once he left, she rushed to Esther's wagon to tell her the news. With the Kesslers, she offered a prayer for those who'd not survived the sinking, and then Esther stroked her cheek with the back of her hand.

"Child, you will have joy in your life at last. How happy I am for you!"

Chapter Sixteen

KIT TOSSED AND turned that night, twisting the blanket around her into a mottled mess. The night air was chilly in the mountains. She had taken the newspaper into the wagon with her and looked at the story again and again. She was afraid she had mistaken something in it. Perhaps not all souls were lost. Perhaps buried in the story would be a reference to one survivor, a Mr. Josiah Carlisle of Boston. But there was no such reference. It was true. She was a widow, had been one for several months, months when she had kept Daniel at bay, kept her own emotions suppressed. Now she was like a bird let out of a cage.

Even the uncaged bird faces risks. When she finally fell asleep, her dreams were tortured. For her pleasure at knowing Josiah was dead, she paid with horrible nightmares. Josiah was there, dripping wet, walking from the pounding surf, laughing at her, taunting her. Don't think you can get away, he cried out in a distant voice. You're not done with me yet. I'll make sure your happiness is short-lived. You can't escape me, Kate Penwether. She awoke in a sweat.

It was just after dawn, with ominous clouds forming and a bite in the air that Kit knew foreshadowed snow or freezing rain. She pulled her shawl around her and poked her head out of the wagon. With a sigh of relief, she noticed that Daniel was still there, dozing by her wagon.

His watch long over, he was catching some much-needed sleep before the day's ride.

The sound of someone walking along the wagons awakened him. Kit slipped her head back into her wagon, but she could hear Mr. Gilmet's voice.

"Mr. Winchester!" he called out before he reached him. "Mr. Winchester, might I have a word with you?"

"Certainly," Daniel answered.

"There's a group of us that wants to take the lower trail, the one you bypassed a day back," Gilmet began.

"That would mean backtracking," Daniel said.

"Someone in our party thinks this is a longer way and harder too. It's already getting cold. We can't risk it." Gilmet's voice was insistent and whiny. It sounded as if he had rehearsed the lines before confronting Daniel. Kit, listening in her wagon, imagined how the "someone" had probably prompted him, told Gilmet he was the best one to approach Daniel. She saw Billy Crane behind this request.

"It's getting cold, that's for sure," Daniel agreed. "But I expect it won't last. And if we get going, we'll be over the pass in a day or two."

"The lower trail will take us less time."

"Not from here. Not with the backtracking."

Mr. Gilmet paused. Kit imagined he had not rehearsed any arguments beyond these obvious ones.

"Well, it don't matter. We're not happy with this way. It's going up higher and we think being at the lower level will keep us safer, lost time or no lost time," Gilmet said at last. "We've got men eager to get to the diggings. They don't want to run the risk of being stuck in a snowstorm up here, blindsided by what happened... "

"It's not going to happen," Daniel said insistently. "The army sends regular rescue teams. Besides, I don't think this weather's settling in. It doesn't feel right."

"No matter," Gilmet said. "We're committed. We'll be breaking off today, going back the lower route."

Kit was relieved. It would be good to see Billy Crane go. It was as if her happiness had come due and it was all being paid up at once. Josiah dead and now Billy Crane leaving. She only wished Lucy Gilmet wasn't part of their group. It would be good for her to separate from that unsavory crew. But Kit knew that was unlikely. The Gilmets had stuck with Billy Crane throughout the entire journey.

"Winchester!"

It was a different voice, a voice Kit recognized— surly and mean. Billy Crane. She heard his footsteps come closer and stop just short of the pair near her wagon.

"Yes?" Daniel asked.

"Billy, I was just telling Mr. Winchester of our plan," Gilmet said, his voice sounding nervous."

Billy ignored him. "My good ox is gone. Stole in the middle of the night. Some damned Indian took it."

"Is anyone else missing any animals?" Daniel asked. Kit could hear the concern in his voice.

"All I know is *my* ox is gone. And you're to blame!" Billy's voice was slurred. Could he be drinking at this hour of the morning? Kate didn't like the sound of this. A gnawing fear began to grow in the pit of her stomach. She nervously grabbed the side of the wagon, waiting and listening.

"How's that, Billy?" Daniel's voice was slow, soothing and amused.

"You were on watch. It was your r'spons'bil'ty," said Billy, his voice louder now. Then, a horrible sound, the sound of metal clicking, a gun being drawn. "It's just like you stole it. Like you's a horse thief!"

Horse thievery was a hanging offense. Kit was wide-eyed fear. *Let him go, Daniel*, she thought to herself. *Let him go.* But in a second, she heard him rise to the challenge.

"I don't think you mean to say that, Billy." Daniel's voice was different, a tone she had never heard before. Serious, cutting, low, and deadly. She heard movement. Probably Gilmet stepping back.

"Now, boys. No need to quarrel. Let's reconcile this."

For what seemed forever, there was silence, and Kate knew Daniel was staring at Billy with an intense gaze. Dread seized her. Everything had been too good to be true. Now it would all end. She wanted to get out of the wagon, to scream for them to stop, but she dared not move. Finally, she heard Billy's voice.

"I reckon I'll look for it," he said.

Kit let out a huge sigh of relief. Thank goodness. It was over. No confrontation, no shoot-out, no—

The crack of a gun split the air, a groan, a dull thud as someone hit the ground. A scream – Kit realized it was her own as she jumped out of the wagon to Daniel's prone figure. Billy Crane stood, his gun in his hand. He was yelling.

"He was drawin' on me! Didcha see? He reached for it! I saw it!" His voice was a high screech. Others started to gather around. The Bartons, Josephus first, followed by Willa with the baby and Mary, the Kesslers, the Culpeppers...

No, no...Blood pooled beneath his body, but his eyelids fluttered.

"Get some bandages." Esther's voice, strong and comforting, came above her. Someone rushed off.

"Now, Billy, what you go and do that for?" Gilmet whined.

Esther knelt with Kit, placing her hand on Daniel's chest. The wound was low in his shoulder, close to his heart. He looked like he was having trouble breathing, bloody foam spilled from his mouth. Kit wanted to scream. She felt herself ready to faint from despair, but Esther laid a hand on her arm.

"Put pressure on the wound, dear. Willa's bringing bandages."

Rev. Kessler spoke. "Billy, you're going to have to answer for this. We'll have to take you to your wagon and keep you there for now."

A scuffle followed, with Billy shouting and Gilmet whimpering protests. But Josephus and the Culpepper boys helped drag Crane away from the scene.

Daniel looked at Kit, tried to say something.

"Hush, Mr. Winchester," Esther said, interceding. "No talking now."

Willa hurried back, bandages in her hands. She handed them off to Esther who packed them around the wound, which continued to bleed. Esther looked up at Willa.

"Where's your baby?"

"Mary's looking after him."

"Go, tend to him. Have Mary fetch Kit's medicinal bag."

When Willa left, Esther looked up at Kit, who was in a stupor of worry. "When the men return, we should get him off this cold ground."

"M-m-my wagon," Kit stammered, her face drained of color.

"Yes. Go get it ready. A clean, soft bed. Some water nearby. Room for him to move."

Kit stood and hurried to the wagon, passing Mary along the way. Without thinking, Kit did exactly what Esther had told her, tugging tight a clean sheet over downy bedding, filling a water jug, dragging her clothes trunk to the edge and sliding it to the ground.

"We can leave this. I don't care," Kit said.

"We'll take it with our things, child," Esther said. "Now, go run and fetch Rev. Kessler."

Kit whirled around, gasping. "Oh, no," she said, thinking Esther meant Daniel's condition was so dire he needed a minister's prayers.

"I need him to help us move him," Esther said, her voice firmer. "Come on, Kit, show your mettle. Stay strong for him."

Kit's eyes widened and she nodded like a child being given an assignment. She went down the line of wagons until she came upon Rev. Kessler, who was standing by the Crane wagon with Josephus, who was holding his gun at his side. She explained what she needed, and Rev. Kessler looked into the wagon, issuing a warning.

"Don't get any ideas, Billy, or things won't go well with you." He and Josephus rounded up a few others—Ira and Paul Culpepper and even Mr. Gilmet—to help move Daniel to the wagon. They followed Kit, who now felt like an empty machine, back to the spot of the "accident."

There, Kit's sensations returned, but in an agonizing way. Esther's two hands were pressed on Daniel's wound but they were bloody, the bandages having soaked up so much that they looked as if they'd been dyed red. Daniel's eyes were closed, and his skin looked like wax.

Kit fell to her knees. She couldn't help herself. She bent over, held Daniel's arms and cried like a wild animal. *Not now,* she prayed deep inside. *Please don't take him now. Give me some more time, a little time is all I ask...*

Her prayer was joined by Rev. Kessler who knelt beside her. He put his hand on her shoulder and led them in the Lord's Prayer, and then uttered a supplication Kit could barely listen to, so dark was her own soul, so lost did she feel.

She wanted faith, and it seemed just out of reach. She turned her wild eyes to Rev. Kessler. His own eyes were closed as he prayed:

"And like the woman who felt too unworthy to be in Your presence, Lord, we touch the hem of your garment with our prayers, knowing You can heal this loved one..."

She turned back to Daniel. *Yes, like the woman who'd touched His hem. That was how she felt. Too faint of heart to look directly to Him for aid. She could only touch the hem of His garment. Let that be enough.*

"We should try to see where the bullet is before we move him," Josephus said quietly after the prayer ended. "How deep it went."

Esther agreed. "I think if we can get it out, we can stop the bleeding."

"I've done a little doctoring," Josephus said. "I can try."

Esther handed him Kit's medicinal bag, and he looked through it for pincers and a small knife. Once he found them, he turned to Kit.

"You should leave, ma'am," he said, placing his hat on the ground by Daniel. To Esther, he said, "I'll need a lantern. The day's too dark to see."

Esther looked at Kit who scurried off to retrieve a lantern from her wagon. She came back with it lit as Josephus was ripping the shirt from Daniel, revealing the bruised and open wound, still bleeding onto his chest. Kit stood transfixed, unable to move. Esther grabbed the lantern from her.

"You shouldn't stay here, Kit, if you don't think you can watch," Esther said with a firm voice. "Go, now!" Rev. Kessler nodded. He knelt next to his wife, ready to help.

This roused Kit. No, she wouldn't leave Daniel. She'd stay by his side to let him know he needed to hang on. She would show her strength to him once again.

She found her voice.

"I'll help." She knelt by Daniel and looked at Josephus. "Tell me what to do."

"Hold the lantern over here." Josephus pointed to the wound.

With the lamp flickering near his face, Daniel stirred. Did his eyes brighten when he saw her? With her free hand, she gently stroked his hair.

"You're going to be all right," she said in a trembling voice. Fearing she sounded too unsure, she cleared her throat and spoke again. "Josephus is going to get the bullet out. We're going to help you."

"I...I'm sorry," he whispered, barely able to form the words.

"Save your strength," she said. While Josephus readied the knife by soaking it in alcohol, she bent close to Daniel's ear. "Stay still, darling. Have faith."

Josephus was ready.

"Give him a good swig of brandy," Josephus told Rev. Kessler. "Several of them."

While Rev. Kessler held the bottle to Daniel's lips, Josephus continued.

"This is going to pain you. But I'll be as quick as I can."

Finished administering the brandy, Rev. Kessler set it to the side.

"Come round here," Josephus said to the minister, "and hold his arm down. You hold the other, Mrs. Kessler. Can you manage?"

"Yes, sir."

Rev. Kessler knelt by Kit and placed both hands on his arm, while Esther did the same on the other side. Kit held the lantern high.

Josephus gave Daniel a twisted cloth and told him he could bite on it, that it was better than grinding his teeth. Kate swallowed hard and rested her other hand against Daniel's cheek.

Josephus began. Daniel's body arched and he let out a strangled gurgle as the older man dug into the wound looking for the bullet. Josephus's eyes squinted, and his face looked grim. He shook his head, disappointed not to find the projectile right away, but he did not retreat and was forced to explore the wound, which he did with sure, small movements. Each one triggered another convulsive flinch from Daniel. He looked at Kit, and she stroked his cheek, mouthing a silent prayer to let it go quickly and heal the wound.

Each probe made Kit's stomach churn as if it were her flesh that was being cut, her skin that was being pierced. How long could he take it? How long could she?

Despite the cold, Josephus was sweating. Daniel's face was also a mask of sweat. He was breathing heavily and Kit could tell when the pain was especially bad because he would turn his head and look away.

It seemed like hours. Kit was ready to scream, to pull Josephus's hand away, to make him stop. It was too horrible, too barbaric. How could a man do this to another man? How could he continue?

At last, at last, the small bullet was brought to the surface. Josephus grabbed it with the fingers of his other hand and sat back, sighing with relief. Daniel's body slackened as Esther and her husband released their grips. Kit blew out the lantern.

"It's over," she said, as if to confirm the obvious. "No more pain."

"Not quite," Josephus interjected. "We have to wash out the wound. It will sting, I'm afraid."

But he did it quickly, before anyone could think about it, splashing alcohol around the bloody opening so fast that Daniel just cringed and said "ah!" and then it was done. With Kit's help, Josephus bandaged the wound, pulling ripped sheeting under his body and around his shoulder. Blood seeped through the layers of cloth, however, leaving a saucer-sized stain.

"Keep an eye on that," Esther said, pointing to the bleeding. "He's lost a lot already. Apply pressure if you have to."

"Yes, yes," Kit said, nodding her head. Anything, she would do anything to make him better.

Josephus looked over at Rev. Kessler. "We need to move him now."

Esther ran off to get the Culpepper boys to help. In a moment they all returned, forming a brigade on either side of Daniel. With Josephus issuing commands, they hoisted him with a grunt. Daniel let out a groan, sounding like a wounded animal, as they shuffled him to the wagon, sliding him onto the bedding Kit had prepared.

"Who'll watch him first?" Josephus asked, but Kit was already stepping up into the wagon. Esther watched her go.

"I'll be back to spell you," she said.

"No need," Kit murmured.

"Don't be foolish," Esther responded. "I'll see if you need help." She turned and walked back to her wagon.

Alone in the wagon with Daniel, Kit leaned over him and placed a soft kiss on his warm forehead. He looked up at her, and his chapped mouth moved to talk, but nothing came out. He was exhausted from the pain, from the loss of blood, from the trauma. Finally, he managed to breathe, rather than speak, a few words.

"Billy?" he asked.

She shook her head. "The men are holding him." How could he have fired on Daniel? Daniel's guns weren't even drawn. She remembered the way his fingers had danced over them, though, when she needed help. She had no doubt that if he'd had to use them, his aim would have been swift and fatal. Billy Crane was just looking for an excuse to fire on an unprepared man. He was a coward, a drunk.... She sighed. That was over. Daniel was still here. Daniel was still alive.

Alive but pale. His usually sun-reddened face was pallid and gray. His breathing was raspy, his pulse weak. Kit resolved to make him well, no matter what it took.

In a few minutes, he was asleep, drained by the morning's events. It was hard to believe that just the night before, they had both been so happy, so filled with anticipation for the future, so sure that nothing but happiness stretched before them. They were close to their destination, the barriers between them had been torn down, and Daniel had talked of courting her properly.

There will be time for that, she thought. She'd not come this far in both spirit and body to have such a blessing taken from her like this. God was kind and merciful.

She leaned back and closed her own eyes.

Chapter Seventeen

DANIEL SLEPT ALMOST all day, only awakening to sip some hot broth and some strong tea Kit fed him after Esther had brought them to the wagon. Neither woman liked the look of him, though. The removal of the bullet hadn't stopped the bleeding as quickly as they'd liked, and he was as pale as the osnaburg cover on Kit's wagon. More unsettling, he was warm to the touch. Josephus said he could just sleep through it and recover nicely, but blood poisoning was always a danger.

She was glad Daniel didn't have to witness what went on that day, though. Because of her conviction that Billy Crane would be unanimously condemned by the company, she was shocked to find that there were some who believed it had been an accident based on a misunderstanding. Sure, he was hasty, Mr. Gilmet explained at a meeting that afternoon. But Billy had thought he saw a movement Daniel made, and mistook it for a move toward his weapon.

Josephus and Rev. Kessler took Daniel's part, but they hadn't been present at the altercation.

When Esther related all these things to her late in the day, Kit reacted with fury.

"There's another witness," she said, rage in her voice. "And he's lying in this wagon!" She pointed to where Daniel slept. "When he is well, I think we ask him what happened. Until then, I think Mr. Crane should be confined."

"On that you'll find agreement, dear," Esther told her, taking the empty soup bowl and teacup back. "The company decided to have him stay in his wagon for the night."

"With a guard?"

"Whoever's on duty tonight," Esther answered. She didn't know who that was to be.

With Daniel laid up, the company talk of splitting turned more serious. It was as if his misfortune had come just in time, giving them the reasons they had lacked before for striking out on their own. The Gilmets and some diggers were eager to move along, sure the route they'd heard about would be faster than the one Daniel had mapped out for them. They didn't like lingering even for the trailmaster who'd left them with a sure hand so far.

Even the Culpepper boys, who had been quietly faithful to Kit's segment of the company, were justifiably, if timidly, eager to set out. Josephus took a leadership role, however, and told them that they needed to stay together for safety's sake, and they would wait until Daniel was up to traveling. He spoke out at a meeting in the evening, gathered around the Barton and Kessler campfire. As Kate looked from face to face from her perch in her wagon, she saw how untenable this plan was. Their destination was within reach now. Would she herself want to linger were it not for Daniel?

They would leave anyway. Josephus couldn't tie them to the train. And that would leave just her and Daniel and those who were too honorable to abandon them—the Bartons and the Kesslers.

"Let them go," she said to Esther, who lingered near her wagon during the meeting. "They won't be any help to us if they're pushing too fast. Daniel will need an easy, slow ride."

Esther agreed and went to have a word with her husband. Kit saw Rev. Kessler speak privately to Josephus after that, and then the minister spoke to the crowd.

"We've made our case for staying together," Rev. Kessler said. "But if you don't agree with our wisdom, then here is how the company ends.... " He proceeded to remind them of the rules in the contracts they'd signed, of how they'd have to pay up their share of fees and the like before leaving, and how he'd get those contracts from Daniel's kit, stored in the Barton wagon, in order to allow a fair tallying.

Heads nodded.

Josephus stood beside the Reverend. "Those who want to leave, come speak with me."

The meeting broke up, and it was no surprise to Kit to see a long line waiting to talk with Josephus. As she expected, all the company but the Kesslers and Bartons would now go on without them.

BY MORNING, Billy Crane was gone. Ernest Gilmet had been on guard duty the night before. Even the members of the company who were leaving looked at Gilmet in disgust and that included his wife, Lucy.

Daniel had done poorly throughout the night. He'd not slept well, tossing and groaning, muttering directions to imaginary travelers, telling Billy Crane to stand down. Kit herself had hardly slept at all, even during the hours when Esther came to relieve her watch, sending her to bed down in the Kesslers' own wagon while the Reverend camped on the ground. How could Kit spend even a moment away from Daniel now?

At breakfast that morning, Kit had barely sipped any coffee. She knew she looked a horror. Wilhemina urged her to eat.

"You've circles under your eyes, and your pallor is pale, my dear," Willa said, urging a biscuit on her. "Keep your strength up for him if not for yourself."

Kit ate.

It was another misty morning, and Kit shivered in her blue shawl.

"What's the matter, Kit?" Mary asked her.

"Nothing, nothing. I'm just a little chilly, that's all." But it was a heart-squeezing fear that chilled her, the fear that Daniel was not getting better. She feared he was getting worse.

THEY SAID GOODBYE to the rest of the company that morning. Despite the fact that Kit was not unhappy to be rid of some of the more unsavory characters, it was a sad parting. They all had endured great hardship together, creating a bond that was not easily broken.

Even the timid Lucy Gilmet felt it, hugging Kit tight as she bade her farewell, and telling her to take care of "that good man." She said she'd pray for him every day for the rest of her life. He'd kept them safe.

Seeing the line of wagons fade from view that morning brought a deep despair to Kit that she found hard to shake. She'd found a shred of faith during Rev. Kessler's prayer the night before, but now it seemed gone with the mist that burned off throughout the day.

Kit spent the day tending to Daniel—Josephus and the Reverend decided they'd rest one more day to give Daniel more time to heal—and each time she stepped into the wagon, she held her breath, fearing she'd find his own breath no more.

How could she revive her faith? What spark would ignite it again? Even when she'd been at her lowest moments with Josiah, she'd always found a sanctuary in her heart where she could call out to God for help. Now that voice was stilled. She didn't know if it was because she didn't think God would want to help her—her sins of deception came to mind as she contemplated this possibility—or that God couldn't help her. Billy Crane was the one responsible for this series of events, after all, not God.

Esther and Willa both spelled her throughout the day, wiping Daniel's brow, which was becoming feverish, and feeding him when he was awake enough to take nourishment. When Kit could stand to be away from him, she found herself walking into the magnificent forest around them, her heart and soul as empty as the woods.

Exhausted in body and spirit by day's end, she could barely murmur an Amen to Rev. Kessler's evening prayer. Esther noticed and approached her before turning in for the night.

"It's a hard time," she said to Kit, placing her hand on her shoulder. "But God will see you through it."

Kit looked down and said nothing, but Esther raised her chin to face her.

"Don't think I don't know your despair," she said, and Kit remembered Esther's story of her dead boy. "The Lord will forgive you your lack of faith, child. He will not hold it against you, no matter how He decides to bring you aid. Pray for acceptance."

Kit kissed her good-night on the cheek and stepped up into the wagon while Josephus put his own bedding together at the foot of the back wheels.

The Lord would forgive her lack of faith...

Why should she even care, Kit inwardly raged, about such forgiveness if Daniel didn't survive....

Why should it bother her at all...

But then she remembered Rev. Kessler's prayer about the woman who touched Jesus' hem. She felt like that woman, unworthy because of her own lack of faith. She couldn't "look God in the eye" right now. She couldn't utter a single prayer.

And yet... and yet the Lord could heal her. All she needed to do was touch the hem of His garment. Just her finger on the hem... that's all she needed to do. No more effort than that. A glancing touch...

She knelt beside Daniel's body and felt his forehead. Hot. Tears welled in her eyes. She picked up the soaked rag she'd dampened after dinner and wiped his brow.

She saw his eyes flicker at the movement. His mouth moved. She bent low to hear him whisper.

"I love you."

It was barely audible—as soft as the flutter of butterfly wings.

"And I, you," she said, patting his arm. "Don't leave me, Daniel Winchester."

His arm, the one on the side where he'd been shot, moved. He reached up and touched the hem of her shawl, reaching out to physically touch the love she'd just professed.

That's all she needed to do—touch the hem of God's love for her and hers for Him. Could she find that crumb of faith?

IN THE MORNING, they headed out, Josephus in the lead, and Rev. Kessler driving her own team.

Even though she had packed clothing around Daniel's body, the wagon wheels still jarred him, every movement a knife to Kit's heart. When he moaned, she inwardly screamed. But she prayed, too.

Ever since Daniel's admission of love the night before, Kit's spirits had entered a serene sense of acceptance. She no longer felt the absence of God, but instead felt His comfort. She didn't know what was in store. Nor did she assume her prayers would be answered. But she no longer felt unworthy of asking for help. As Esther had said, He would forgive her lack of faith in such a dark moment. She felt at least capable of belief once again, even if she sometimes felt she was mouthing prayers empty of a full measure of faith.

Her world became the inside of that wagon. Throughout the day, she tried to keep up a constant flow of prayer, song and talk. The prayers were silent. But she sang hymns and folk songs, which Daniel seemed to enjoy if his squeezing of her hand was any indication, and talked to him of the life they'd have together in California, of what a good job he'd done leading them through the trails, of her own happy childhood at Blue Hill.

Her singing and talking was but a distraction, however, from the hard reality of the situation. As they traveled up and up into chilly air and snow-scented mountains, a brushfire of fever began to slake through Daniel's body. The wound turned puffy and red, and more often than not, he tossed in delirium, fighting imagined dangers on the trail, calling her name, or telling Billy Crane to get back.

Near the time for their evening stop, Kit herself stopped, sinking back into a delirium of her own as she tried to parse out her inner feelings of both helplessness and rage.

The rage sometimes flooded her like a fever, too—rage at Daniel for taking chances, at Billy Crane, at Josiah, at her own stubbornness.

It was her stubbornness, after all, that had led her down the wedding aisle with Josiah Carlisle.

"The one she loved above all others." That was what her father had asked her before he agreed to give her hand to Josiah Carlisle, a man of whom he clearly didn't approve. But she had been persistent, telling her father what a good man Josiah really was and how he'd prove a good husband and son-in-law.

Her jaw tightened at that thought. Her eyes shut tight.

A good husband—on what had she based that grand supposition, she who'd known nothing of men but the compliments they'd paid her! And Josiah had bested everyone at that exercise.

Josiah Wendell Carlisle, youngest son of one of the most distinguished families in Boston—how could she have known what a wicked man he was? Maybe the clue had been in the obsequiousness of his courtship. No man could have meant everything he said to her. No man could have meant everything he'd done for her. She'd believed his falsehoods because she'd been a vain, stupid girl in love with his love, not with him.

He'd filled her dance card at the spring cotillion, sent her bouquets of fresh flowers and little presents, escorted her to church suppers, made a public display of his adoration by asking for her hand in marriage on a crowded Boston street—the final curtain in one long act.

No one in Boston had suspected that the great Carlisle Shipping Company was debt-ridden and on the verge of collapse. No one had known that the older Carlisle brothers were in Europe to avoid debt collectors, not scouting out new business or dealing with Asian traders. No one had known that Josiah had decided to save his skin by marrying into a moneyed family where a generous dowry would pay off his debts and a yearly income would allow him to live in style.

Josiah had told Basil Penwether that his heart "ached for the soothing balm of her gentle smile."

"What kind of man uses such vainglorious language?" her father had mused.

Vainglorious, she'd questioned?

"It's as if he loves the sound of his own voice," he'd answered.

That's what her father had said to her when preparing her for Josiah's imminent proposal. She had sat in front of the fire sewing, pulling the thread through the cloth but having a hard time concentrating. Her father often let her sit there in the evening while he worked on some papers or read. She had known Josiah was going to talk to him. She had suspected it was that day. Her father had finished reading some letters and then come over to her, sitting in the wing chair opposite the ottoman upon which she sat, ramrod straight. He had lit his pipe, taking his time, excruciatingly slow because Kate knew in her heart that he would reveal Josiah's proposal to her.

"Is he the one?" he finally had asked. "The one you love above all others?"

"Yes, of course," she had said quickly. But the question had bothered her. It had forced her to think of the "others." Surely she had loved—or thought she loved—Josiah more than any of the young men who had courted her that spring. She had lit on his dashing figure and beguiling ways immediately, and had felt favored that he had chosen her on whom to shower his attention. But what about her father? Had she loved Josiah more than she had loved him? Even when Josiah had proposed, the thought of leaving her father had cut her deeply. She'd visited him almost every week after he'd moved into his home in Boston, only forgoing visits when her bruises would have made him suspicious.

Now she knew what her father had meant. She had to love a man enough to want to leave her family for him. She had to love him "above all other men in her life."

She looked at Daniel. If Blue Hill were still whole, if her father were still alive, she would still follow Daniel.

He was sleeping again. But his breath was ragged, which disturbed her. And there was fresh blood on the bandage. She needed to change it. Better now than never, she thought. She gently prodded him in the arm.

"Daniel. Daniel, wake up. I'm going to change your dressing."

But he would not rouse. Her heart thumping wildly, she shook him a little. Still no response. She leaned over and listened to his heart. Still beating, but weak. *Oh no, he's come so far.* He was doing so well, just talking a little while ago.

Her nervous fingers found her embroidery scissors and slashed through the cloth that bound his shoulder. As she lifted him gently to pull the bandage from underneath, he moaned a little. She worked quickly to ease the pain. When she got to the bottom layer, she pulled the cloth swiftly so it wouldn't hurt him.

She took in her breath at the sight. The wound was still wet and the skin around it was swollen and red. Worse, there were red streaks emanating from the swelling. She knew what that could signify. Blood poisoning. *Oh Daniel*, she murmured to herself. You have to hold on.

She rummaged through her medicinal kit, finding the bottle of alcohol and a fresh cloth. She poured a little alcohol on the cloth and started to wash the wound. He flinched as she worked, and his hand moved to pull hers away, but other than that, he did not awaken.

His skin was on fire, so warm to the touch that she thought at first that she had left a hot mug from their midday meal in the bedding. With horror, she realized his shoulder and head were giving off the radiant heat.

"Not so fast," she whispered to him, finding the stubbornness that had led her to both foolishness and redemption. "Not so fast, Daniel Winchester. Give me some time, some time to show you what real love is."

She bathed the wound and rebandaged it, then forced him to drink more water.

When she was finished, he started to tremble and shake. He pulled the blanket loosely over him. As he sank deeper into trauma, he said things, most of which she couldn't understand. Only a few words were intelligible. She heard her name a few times and reassured him she was still there. And he must have been reliving the moment with Billy because she saw his hands reach as if for a gun and he muttered "stupid... not watching... ah... " Then later, "can't hurt her... " "never again... " And then she heard him murmur the beginning of the Lord's Prayer.

What had he told her—that he'd given up on praying after his Jane died?

He wasn't giving up—neither should she!

She finished his prayer for him, then bent low.

"I'm here, Daniel," she kept saying. "I'm here. I love you. I won't leave you."

HE KNEW THEY'D stopped. He knew it was dark. He heard voices. Kit had left him. No, not left. Gone for water. Why was he so cold, so hot? He blinked and tried to speak. Nothing came out. She needed to know...

Needed to know...

Go on with the company. Don't wait for me...

Had she heard?

He tried to raise his head. Something pushed him back. It was something in his shoulder. What was stuck there? Something like a knife.

He looked down. Nothing but a wad of bandages. But it felt... like a knife was jammed in the flesh.

With his other hand, he tried to pull it out but couldn't get a grip.

The pain was fierce.

It rippled through him, making him shudder.

Dear Lord...

You take care of her, Lord.

No more hurtin' for her.

You...

She was there, saying something, pushing his good hand away. Fussing with the bandages.

He looked at her, smiled.

Have to go now...

He dove underwater.

"The Lord is my Shepherd," she was saying...

Billy Crane was there, swimming toward him in the North Platte, gun in hand.

Daniel's hands wouldn't move; they were stuck to his side. And his heart raced as he saw the flash of the gun and felt a stabbing pain and heard Kit's voice telling him he would be fine.

He had his hands around Billy's neck strangling him, beating him, but then Kit appeared and told him to stop.

She was in the river, too. *Kit, Kit—get to dry land, woman!* Her head bobbed up and then down, like Peter Crane's. *Hold on now. I won't let you drown.* But she didn't hear. She was turning, looking around for him. Why didn't she see him, hear him... she was looking wild and lost and then let herself sink like a stone to the bottom. No! Her hair spread out in the water like an angel's halo and her eyes opened wide, staring straight ahead, her arms at her side, her dress ballooning out, her feet pointed down to the sandy river bottom

No, Kit! No! Don't give up!

He swam, but the water was like mud. He made little progress. Still, she floated just out of reach. If he tried harder...

He'd reach her if he tried harder. Closing his eyes, he pushed with all his might, thrashing the water with his arms and legs.

Kit, hold on!

IT SEEMED AS IF a hundred years passed instead of just the week it took them to come down through the mountains. Days of jostling and rumbling over rocky paths, nights of dark cold, and always Daniel in and out of fever, eyes glistening when they were open, body shivering and thrashing.

Kit passed those days in her own stupor, spelled by Willa and Esther for a few hours here and there, but more often not, Kit wouldn't relinquish her post.

She prayed regularly throughout this travail, but she had to admit to herself that sometimes her prayers were empty of true faith. In those dark moments, she'd remember the story of the woman touching the Lord's hem. That had to be enough—just that slight gesture of faith.

The camp was quiet with little conversation amongst the travelers and certainly no singing or joyful banter. A somber mood fell over all of them, and sometimes Kit angrily suspected Josephus or even Rev. Kessler acting as if they were on a death watch, waiting for the moment when Daniel would...

She couldn't think on it.

The weather, too, reflected her mood. Day after day, gray clouds hung over them, sometimes spitting cold rain or light snow. It made her feel as trapped as she'd felt on the desert crossings—but instead of relentless sun and heat, they were now caught in cold and shadows.

She didn't know how much longer she could stand it. But she couldn't give up—here her stubbornness served her well.

"No, Daniel Winchester, I could no more give up on you than I could on life itself," she said, climbing into the wagon for yet another evening of watching over him.

That night, fatigue overcame her and she fell into a deep sleep, so deep, in fact, that when she awakened in the early morning, her heart thudded as she wondered if she'd missed helping Daniel, if he'd needed a drink of water and been unable to rouse her.

Something felt different. With growing unease, she looked at him.

Pale, waxen, his mouth ajar... *No!*

Chapter Eighteen

"DANIEL?" HER VOICE was a whimper as she touched his good shoulder and shook him just a little. "Daniel?" she cried.

She pulled her hand back to her mouth, gulping in a sob.

Daniel.

His eyes flashed open. His parched lips moved.

"Kit?" he whispered.

"Yes?"

"I'm hungry."

She nearly tripped over herself leaving the wagon. She nearly shouted for joy as she clattered around the campfire, looking for the kettle, the pot.

"Kit? What's the matter child?" Esther came toward her in the blue dawn, hugging a shawl over her nightdress, a long brown-gray braid down her back.

"Breakfast," Kit said, so excited she couldn't think straight. "He wants some food."

Esther rushed toward her. "Praise the Lord!" She took the kettle from Kit's hands and poked up the fire, throwing on another log.

"Let me do this," Esther said, busily beginning the meal preparations. "Just a little will be best. We don't want to strain his stomach now." She turned and looked at Kit and laughed.

"You look a fright, dear. You go wash up. I'll tend to him and the breakfast."

HE NOT ONLY ate a breakfast of tea and cornmush that morning. He drank a full mug of broth at midday and asked for some bread. Although flushed in the evening, he still wanted food, and she served him a feast of biscuits, beef stew and a few bites of apple cobbler. Willa and Esther cooked the meal, and Daniel insisted on being helped from the wagon to warm himself by the fire and eat with the rest of their small company after Josephus helped him wash and later, shave the bristle from his face.

He looked pained to sit at their small table for too long, but no group could have been happier to have him in their midst. Young Mary asked if they could sing songs around the campfire, and Daniel, despite his fatigue, agreed to one tune before retiring for the night.

It was a rousing rendition of My Shepherd Will Supply My Need that wafted with the smoke into the crisp air that evening. Before helping Daniel onto newly-cleaned bedding, Kit looked up at the sky.

"Stars," she murmured. "We've not seen them for nearly a week—it's been so cloudy."

"It's a good night," Josephus added, his gaze lifted as well. "And tomorrow will be a good day."

JOSEPHUS WAS RIGHT. The next day was good. And the day after that. And after that.

Now that Daniel's fever had broken, he was able to sit beside Kit on the wagon bench while she guided her own team. After consulting with Josephus, he discovered they'd taken a wrong turn, and he quickly corrected it by leading them along another route, one offering what seemed to them, after such a hard journey, a gift from God Himself.

In the distance, at the far edge of the meadow, mountain peaks soared upward to touch the sky. At the foot of these, a dark green grove of pine trees looked small, while immediately in front of them, spread like a beauteous blanket, were tall grasses speckled with wildflowers. Kate saw spikey, rose-purple paintbrush, deep blue penstemon, and daisy-like pink asters dotting the landscape along with delicate mariposa lilies and alpine goldenrod. Butterflies were attracted to the flowers and added their own flashes of color—orange and blue. It was a painter's palette stretched before them. The frame itself was the mountain range beyond, rugged and masculine, holding in the gentle beauty of the meadow flowers like a father gently embracing his child.

Daniel looked over at her and smiled.

"You knew this was all here," she said, wonder in her voice. "You've seen it before."

"Yes. But there wasn't anyone to share it with." He flicked the reins, and the animals picked up their pace on the flatter stretch before them. Their wagon was in the lead now as Daniel charted the course.

She grinned at him. "You should rest. You've been driving the team all morning."

"It's good for me. Tomorrow I'm riding my horse."

"No!"

Daniel burst out laughing. "I'll stick to this," he said, chuckling. "I just wanted you to know it could be worse"

She grumped, but her heart wasn't in it. She couldn't stay mad with him. Ever since his turnaround, she couldn't stay angry with anyone. Each day she awoke with a song of praise on her lips. Soon they'd be in San Francisco and then...

They'd not talked about it, at least not beyond the "courting." In fact, Daniel seemed to have gotten a start on that, doing small kindnesses for her as his strength allowed. He let her take the reins in the afternoon so he could rest, but in the evenings he accompanied Josephus to water the animals for her, and he helped her clean up after the evening mess. He also insisted she sleep in her wagon again while he bedded down on the ground. But she'd hear none of that. Josephus settled it by constructing a tent in which he and Daniel camped out.

These things lifted her heart and endeared him to her. No foolish flattery or empty compliments came from him, just steady admiration and respect. That was a pleasure after Josiah. She reveled in his glances.

At the midday break, she couldn't contain her joy and ran through the meadow with Mary, gathering wildflowers.

This was nature's cathedral, she thought, staring up at the enveloping sky, the magnificent mountains.

When she returned to the wagons, her arms filled with blooms of yellow, blue and pink, she noticed Daniel talking seriously with Josephus and Rev. Kessler. Her smile left her. Was there a problem?

"Go on to your mother," Kit said to Mary, handing her some of the flowers. "Take these to her."

She took her own gathered flowers to her wagon, pinning some of the more fragrant of the bunch to her dress. As she passed the men on her way to help Esther with the noon meal, she caught a snippet of what Rev. Kessler was saying to Daniel.

"We won't stand in your way."

What was he talking about?

He saw Kit and smiled. Looking at Josephus, he nodded and suggested they get back to their chores. With that, Daniel turned to look at her.

"You're a sight for sore eyes," he said, devotion in his gaze.

"Are you flattering me, Mr. Winchester?" She stood directly in front of him.

His right arm was still bandaged, resting in a sling to take the pressure. His color was nearly back, but dark circles still shadowed his eyes. She guessed it would be a month or more before he was completely back to normal. But every day was a step in that direction. This filled her heart with inexpressible joy.

"Just telling the truth, ma'am." He took off his hat, a gesture of respect. "May I take you for a stroll?" he asked, cocking his good elbow toward her.

She looked over her shoulder at the camp.

"Don't worry," he said. "I already talked to them about my intentions. No chaperone is necessary."

She blushed. Taking his arm, she let him lead her back into the meadowland.

"You know my intention was to court you proper," he began, placing his hat back on his head.

"Yes. And I will be holding you to that, Mr. Winchester," she teased.

He looked down. "Then you'll be disappointed, I'm afraid."

She stopped, her heart pounding. Was he telling her he'd reconsidered and wanted to stay on the trail? That was why he'd been talking to the other men—letting them know his plans. And they'd agreed, from what she'd overheard. They'd told him they had no objections.

All right. She'd accept it. He was alive. That's all that mattered. He'd said he loved her. That would be enough. It would have to be.

"Daniel, don't trouble yourself," she said, staring into his eyes. "I can understand how what you have been through might shift your view of things. I'll be content to go on with—"

"Go on where, Kit?" He peered at her, confusion in his own eyes. "Hear me out, now."

She opened her mouth to speak, but his serious look stopped her.

"I spoke with Rev. Kessler this morning. Both he and Josephus agree that my promise to court you proper can be set aside."

"Yes," she said, nodding. "I won't hold you to—"

"Listen to me," he said, interrupting. "I do want you to hold me to something, and that's the promise such a courtship leads to. That's what I'm trying to tell you, Kit. I'm asking for your hand in marriage now. It's sudden, I know. But like I said, Rev. Kessler thinks it's all right to do it this way. He thinks we've been through a lifetime already—or what counts as such in some people's view. These last weeks, and all we've been facing, they've made me realize... well, I don't want to waste no more time, Kit. I want to skip over the courtship and ask you now...." He held her hand with this good one. "Will you marry me, Kit?

A gurgle of joyous laughter sprang from her as her hand fluttered up her chest.

"Yes. Yes, Daniel! I will marry you!"

Chapter Nineteen

TO SEAL THEIR engagement, Daniel presented her with a reed ring that evening, something he'd woven from grass blades on the meadow.

As tempting as it was, they did not linger in that beautiful spot. To Kit, time no longer mattered. She felt like she was walking on air. The pain, the aches, the worry of the past few months—even the past few years—lifted off her, and she began every morning with a prayer of thanks on her lips. Her energy, which had flagged during Daniel's infirmity, now multiplied tenfold. With Willa's help, she began turning a dress of a rosebud pattern, ripping out seams and re-sewing it inside out, the now-fresh side clean and bright. It would be her wedding dress.

Daniel told her one evening that he had some land down the coast, near the Salinas Valley, and he'd always dreamed of starting a ranch there when he'd tired of the trail. They'd head there after a stay in San Francisco, after the wedding.

Their small band all joined in the wedding preparations, with Mary excitedly sewing a lace handkerchief for Kit as a gift, and Esther and Willa both giving her treasures from their small inventory of belongings. Esther presented her with a blue-china teapot, while Willa bestowed on her a delicately-sewn quilt. Kit protested she couldn't take such fine things from them, but they'd hear none of it. It would make them happy, they told her, knowing she had these things in her new household with Daniel.

The men, too, gave Daniel presents. Josephus presented him with a saddle blanket, and Rev. Kessler gave him a book of hymns he was "sure Kit would use to soothe him with."

They were a merry group as they came down from the mountains, and hardly anything seemed capable of dimming the sunshine of their bliss.

WHEN THEY FINALLY approached the outskirts of the young and wild San Francisco, they all tensed, becoming quieter with each mile. Daniel, who was now out of the sling and riding his horse part of each day, checked his guns every morning. Josephus and Rev. Kessler kept their rifles close at hand. The city had a reputation for bad characters.

As they started down its hilly streets, the first thing Kit noticed about San Francisco was the absence of women. Men were everywhere—miners in town for a spree, shopkeepers, ranchers bringing in beef, hunters toting game, restaurateurs catering to this ever-changing populace. Gambling places abounded, and in the doors of those, Kit glimpsed a few members of the fairer sex. But they were women of Billy Crane's liking, dressed in gaudy satins and filmy silks with ruffles barely concealing their deep-shadowed bosoms. Glittering jewels were at their throats and ears, and feathers decorated elaborate hairstyles of ringlets and waves. Their faces were covered with rouge and lip paint and some even had a sooty line around their eyes, giving them an eerie, cat-like look.

Most of the women appeared exotic—Mexican or Chilean ladies. But one woman who stared straight at her as they passed by in their wagon was not. She was tall and buxom and wore a deep purple satin and velvet dress with vertical stripes at the bodice, and a tuft of black lace falling gently over her breasts. Her corn silk yellow hair was smoothed back from her face into a bun at the crown of her head, into which she had pressed black lacquered combs. A beauty mark was painted on one of her rouged cheeks, and red glass earrings dangled provocatively below each earlobe. When she saw Kit, their gazes locked, and then the woman hurried back inside a saloon, as if on an errand to tell someone what—or whom— she'd seen.

Kit shivered.

They would stop in San Francisco only long enough to do three things, Daniel had told her as he whipped the reins on the team and guided them towards Kearney Street, the site of a new four-story brick hotel called the Union. They would formally marry. Daniel would retrieve his savings from the vault of the San Francisco Bank. And they would replenish their supplies and head south. There was a chance the Bartons and Kesslers would travel that way, too. The Bartons were looking at a homestead south of San Francisco, and the Kesslers' son had a ranch just north of Monterey in a farming town.

None of them were eager to stay too long in the city. It was too risky—too many bad types around and certainly not a place for good women.

At the hotel, Daniel helped Kit down from the wagon and walked with her up to the front of the brick building.

"I'm going to register myself," he said, "but you're going to stay with a preacher's family."

"Why?" The thought of being separated from him suddenly filled her with cold fear. "We don't need to do that. Esther will serve as chaperone."

But Daniel ignored her. "Rev. Kessler says he knows a minister who's moved into town, settled in, holds services every week. The Reverend is taking Esther there, and you'll go along with them."

"What about Willa and Josephus?" she asked, looking over her shoulder to where they waited in their wagon.

"They're going to an encampment on the southern edge of the city."

"They won't be here for our wedding?" Kit couldn't keep the disappointment from coloring her voice.

Daniel smiled. "They'll be there. They're delaying their journey for our sake." He looked over at the wagon, too. "Why don't you go on and sit with Mrs. Barton and Mary for a spell? Josephus and I need to buy some supplies and it won't take but a few minutes."

She obeyed him, hurrying to the Barton wagon to join the girls, while Josephus headed toward Daniel. She watched as they first went into the hotel, then reappeared a few minutes later, disappearing into a general store not far away.

The sounds of piano music drifted up the street on the morning air, and sometimes men would pass the wagon and give them uncomfortable looks.

"I do hope we can settle close by," Willa said to Kit, patting her hand. "I'd be more than pleased to have you as a neighbor."

"I share that hope," Kit responded, nervous as they waited for their men to return.

The baby in the wagon started to awaken, so Kit went back to soothe him as Willa instructed Mary on how best to handle some stitches on her wedding gift project.

For the next quarter hour or so, Kit contentedly rocked the baby, glad to be out of sight. Something about San Francisco unsettled her—it was as if someone were watching her, tracking her movements.

The baby had just fallen back asleep when she heard the men approaching. Although she didn't try to overhear their conversation, it was impossible not to as they came closer.

"I'm sure of my eyes, Dan'l," Josephus was saying.

"I don't doubt that. But a lot of men look like that." Daniel's voice was tight.

"That's true. But be cautious. That's the only reason I'm telling you."

"I understand. And I'm grateful for it.'

What did they mean? Who had Josephus seen? Kit put on a smile as she came out of the Barton wagon to rejoin Daniel, but her heart was thudding with fear. She could think of only one man Josephus would see fit to warn Daniel about—Billy Crane.

THE AFTERNOON WAS spent settling in. Daniel and Josephus took their women to the house of Rev. Charles Quimby and his wife, Ellen, where they reunited with the Kesslers. Rev. Kessler directed the men toward a nearby stable and corral in which they could board the animals and leave their wagons for a spell. Willa, Mary, Kit and the baby, meanwhile, were welcomed into the Quimby household where they'd enjoy an evening meal.

It was one of the few family homes in this city of stores and banks and hotels and saloons. A large frame building, it sported a bedraggled garden by the front steps that appeared to be losing the battle between its caretaker's ministrations and the trampling of careless miners who strode past it every day.

When Rev. Quimby had opened the door to them, his face had immediately lit up with a large grin and he practically pulled Daniel and Kit into his house.

"My goodness, you must be Daniel Winchester! I'm so pleased to see you. So glad you've made it through. Andrew has told me a great deal about your good counsel." Then looking at Kit, he said, "And this must be your betrothed. How honored we are to have you stay with us, Miss Austen. Please do come in."

The Kesslers stood in the parlor smiling at them as they entered.

The inside of the house made up for the wildness outside. It was a temple to orderliness, with crocheted cloths on tables and chairs, polished wood floors, the scent of just-baked bread, bright white cotton curtains at the windows, and a warm-hearted host and hostess.

Rev. Charles Quimby was a Georgia-born gentleman, long and straight, with a shiny bald pate and a dusting of wiry gray hair above his ears. His facial features were small and birdlike, but his cheerful eyes danced with good will behind wire-framed spectacles. When she heard her husband's voice, Ellen Quimby came out of the kitchen at the back of the house to see who was visiting them. She was short and plump. Her hair was brown, streaked with gray, pulled into a bun at the nape of her neck. Her hands were pudgy little pincushions of flesh, always moving, grasping each other and fidgeting, pulling at a spotless apron of white starched cotton.

Staring at Kit and Willa and Mary, Mrs. Quimby's eyes watered. "My, my—it's so wonderful to see so many women!"

This was followed by hugs and an interrogation as to sleeping arrangements. When Willa said she and Josephus were camping south of town that night, Ellen Quimby shook her head and stomped her foot.

"No, my dear. You will do no such thing. You have not slept in a real bed since taking to the trail, and it might be weeks or months before your husband is able to build you one. You shall sleep in one tonight. And the next and the next, God willing, before you take up your journey again."

Before Willa could respond, Rev. Quimby laughed. "Now, don't be thinking you'll change her mind. You might as well accept her invitation now, instead of after hours of trying to tell her otherwise."

It was settled. Willa, Mary and the baby would share one of the three bedrooms, while Esther and Kit would take another. The rooms, the Quimbys explained, were for just this purpose—taking in travelers who needed respite.

What a jolly afternoon and evening they all had together. The four women took to the kitchen and lent their aid in preparing a true feast—rare roasted potatoes and turkey, fresh tomatoes and lettuce, green beans and corn, beaten biscuits, apple butter and even two pies—a dried cherry and something Ellen Quimby called shoofly.

While they worked, they talked. Or rather, Ellen Quimby talked. She and her husband had heard the calling to go west to minister to those settling in the state much the way the Kesslers had. The Quimbys' five children were grown and settled in Georgia, Louisiana and Texas, and they'd been hard-pressed to say goodbye to them, even if they only saw them but once every few years.

"I never felt so right about something as I did the first day we took to the trail west," she said as she removed a tray of biscuits from her oven. "It's been a blessing ever since. Hard, yes. But a joyful hard."

Her husband had set up a small church around the corner, and they rejoiced every time some rowdy boys from town came in. Some of them kept to it while others only found redemption in one morning of church, sliding back into troubled ways the next week.

"But we are grateful for every soul that comes our way," Ellen said. "And Charles keeps his eyes on who's coming into town and what they might be needing—or fixing to do."

This reassured Kit, that the Quimbys would be so knowledgeable about new arrivals.

They crammed around the Quimbys' dining room table, and Rev. Quimby said the grace. After that, it was a feast of laughter and good food, as the men recounted stories of the trail, sometimes exaggerating their heroics and politely setting each other straight.

At one point, Kit sat silent and smiling, looking around the table at the happy group, people she now counted as her friends, glancing across at Daniel who winked back at her and thinking of how far she had come. Not just in miles, but in distance from her past heartache to this new happiness. How blessed she felt!

After the men had bid farewell and the women were finished cleaning, Kit lingered in the kitchen to talk to Ellen while Esther and Willa made ready for bed.

"You said your husband keeps track of new arrivals," Kit said.

"Why, yes, dear. It's not that big a city, and easy to see when new companies are coming in."

"Would he know them by name—people who've recently arrived?"

Ellen folded a dishtowel and leaned on her kitchen table. "Who are you looking for?"

Kit swallowed. "A man named Billy Crane. He... he caused trouble on the trail and left the company."

Ellen came over and squeezed her arm. "Don't fret about it, dear. I'll ask Rev. Quimby if he's seen such a man. If Mr. Crane has come through in the past month, my husband will know."

FOR SEVERAL DAYS, they lingered in San Francisco. It was longer than they'd originally planned, but the Quimbys' hospitality made any anxieties Kit had felt when entering the town disappear. Their delay was caused by some problems with the Bartons' wagon and preparations for the wedding, which would be held in the parlor of the Quimby house.

These days, just like the time after Daniel's recovery, were dream days for Kit. She and Esther shared a room that brightened their spirits just to walk over its threshold--rose-patterned wallpaper, a wrought iron bed covered in downy blue quilting, large feather pillows at the head, a hooked rag rug on the floor, a maple chest with a marble top, a matching lady's dressing table, and a rocking chair in the corner by the window. At the sight of such comfort, Kit had felt the miles drop away.

Comfort multiplied with each meal they shared together. The Quimbys were beyond generous with their food and Mrs. Quimby was a magnificent homemaker with a pantry full of preserved fruits and vegetables and a garden bursting with harvest's bounty.

She also was an accomplished seamstress, a skill she put to work the morning after their arrival when she came into Esther and Kit's room burdened with so much clothing that Kit almost couldn't see her head over the piles of frothy fabrics, some in gaudy colors but all made of rich materials—satins, silks, velvets, fine linens.

"What is this?" Kit asked as Ellen threw the clothing on the bed.

"The remnants of sin!" exclaimed Ellen with a giggle. "Over the last year, my husband and I have had some modest success in converting some of the foreign girls to the Lord's way," she explained. "We help them learn to read and I teach them to sew, to tend house, and then we give them enough money to make it to Sacramento, where a friend of ours, Reverend Mandrake, runs a boarding school for girls. When the girls leave us, they leave these behind. I tear them up and use them for quilts and pillows and whatever I can think of... But somewhere in here might be something for you, something we could alter just a tad, for a proper young lady to wear on her wedding day...."

"What wonderful work you do," Esther said, helping sort through the pile. "You are providing me a great example, Ellen Quimby. I hope I am able to accomplish half of what you and your husband have done here."

They began rummaging through the clothes, and Kit smiled at the sight of the stout little woman paddling through the sea of silk. She seemed to be looking for something in particular and finally pulled it from the group.

"Oh my, oh my, here it is," Ellen said and pulled from the stack of discards a pale dress that stood in stark contrast to the richer-hued garbs on the bed. "This might seem a bit garish at first, but I know what to do."

She held up the dress. It was a very pale pink shade of light silk, so light that it seemed to float in the air when Ellen offered it to her. Despite her reluctance, Kit reached out to touch it. It was like a cloud. But its color and fabric were the only demure features to the dress. The front was cut so low as to be immodest. Large bows, edged in shiny black satin, decorated the sleeves and the back of the dress. The black satin edging continued around the hem as well.

"I know what you're thinking, my child," Ellen said, holding the dress up in front of her. "Do you really want to wear something that was used to... well, in the service of temptation? But if the person who wore this can be redeemed, I see no reason at all why the dress itself can't be born again!"

They all laughed. Esther immediately began making suggestions. "If we remove the satin border—"

"And sew a lace panel here," Mrs. Quimby said, pointing to the décolletage.

"Yes, that would be perfect." Esther turned to Kit, smiling. "Of course, perfect if it's what you want."

Kit thought of the simple rosebud-patterned dress she'd turned inside-out on the trail. This dress would be far grander—she could hardly wait to see Daniel's reaction when he viewed her in it.

"It's more than what I want! But you must let me help."

Willa, who'd been tending to her baby, came in the room. "If there is work to be done, please let me join in."

Ellen Quimby put her hands on her hips. "We'll have a sewing bee today. I've almost finished embroidering some linens and knitting a scarf. We'll sit round the parlor—making sure no menfolk come in—and prepare for the wedding."

GETTING READY FOR the wedding and getting ready to leave occupied every moment of the days ahead. Daniel came round in the evenings with the other men, and it was as if he and Kit were real courters now, with their chaperones watching over their ardent gazes in the parlor room after dinner. Kit felt like a girl again.

So profound was her step into happiness that she began shaking off any residual fears. She would have let them go entirely were it not for an uneasy feeling of being watched. Sometimes in the kitchen, she would glance out the back window and swear she saw a shadow disappearing down the byways. Like the gaze from the woman in the saloon, it rattled her. But she shook it off, telling herself she was in the habit of worry and would have to learn to discard it like any other bad habit.

More unsettling news followed that evening, though. After they'd cleared the dishes away, the men sat at the table talking over travel plans while the women washed up in the kitchen. But in between their own chatter, Kit overheard disturbing news.

Billy Crane was in town.

Rev. Quimby explained to Daniel how Kit had asked his wife about the man. It had taken him a few days to track down the fellow, but he'd eventually found him in a saloon on the main street.

Probably the saloon where Kit had seen the woman rushing to tell someone of their arrival!

"He was with a rowdy bunch of no-goods, as far as I could tell, hootin' and hollerin' on a spree," Rev. Quimby said.

"I was afraid of that," Josephus said. "I thought I'd seen him—and he saw me—when we went for that gear our first day in town."

Rev. Kessler spoke. "This Crane fellow is a bad sort. He shot Daniel on the trail."

"Ellen told me the story. Your wife explained the history to her."

"What else did you learn about him?" Daniel's voice, as hard as iron.

Rev. Quimby continued, "Like I said, he's with a bad crowd, not hard to find in this city. A small group of men who, unfortunately, feel they can get away with almost anything. They'd planned on heading back East awhile ago, but changed their minds and now harass newcomers, selling them snake-oil medicines and equipment they don't need."

The men talked some more, but Kit couldn't make it all out as Esther asked her to put away some dishes in a far cabinet. When she returned near the door, she heard a man's fist crashing into the table, and then Daniel spoke.

"It's not done with Billy. It won't be done until he's..."

"Don't say it, Daniel," Rev. Kessler said. "Vengeance is the Lord's."

"It's not vengeance I seek. It's safety."

With that, Kit rushed into the room, towel still in hand.

"Please, Daniel, heed their advice. We'll be leaving Billy and this town behind soon...."

"As long as he's got an eye out for either of us, we'll never leave him behind, Kit." He stared at her with dark intensity, his brows furrowed.

She fell at his knees, looking up to him, pleading with him. "But there's no point in seeking out trouble.

We're so happy now. Please, Daniel, I'm begging you. For my sake, leave him be."

Rev. Kessler agreed. "Listen to her, Daniel. You have her to think of as well now."

"That's who I am thinking about!" Daniel said, his voice rising. "I've come across the likes of Billy Crane before. They don't stop until they've—"

Rev. Quimby reached over and patted Daniel's arm. "Hush now," he said, nodding his head toward Kit. "There's no point in stirring up trouble."

Daniel let out a long sigh.

"I won't go seeking trouble," he said at last. "But I won't run from it should it find me."

Chapter Twenty

WITH ONLY ONE DAY until the wedding, Kit pushed aside any worries about Billy Crane by reminding herself of Daniel's words, that he wouldn't go seeking trouble. Soon, they'd be far from any trouble. Once they left San Francisco, Billy Crane would be behind them. It was unlikely he'd follow them beyond the city now that he'd found a new group of "friends" and San Francisco offered so many temptations.

She told herself—and Esther helped remind her—that there was no point in imagining troubles that didn't exist. Billy Crane had not found them at the Quimbys, and if he knew they were in town, he surely knew this was where they were staying. Perhaps his flame of resentment had burnt out, and they'd be left alone.

Kit's wedding day dawned misty, with the sun occasionally cutting through the clouds that rolled in from the sea. Ellen fussed around her all morning, bringing a tray to her room with tea and cakes and a vase with red flowers.

"Don't worry, child," Ellen told Kit. "The weather will be fine. A bright, cheerful day to remember all your life. The fog always rolls in in the morning."

Kit cared little about the weather. Or about the food set before her. She couldn't eat this morning. She was too nervous, too restless. She just wanted Daniel to walk through the front door, to start their life together. They were to be wed at noon.

Mary kept running into her room asking when she'd be putting on her dress, and Willa scolded her. But Kit didn't mind the distraction. The girl's giddiness was infectious.

To Kit's delight, Ellen's prediction came true and by midmorning, sunshine drenched the city, with a cool breeze blowing in from the ocean.

While Willa dressed Mary in a new frock sewn from plaid taffeta found among the discards, Kit let Esther slowly brush her hair. In the other room, they could hear Mary asking her mother when she'd be old enough to get married. Both women smiled.

"Don't fret about anything, child. This is a day for nothing but happiness."

Kit smiled at Esther and reached up to pat her hand.

A knock at the door was followed by Ellen blustering in, then by Willa and Mary, whose hair was only half-braided. In Ellen's hands was the dress. Gone were the garish black-edged gewgaws. Gone was the revealing neckline and inappropriate back. In its place was a splendid gown, fit for the best society ladies, a pink confection with white gauzy silk in creamy layers at the neck, a plain hem, and some more of the gauze at the sleeves.

"Oh, oh, it's too lovely. My word! I don't know what to say!" Kit stood and went to the gown to touch it, its inviting softness calling out to be felt. She'd seen them working on it, of course, but Ellen had been secretive about the last bits of tailoring. "Thank you, all, thank you so much!" Kit leaned over and hugged each woman in turn.

"Now, now, don't make me weep," Ellen said. "It was no trouble, no trouble at all. I have some flowers for you too, some white hollyhocks. Would have more but some bumbling oaf stumbled into my garden last night."

"Oh, yes. I saw how your poor garden suffers," Willa said. "You'd think passers-by would take more care."

"No, no, not the front one. I've given up on that one, my dear. My back garden! Can you imagine? It's not bad enough that they fall all over the front in their drunken stupors. But to come all the way 'round back! Why, they must be blind with the demon rum, just blind! But this isn't the day to think on such things. Let me know if you need my help, Kit. I'll be right downstairs. Just fixing up a little fruited punch and some biscuits. Maybe a tart with blueberry jam. You have to have some sort of wedding feast!" She was gone from the room in a bustle of energy.

But the woman's bubbling effervescence wasn't enough to keep a nagging worry from entering Kit's thoughts. While Willa insisted Mary go back to their room so she could finish the girl's hair, Kit went to the window and peered below into the Quimby back yard. It was a small plot of land that Mr. Quimby had surrounded with a fence, an Eastern-style picket fence painted white.

Yet inside this little piece of Georgia garden, with its blooming flora and trimmed bushes, was a clear indication of a nighttime intruder. Long-stemmed delphinium had been bent by some heavy foot. Tall lamb's ears had been trampled and ruined. Nothing had been stolen—a hoe and shovel still leaned against the southern fence.

With a shiver of fear, Kate noticed yet one more piece of damage. A trellis, with a winding vine of the red flowers Mrs. Quimby had brought to her that morning, rested against the house. One or two of its latticework rungs were broken. Someone had climbed it in the night. It stopped just short of her window.

"Esther," she whispered, and the woman came up and put her hands on her shoulders.

"Don't think on it," Esther repeated. "You don't know if it was him."

So even Esther had assumed, like Kit, that it had been Billy.

DANIEL ARRIVED. He was early. As Kit heard his voice in the vestibule below, relief rushed through her. She felt safer and happier knowing he was there.

"You didn't think he'd not come, did you?" Esther teased, seeing Kit's big grin.

Kit laughed. "I knew he'd come. I'm just glad to be able to get on with our lives now." Get on the trail again, away from San Francisco, away from Billy and his friends.

She sat at the dressing table, and admired Esther's work with her hair. Gleaming from a good wash, it was braided and coiled in a bun at the crown of her head. Esther had even woven some delicate white blossoms through the strands, after helping her into the pink gown.

Esther herself had changed into a robins-egg blue dress with eyelet lace at the neck.

"I've not see that gown, Esther. Did you sew it from Ellen's materials?"

Esther smiled and shook her head. "I'd saved it on the trail—to wear for my husband's first Sabbath service once we'd settled. But this seems like just as worthy a celebration."

"I'm honored, Esther," Kit said, thinking of how she'd tried to spare a dress to wear once they'd reached

California, but had ended up using all her small store of them as the days had worn on.

"If you don't need me any longer, I'll go see if I can help Willa with the baby," Esther said.

"Go along. I'm fine. Thank you for all you've done." Kit stood.

Esther stared at her, biting her lip. Then in a rush, she came forward and embraced Kit.

"You are the most beautiful bride I've ever seen, dear." She wiped a tear from her eye as she stepped back, admiring Kit.

After Esther left, Kit opened a small wooden box from her bag. From it, she pulled the grass-woven ring Daniel had given her in the high mountain meadow. It was faded and starting to dry now. She slipped it on her right hand.

Closing her eyes, she murmured, "Help me to be a good wife, Lord. You have seen us through so many trials, when my faith was often low. Now it is strong. Keep us safe."

In a few minutes, Ellen came to her door to fetch her. But Kit was ready and waiting before the door even opened. When it did, Ellen Quimby raised her hand to her mouth and suppressed a cry.

"Oh, my child, my child! You are a princess. I knew that dress would suit you. You have the coloring for it, the figure. You look like a dream. My, my, your gentleman will be so pleased."

Ellen herself had donned a dark, hunter green frock of heavy watered silk. At her throat was a lace collar, and a tiny cap of matching lace adorned her head. A silver filligreed pin with an onyx center was affixed near her shoulder and she carried a lace-edged handkerchief in one hand and a nosegay of fuchsias in the other.

"They're ready for us, dear," she said. "I'll go down first. You follow." Clearly, the woman had thought out the ceremony as if it were being held in a cathedral.

No fear clutched at Kit's heart as she walked down those stairs, following the straight back and deliberate pace of Ellen Quimby. She breathed easily, her heart beating out a steady rhythm leading her to the moment when she'd be united with her beloved.

An uplifting joy Kit had never experienced before squeezed her heart as soon as she saw Daniel's hat hanging on the post by the door. The house was silent except for the ticking of a clock, the muted sound of their footsteps on the stairs, and the gurgle of Willa's babe.

Daniel saw her midway down the stairs, through the arched entryway to the parlor. He took in his breath at the sight of her, and his gaze locked on hers. Did she hear him speak or did she hear his thoughts—*I love you. Forever.*

Kit swallowed as she took in his appearance. She had never seen him in anything but utilitarian trail clothes, and she smiled at what a fine figure he cut in his dark black trousers and new white shirt, gray vest, and black tie. Charles Quimby stood in front of him, holding a prayer book to his chest. It all seemed slowed down, as if they were moving through water, each step taking longer, each breath a conscious effort, each moment an hour, a blessed hour. She wanted to stay locked in this moment. Every moment with Daniel was a blissful eternity. *Forever. Tomorrow.*

She was beside him. Charles Quimby was raising the prayer book, clearing his throat. Ellen was standing to the side, a handkerchief already at her eyes. Willa, Josephus, the Kesslers, Mary—they all gathered around. She noticed Willa and Esther held flowers—Ellen had probably picked them for them. Such a thoughtful woman.

Charles began the ceremony, the familiar words, *do you take this woman... do you take this man... love, honor, obey... till death... the ring...*

To Kit's surprise, Daniel had a ring. He pulled it from his vest pocket, a small gold band with a coral cameo. She looked into his eyes, her own eyes glistening with unshed tears of joy. As he moved the ring over her finger, she felt her body sway from the intoxicating moment.

I now pronounce you...

Daniel leaned towards her, brushed her lips with a kiss that felt like a bolt of lightning striking her heart. *I love you, dear*, she thought. And heard his unvoiced answer.

Mrs. Quimby was crying in full force now, while Esther sniffled and Willa told Mary how good she'd been. The ceremony over, Mr. Quimby turned to her and comforted her. "Now, now, Ellen. Don't make them worry over your goings-on."

Esther suggested they sing a hymn, so they all joined in song of praise and gladness. Their spirits as bright as the sunshine outside, they moved into the dining room where the women insisted Kit sit with her new husband while they fussed with serving them.

Daniel looked over at her and squeezed her hand.

"We'll leave at daybreak," he whispered.

It was exactly what she wanted to hear. One more night in San Francisco and they'd be on their way.

"Have you told Mrs. Winchester about your ranch plans, Daniel?" Josephus asked. Kit blushed at the use of her new name and smiled.

"She knows I have some land." He turned to her. "I'm giving some acreage to the Bartons and Kesslers in exchange for help with setting up a cattle herd."

"And building a proper house," Rev. Kessler pointed out.

"We'll all be helping each other on that," Josephus said. "But your house, Mrs. Winchester, will be the first raised."

Daniel smiled broadly. "And you can tell us how you want it planned out."

Kit's heart soared. At first she thought of her home back in Boston—could they build another Blue Hill here? Then she remembered some of the long, low Spanish buildings Daniel had described to her, those he'd seen in Monterey. That's what she would want. Not another Blue Hill. Those days were over.

They feasted on Ellen's wedding banquet for a good portion of the afternoon, even joining in to sing songs and hymns together the way they used to around the campfires. By the time Daniel suggested they head out together, it was nearing sunset.

"We'll be back in the morning to say farewell," Daniel said to the Quimbys at the door.

"And to fetch our wives," Josephus added, as he too left.

One wife wouldn't need fetching. Kit was joining Daniel that night at the Union Hotel.

"You can still consider staying here for the winter," Rev. Quimby said. "The rains will come soon and the roads will be tough going for a wagon. Don't want to be stuck in the mud all winter. We would welcome the company."

"If we begin tomorrow, we'll surely beat the worst of it," Kit said. She didn't want to linger here, as wonderful as the Quimbys had been. "We've been through hard trails. It would be good to be settled before the spring."

Daniel smiled. "I guess I'm already learning my wife wants a say in things. But I do say I agree with her."

They parted ways, Daniel driving her in a borrowed carriage into town.

"I didn't know Mrs. Quimby would plan so much food," Daniel said, flicking the reins. "I'd planned on treating you to dinner at the Sutter Restaurant this evening."

Kit laughed, feeling warm and comfortable next to her new husband. A bright future stretched before them, and her spirits felt as light as the air.

"To tell the truth, I could hardly eat a bite at the Quimbys."

"Same with me." Daniel chuckled. "Too much excitement."

They supped that evening at the Sutter Restaurant, where they had roast duck for an exorbitant five dollars, precious potatoes and even some late green tomatoes. The dining room was bright and comfortable but crowded. Even a high quality establishment such as Sutter's attracted diggers and gamblers. Everyone ate in restaurants in San Francisco.

It didn't matter to Kit and Daniel, though. They were alone in their own universe. Finally able to talk in private after days of wedding preparation, they shared their observations and thoughts, their hopes and dreams.

"So what kind of house would you like, Mrs. Winchester?" Daniel asked at the end of the meal. "Some grand mansion with pillared drive like they have down south?"

"No, I was thinking more of the types of houses you've told me about—haciendas?"

He nodded. "That's the word. They're cool in midday heat, and open to the outdoors."

"I can hardly wait to see one."

He smiled, and it felt as if she'd lived here forever, with no past, no connection to anything but this sunny land.

"And don't be calling me Mrs. Winchester," Kit chided. "We're in a new place, with new customs."

"What should I call you, then—your given name, Katherine?"

She shook her head vehemently. "Never. Katherine is gone. Call me Kit."

"Kit," he whispered.

"I wish we could leave tonight," she said, staring into his eyes. "I want so much to just start our life together."

"We've already started that life," he said huskily, his hand reaching out for hers on the table.

They finished their coffee and wandered out into the moonlit night, holding hands like schoolchildren.

"Unusually bright," Daniel commented, looking at the full moon that shone through wispy strands of clouds.

"Which is why we could set out this evening," Kit added.

Daniel chuckled and slipped his arm around her waist. "You don't give up, do you?"

"You should know that by now, Mr. Winchester," she replied.

He leaned over her and brushed her lips with a kiss.

With giddy anticipation, they walked the few blocks to the Union Hotel. Inside the lobby, the clerk looked up and called them over before they headed upstairs to their room.

"Mr. Winchester, a man came by to see you, left a message." He handed Daniel a folded slip of paper.

Daniel opened it at the desk, letting Kit read over his shoulder.

"Dear Daniel,

The Mrs. and I will be leaving at first light. Would be much obliged if you could stop by the stable this evening to help me with troubles. It won't take long. Sincerely, Josephus Barton."

"Josephus wasn't happy with the way his wheel axle was acting," Daniel said, tipping his hat back. "He and I wrestled with it yesterday." He looked reluctant to leave. "I could see to it in the morning."

"He said it won't take long. Go on now," Kit said, understanding Daniel's need to still see to his travelers' problems. "Josephus is a man of his word." And he wouldn't have contacted them on their wedding night if it weren't serious, she thought. She could spare her husband for a little while.

Daniel looked at her, and then at the broad staircase leading to the rooms upstairs. He grimaced. "If it looks to be a lengthy job, I'll tell him I'll get to it in the morning and we'll just take off a little later." She touched his arm, proud of his loyalty to their friends and his respect for her.

He accompanied her to their room. She was touched to see he'd placed some flowers there—Mrs. Quimby's idea, he shyly admitted—and had already stowed her bag in the armoire.

"I won't be long," he said after a deep kiss. "Nothing could keep me from you, my Kit."

AS SOON AS HE was gone, Kit lit the kerosene lamp by the bed and set to looking through her bag to make sure she'd not left anything at the Quimbys. Her mind had been such a muddle when she'd packed, she was amazed she hadn't forgotten the most rudimentary items. Done with that task, she took great pleasure in folding Daniel's shirts and placing them in his leather satchel.

After tidying up a few more items, she walked over to the chevalier mirror to take one more look at herself in her wedding dress. As she watched the fabric undulate with her slightest move, she was grateful to Ellen Quimby for suggesting she wear it. She would save this dress, just as Ellen suggested, perhaps use it for a fancy ball if they ever attended such a thing together. If not, it would go to a daughter. A daughter, she thought, happy with the idea of bearing Daniel's children. So much that had once seemed impossible, seemed possible now. Maybe she could still have children....

A click and a footstep. Had Daniel forgotten—

As she turned, her body shook. Her blood ran cold..

A voice from the past penetrated the room.

Not the voice of Billy Crane. A voice that sent dread through her whenever it had echoed through the halls of Blue Hill.

No, no, this couldn't be happening. He was dead!

Her fear came flooding back, and her knees went weak. She thought she would topple, so she reached out for the nearby dresser for support.

"My, my, you do have a glow about you." It was a voice that choked her, that sent ice through her veins.

"You always were an attractive woman, Kate. That's why I married you. No use hitching up to one of those prune-faced biddies past their prime when I could have you—young and fresh and so eager for me."

Holding her breath, she forced herself to stare at him. Josiah.

How could this be? He was dead! How could he be standing here?

She blinked fast, trying to make his image go away. The familiar sensation of feeling guilty, of wondering what she had done wrong, came back with the sound of his voice. A scream caught in her throat, strangled. She couldn't move. She couldn't speak. *Lord, have mercy...*

Josiah, in the flesh, no more dead than she was. Her feet were heavy blocks of wood even though she wanted to run. Her hands were like icicles, still clutching at the dresser.

He had changed little. The same broad-shouldered build, those muscles holding a coiled strength that she knew all too well could harm in an instant. The same dark brown hair, straight and loose to his shoulder, the same square face with its thin straight lips and coal-dark eyes. But he was wilder-looking somehow. His face sported a day-old growth of beard and his eyes were bright with wickedness. There was something more reckless about him, as if California were a place where he need not hide his penchant for roughness and malicious treatment. In his hand, pointing at her heart, was a gun.

She found her voice. "What do you want?" Under her breath, she thanked God that Daniel wasn't there, glad he was away from this fiend, this part of her life she wanted to forget. It was a stroke of good fortune he'd been called away. He'd be safe at least.

"You look mighty fine in that dress, Kate."

She wanted to get him away from here, away from Daniel. Keep Daniel safe from this monster. *There's no need for his life to be destroyed by it.* Why had she thought she could escape? Now she would infect Daniel with this poison if she didn't get him away from the room. Best to do what he said as quickly as possible.

"If I had time," he said in a low voice, "I'd do my husbandly duty."

She inhaled sharply, trying hard not to let him see.

"But that raises an interesting point. You now seem to have two husbands, Kate, something I'm sure the authorities would be interested in learning."

"I thought you were dead. The Eustace Marie... it sank."

"Why, yes, it did. Sank like a stone. Good thing I lost my ticket in a poker game the night before. I was the luckiest loser at the table and didn't even know it!"

"Take me to the authorities. I'll explain."

He laughed. "I'm sure you would." He shook his head slowly. "No, Kate. I don't want you as my wife, any more than you want me as your husband."

She was confused but heartened by this news. Maybe all she needed to do was reassure him. "Then let me go. I'll divorce you. I won't care what people will say."

"What people will say? Kate, you're in San Francisco. People out here don't care one way or the other. There is no society. No old families. No rules."

"Then... I-I have money. Do you need more money? Is that it? I have some... here in my bag." She gestured toward the carpet bag and took one step toward it. But then he raised the gun, and his mood changed.

"Stop! I'll get that soon enough. What I want is to marry again, a real woman who's been piling up a fortune to rival yours. I could have borrowed it away from her, whittled it down little by little. But a man doesn't like to ask a woman for money. Better to own it outright as her husband... "

Her thoughts raced. If he wanted to be free, then he could be free! "I told you—I won't stand in your way!" She was relieved to hear he had a new woman in his life, even though part of her felt a measure of sympathy for this latest victim.

"I know you won't stand in my way, Kate. In fact, you've provided me with the perfect plan. Kate Carlisle is dead. Isn't that right? Died in that horrible fire back east? That's what Mr. Crane told me. You remember him, don't you? He said you were the talk of the wagon train. And although you might not have presented him with all your secrets, they found their way to his ears nonetheless."

Her shoulders slumped. Billy Crane. So Josiah was part of the rowdy crowd Billy had linked himself to. Of course. One bad sort attracted to another. It hadn't been Billy stalking her at the Quimbys. It had been Josiah, on Billy's counsel. Daniel had been right. They weren't done with Billy. Hopelessness swamped her, and she nearly swooned.

"It was a good plan, Kate. I tip my hat to you. I just need to finish what you started." He moved closer to her and grabbed her arm. She winced. "We're going to leave now, and remember, I'll have this gun pointed right at your back the whole time we're walking down the stairs. You try to run and I'll shoot, and don't think for an instant I wouldn't do it. No sheriff would put me away for killing a double-crossing vixen who ran off and married two men!" He pushed her forward toward the door thinking what to do, what to do. If they left the room, at least Daniel would be safe when he returned.....and he'd look for her.

"There's just one thing I want you to do before you leave," Josiah instructed. "Pull out some of your fancy writing paper. Write what I tell you to."

He had her pen a note about how she was "taking a stroll in the moonlight by the harbor." He laughed as he watched her write what he said, telling her, "The harbor's a dangerous place, Kate. Lots of ships there all burnt up but nobody wants. Terrible accidents can happen there."

Her heart raced. In a moment of desperation, she signed the note, "Kate." If Daniel found it, he'd know she was in jeopardy. She'd told him Kate was her past.

"Kate Carlisle is dead," she said hurriedly, before he got her out the door. "But Kit Winchester is alive and someone will know. *He'll* know. He'll come looking for me."

Josiah laughed again, a full-throated laugh that turned Kate's stomach. "Kate, you naïve girl. Your new groom is probably dead himself by now. I had you write that note so your friends will know where to look for you."

Her breath caught. *Oh, no... no....* The note from the Bartons—of course it wasn't real. She fought to keep the tears burning at her lids from coursing down her cheeks. *Don't let him see how much he's hurt you,* she thought. *That's when it's the worst, when he knows.*

Suddenly, she was back in her old world again, the world where Josiah ruled with an iron hand, where she had to think twice about simple reactions, where the chance gesture, the ill-timed remark, were all excuses for brutality. She closed her eyes and let him lead her. She became dead inside.

JUST TWO BLOCKS away, Daniel stood in the pearly moonlit night, staring at the stables. The note from Josephus bothered him. Not because of the trouble the man mentioned. Daniel knew Josephus had concerns about his wagon. No, it was so unlike the man to bother Daniel on such a special night. Josephus Barton didn't have a selfish bone in his body, and he'd never put his own needs over Daniel's happiness. He smiled to himself. Maybe this was some trick, some last-minute gift or other treat Josephus had planned? Daniel approached the stable door with a lighter step. He'd enjoy telling Kit about it after.

Just before entering the stable, he encountered a man, another settler, leaving. It occurred to Daniel he could turn the tables on his friend by surprising him instead.

"Excuse me, sir. I'm looking for a Josephus Barton," Daniel said to the man, who stopped and looked uncomfortable.

"I—I don't know anyone by that name, sir," he said.

"I was supposed to meet him inside," Daniel prompted pointing to the stable. "Has he arrived yet?"

The man scratched his head. "Well, I don't know his name, but there's a feller in there—a thin man, about your height... "

"About my height?" Daniel's smile left him. Josephus was a good four inches shorter. "You sure?"

"Yes, sir."

"What else about him?"

The man shrugged. "Kind of nervous, dirty clothes..."

"Brown hair, dark eyes?"

"I don't know. Didn't look that close."

Daniel grit his teeth. "Thank you kindly." He touched his hat and the man went on his way.

Josephus wasn't in the stable. Billy Crane was.

And Daniel knew he was dealing with a man whose temper was tenfold larger than his mind. He patted his guns. He drifted into the shadows, where he wouldn't be seen from the stable windows facing up the street. As soon as he passed the end of the building, he crept around the back past a closed sutler store, and reached the side away from the street. He crouched down below the height of the windows and stealthily approached closed back door, drawing his right gun as he walked. All the while he thought to himself, *Billy Crane, you stupid, stupid mule. If this is the way you choose to die, then so be it.*

Chapter Twenty-One

As Josiah led her through the lobby, Kit seriously considered making a run for it. If Josiah was telling the truth and Daniel had already been lured to his death, then what reason did she have to live? So that Josiah could abuse her one last time before ending her life?

Now she found hope in Josiah's cruelty. He told her Daniel was dead because he knew it would hurt her. But Daniel could very much be alive. After all, he had been prepared to encounter Billy Crane for some time—ever since discovering he was in San Francisco with them.

It was possible, very possible, that Daniel was still alive. She'd had faith before, and she would find it again. She dug deep into her soul and dredged up the remnants of hope. Daniel would expect her to try. Daniel would demand she hold fast and fight.

She allowed Josiah to push her through the lobby, the cold barrel of his gun shoved against her side, hidden under her shawl.

The clerk looked up. Recognizing her from earlier when Daniel had escorted her upstairs, he leapt to the wrong conclusion.

"I don't want none of that business in my establishment," he said sternly, looking at her. "Take it over to Betsy's or one of those other houses. This is a respectable hotel!"

Josiah chuckled under his breath and pushed her outside. "You do look the part. I'd make a pretty penny on you at Betsy's."

"Where are you taking me?" she asked as he shoved her down the street.

"Out for a moonlight drive to the harbor, my dear," he said. "Just as you wrote in your letter."

In a few moments, they reached a dark side street that ended in an open field. There, a flat back wagon was hitched to two horses who were tethered to a small tree. He picked up the pace as they neared the wagon and, by the time they reached it, she was out of breath. Keeping the gun trained on her, he reached into his pocket and pulled out a blue bandana and quickly looped it around her wrists, tying them so tightly that she felt the circulation to her fingers cut off. While he was occupied thusly, she thought of running away, and stealthily started moving down the side of the wagon to keep him from noticing the beginning of her flight.

He yanked her back by her hair, pulling out the fine braid Esther had set for her earlier.

"Not as fancy as a wedding carriage, I'm afraid," he said, pushing her into the seat and following. He picked up the reins and clicked the horses forward. "But it will do. Don't think of trying anything silly now, Kate. I've got the gun right beside me. And you know how fast I can react."

The wagon started off down the road toward the bay. The moon was full and bright and provided ample light to see a path to the gleaming water, where the masts of hundreds of ships cut into the sky.

Kit felt as if she were entering some strange foreign place where everything was the opposite of what it should be. Josiah was supposed to be dead. He was alive.

She was supposed to be with Daniel. She was with Josiah. She was supposed to be safe. She was in mortal danger.

DANIEL STOOD BESIDE the back door to the stable. Billy would expect him to enter from the front, where he'd have a clean shot at a silhouette outlined against the moonlit street. Daniel would have to lure him outside, into the open, where it would be a fair fight, where he could offer Billy a chance to surrender. He turned and kicked lightly at the open back door. Thud, thud, thud. He heard horses neigh.

"Josephus!" he called into the blackness. "Josephus! Are you there? It's Daniel. This door is stuck. Can you fetch it open for me? Josephus?"

He waited silently, standing beside the door. He knocked again and waited some more. He knew Billy would come eventually. He wouldn't be able to resist his chance to get Daniel. Malicious intent would win out over wisdom.

In a few seconds, Daniel heard muffled footsteps moving slowly through a hay-strewn corridor. He held his breath and listened closely, estimating where Billy was in the stable by how close he sounded. Billy was being cautious. His gait was tentative. Daniel smiled, imagining the foolish boy trying to figure out what to do. Billy wouldn't have planned for anything but the plot he had constructed himself. He wouldn't know how to react if there was a change in the situation.

"Josephus!" Daniel shouted impatiently. "What in tarnation is taking you so long? I've got a young bride to get back to!" His good-natured goading was enough to do the trick. He heard Billy's pace pick up, then the stable door began to creak open, and Daniel saw the tips of Billy's fingers on its rough-hewn planks.

It was open just a crack, just enough to move into action, to grab for the figure behind those dirty fingers. Daniel half-rolled, half ran, forward, reaching for Billy's hand and holding fast.

"Billy Crane! Come out, you lying coward! Come out and face your fate like a man!" He heard a sharp whimper, like a dog who had been kicked. Then, Billy wrenched free and ran in the opposite direction to the other door. With equal speed, Daniel tore to the street side of the stables and got there just as the quivering Billy opened the door and ran out into the open. His right hand clutched his chest, and his left held his gun, pointed at the dirt.

"Billy! Stop it right there! Drop the gun!" Daniel slowly walked forward toward the trembling man. He saw Billy's eyes narrow—saw him consider whether to run. But Daniel was too close and could get off a fatal shot in an instant. Billy was stupid but he wasn't that stupid. He stayed where he was and let his gun fall out of his hand.

"Kick it over here, gentle now," Daniel said.

Billy did as he was told and Daniel slowly reached down to pick up the gun, while keeping Billy fixed in his sight. Billy was a menace and Daniel had a mind to end it all right now, to get this plague out of his life and out of Kit's.

"Two choices, Billy. We can shoot it out right here, right now, or I can take you to the local sheriff. But I'm not letting you go this time to come prey on me and Kit any more."

Billy sucked in his breath and rubbed the hand that Daniel had squeezed on the door. "Now, Daniel, I didn't mean no harm, no real harm... just wanted to scare you, that's all, wasn't going to do nothin', honest. Just wanted to scare you like I was after Pete's death...." He sounded like a spoiled child who had been caught stealing candy. His voice was so pathetically whiny that Daniel almost laughed.

"No harm? Then I guess this gun here's not loaded." He raised Billy's gun and pointed it at his heart.

Billy's eyes grew large as Daniel squinted his eyes to aim.

"Wait! Wait now, Mr. Winchester. Daniel. Wait a minute... I don't want no trouble. Serious now. I can help you. Yes, I can. We can help each other...please, Mr. Winchester."

Daniel smiled in the dark at Billy's persistence. "Help me, Billy? Now, how you propose doing that? Driving a wagon for me? Don't have no need. Working a ranch for me? Wouldn't trust you. No, I don't think you have anything you can help me with."

"Yes, I do, sir. Yes, I do. I can help you find your new wife. Yes, sir. I know where she is."

Daniel's blood ran cold at the mention of Kit. Why would Billy be talking about Kit, offering help to "find" her? A lump appeared in his throat and he swallowed hard before speaking again. His voice was dry and his tongue stuck in his mouth as a fear he had never felt before clutched at his heart and squeezed it.

"What do you mean? And remember—there are lots of places to shoot a man without killing him."

"He's... he's taken her somewhere. I can help you find where. You see, his mine's a bust. That's why the feller is so eager to git out of diggin'. He's got a new gal, see... and when he heared his old wife done and pretended she was dead, it gave him an idea... "

"What fellow?" Daniel interrupted him, his nerves on fire to find Kit. "What fellow are you talking about, Billy?" His voice was hard and quick.

"The Easterner. Josiah's his name."

Another stabbing fear gripped Daniel. His hand shook and he was glad it was just dark enough that Billy wouldn't be able to see it. "Josiah Carlisle?" he said in a half whisper.

"Yup. That's the one. A mean feller. Done beat up his gal. She's black and blue from it."

"You know where Josiah took Kit?" Daniel asked, ignoring Billy's nervous chattering.

"Yes, I do, sir. And I can lead you there sure as day."

"Tonight? Right now?"

"Well, it's hard going'. Mornin' would be better," Billy whimpered.

"We're going now!" Daniel shouted at him with anger and derision. "Get going in front of me. I've got the gun on you every second. We'll fetch horses. And if you're lying, Billy, or if anything happened to Kit, you're a dead man. I wouldn't think twice about it, do you hear?" His voice held a trembling conviction. Daniel wasn't a man to be toyed with right now. And Billy Crane knew it. They walked through the stables to Daniel's horses.

THE BUCKBOARD SHOOK and creaked as it moved down the hilly paths over rocks and dry mounds of dirt. The road was so rough, in fact, that Kit thought for sure they'd be hindered by a splintered spoke or broken wheel before their journey's end. She prayed for such an event. She thought of rolling off the seat and running. She thought of screaming into the night, hoping some one would hear her. But she abandoned each plan as its drawbacks became clear. He'd jump off after her if she fled now. When she had a clear path to escape, she would take it.

He occasionally talked to her as he drove the team forward, taunted her, asked her if her new husband "knew how to handle her." He talked about his new love, Betsy Macrae. Kit cringed as he boasted of keeping "his woman" in line, of how she'd been so used to rough treatment that he found he needed to be tougher still. He talked about it as if it were a tiresome responsibility he had to shoulder. Kit shuddered with pity for poor Betsy Macrae. How could Betsy think so poorly of herself that she would take what Josiah doled out? But then Kit remembered that for a while, she, too, had thought it was her lot in life to accept the slaps and punches and kicks of a mean man. She turned her face away to the side of the trail so he would not see her tears.

After a short ride, they stopped. In the gray moonlight, the ships in the harbor loomed before them. The air smelled damp, of dead fish and rotting wood, and some of the ships creaked at their moorings as they floated in the lapping water. She wondered if Daniel were alive. Of course he was. She would know if he wasn't. She would feel an emptiness, a void. She felt no such sensation. He had to be alive. This thought comforted her. At the same time, she felt shame for having put him in harm's way. Perhaps Josiah hadn't even bothered to deal with Daniel, she thought, but merely lured him away. Yes, he would do that. He was a lazy man. He wouldn't go out of his way to kill a man he didn't need to waste either time or effort on. He only wanted to dispose of her. Daniel was safe. *I love you,* Daniel, she thought to herself. *Know that I always loved you. Tell him, Lord.*

"All right, girl. Time to get down!" Josiah reached up and grabbed her arm, forcing her off the wagon. "Just go on ahead there." In one hand he held the gun, in the other a lantern and some items Kate couldn't make out. Something that looked like coiled rope was among them. He pushed her toward the ominous-looking ships along a narrow wooden walkway by the water. Halfway along its planking, he stopped her. The lantern cast flickering shadows on the sides of an empty ship. She could barely make out its name. *Caldonia*, she thought it said. A sense of doom settled over her. *What will happen will happen. At least Daniel is alive*, she thought as Josiah pushed her towards a gangplank and the ship. *I know it.*

BILLY CRANE SAT BENT OVER in the saddle, his hands tied behind his back, his neck straining forward to peer into the distance. Daniel was right beside him, the barrel of his gun resting on his own saddle and pointed in Billy's direction. They had ridden hard for twenty minutes and now Billy was having second thoughts about their path. They were by the harbor, but all the ships looked the same in the night. He couldn't make out the one Josiah had pointed out to him earlier that day—the one where he'd told him to leave the powder keg and the kerosene.

Daniel used all his self-control to keep from reaching over and grabbing Billy by the neck. All he could think of was Kit. Kit was with Josiah. He knew Josiah intended to kill her, even if Billy was too stupid to put it together. Billy had revealed, early in their journey, that Josiah had a "new gal." Daniel knew what that meant. Josiah wouldn't want Kit around to interfere with his life now. He just prayed he hadn't harmed her yet, hadn't touched her. And he cursed himself for going out into the night after receiving the note from "Josephus." He should have stayed with her! It was his job to protect her.

He gagged at the thought of Josiah with Kit. He knew what it would do to her, how it would kill her inside. *Lord, keep her out of his clutches.* Just a little while longer, he silently prayed.

"Come on, Billy! Which way? And don't tell me you don't know! Think, man!" He reached over and slapped Billy's thigh with the gun for emphasis. Billy jolted upright and looked off to the left at a nest of ships. There was one, its mast thicker than the rest. Yes, that was it.

"Th-that's the way. Yup. I'm sure of it. That's the one."

"Which one?" Daniel asked.

"The one with the big mast there…between the other two … Are you going to let me go then, Mr. Winchester?"

Daniel didn't answer, just kicked at the side of his horse and took off with Billy in tow. As they moved into the blue-white darkness, a revelation came to him. She was still alive. He would know if she was dead. He would sense it. I'm coming, Kit. Wait for me....

"THEY BRING THESE ships here and just leave them to rot," Josiah said as he pushed her up the gangway. "Everyone thinks they're an eyesore. They'll be happy when they're gone." He laughed a little. "Hear that, Kate? We're going to make a whole lot of folks happy tonight."

They were on the ship's deck and Kate's stomach turned at the gentle rolling of the waves and the stench of rotted wood, stagnant sea water deep in the ship and the thought of what Josiah would do next.

"Through there," he commanded her, pointing to a ladder leading down into the ship itself. If she ran now, where would she go? Back down the gangway where he would have a clear shot? No, better to keep going, keep thinking. She held her breath and clutched at the ladder rungs with her tied hands as she made her way into the stinking bowels of the ship. The air below was thick with the smell of slime. She kept her focus on her feet, stumbling several times on the slippery rungs, the limited light from the lantern not spreading far enough ahead for her to really see where she was going. When the ladder stopped, she found she could not stand upright. Her hair brushed against something above her that sent shivers down her spine. Josiah clambered down the stairs with agility, keeping the gun pointed in her direction. He came beside her and pushed her back into the ship, the gun at her side. At one point, he made her stop.

"That idiot!" he said. "Where did he put those things? I told him... There they are. Let's go." They moved forward toward a small barrel, a keg of blasting powder. It became clear what he was doing. He was setting up a blasting powder arrangement. Her mind raced. He was going to blow up the ship with her in it. If she wanted to live, if she wanted to see Daniel again, she would have to act and act soon.

DANIEL SLOWED HIS pace as he neared the ship. The few clouds in the sky had drifted away and now the entire landscape was bathed in bright moonlight, making the sky a deep blue and everything else shades of gray and black. In the near distance, he could see the ship with the broken mast that Billy had mentioned. More importantly, he saw a wagon drawn up nearby, but no evidence of Kit or Josiah. They had to be there. He got off his horse and ordered Billy to do the same. Taking a bandana from his saddle bag, he wrapped it around Billy's mouth as Billy sputtered and cursed.

"You're waiting here. Don't want you 'accidentally' giving your friend a warning," Daniel said as he pushed Billy to a sitting position near a wharf post and looped some rope around Billy's hand and the timber. Billy might be able to wriggle free, he guessed, but it would take him awhile, longer than what Daniel needed. He gave Billy a parting smack on the head to remind him who was boss and crept off into the night, making sure his footfalls would not be heard as he walked along the dock toward the hulking ship.

THEY HAD GONE down another ladder to another deck, this one more foul smelling than the one above. The roof, or whatever sailors called it, was so low here in this tiny space that they had to bend nearly double to fit. Josiah was breathing hard from the effort and sweat slicked his face. Looking at him in the lantern light, she saw, to her dread, the same look in his eyes she had seen many times before—the cold gaze of the hunter ready to pounce on his prey. Why, he was practically drooling as his gaze scanned her.

"We have some time," he said slowly. "No need to rush. Don't want you leaving this world without thinking of me...and how it used to be."

So this is the moment, she thought, watching him. He was putting the lantern down, reaching for his belt buckle. She closed her eyes briefly, steeling herself for his touch, trying to put her mind in a separate place, reminding herself that it would soon be over, that his passion was always quickly spent.

What could be worse than this, she asked herself as he moved forward towards her. She could smell his alcohol-laden breath, his filthy clothes. At least in Boston, he had been meticulous about his dress. His slovenliness out here was a sign that he had sunk to new levels of degradation. "I think we have time for a little taste of our former married bliss," he said malevolently.

Nothing could be worse than this, she thought, nothing. He was going to kill her anyway. Why should she go without a fight? The rage that had filled her in their previous couplings now bubbled to the surface like a churning geyser. There was nothing inadequate or lacking in her. Why had she thought there ever was? She was worthy of a good man, of love. She deserved happiness. She deserved to be treated with respect, to be treated humanely.

He would *never* beat her again!

With a strength she didn't know she had, she raised her tied hands and slammed her fists under his chin, driving his head up into the low ceiling with a sickening thud. Caught off guard, he reeled backwards, and she used his imbalance and surprise to her advantage, pushing him again on his back and struggling to climb past his prone body in the low space. She felt him grab for her, but she kicked and kicked, a wild mare refusing to be broken. She heard him cry out, his voice a roar of mad fury. She would have to get away now. His anger thus fueled, he would surely inflict on her a brutal beating if he caught her.

She ran toward the spot where the ladder led to the upper deck, barely making out its shadow in the dark hold. She pulled her hands up to the first rung and felt a sharp nail scratch her wrist. Moving her tied hands to the nail, she yanked and yanked with a ferocity unknown to her. Finally, the ties shredded and broke. Wrists bleeding from her frenzy, she reached for the rung above her.

"Kate, you witch!" he called after her. "You'll pay now, you'll pay!"

She heard him scrambling after her with the energy borne of anger. *Please, Lord, please,* she prayed, *help me.* Her feet slipped on the rungs.

"Come here!" He pulled at her hem. He was right beneath her, clawing after her. Her heart was pounding, but she kicked at him, feeling her heels dig into his face.

"I'll kill you!" he screamed. "You'll pay, you'll pay! It'll be like you never felt it before, Katie!" To her amazement, he laughed, a loud raucous sound that sent a cold vise around her heart. He enjoyed this, she realized. He liked it rough. Then give him more, she thought. This is what he craved. This is what he wanted. This was his weakness. She kicked again when she felt him gaining on her, and he cursed. He gripped her leg when she threw it out to greet his face, and then she tumbled back on top of him. He clawed at her, then stopping and taking his hand back to slap her across the mouth. His other hand grabbed her waist, but she noticed something... The gun, the gun was gone. He wasn't holding the gun.

"Ouh...uh!" she cried as she tasted blood on her lip. It didn't matter. He didn't have the gun and she could fight her way free. If this is what he wanted, it was what he would have. She wrestled herself from his grip and managed to pull away just enough to set her heels in his side, kicking and pushing him across the dusty, stench-filled deck.

"Never again!" she cried out as she heard him groan. She raced again to the ladder, but he was too quick, wrapping his arm around her waist, pulling her down. She didn't kick this time, but pulled his hand up, up, across her breast, fighting the bile that formed in her throat, up to her mouth, where she bit his fingers so hard she thought she heard the bones crack.

This pain did not amuse. He cursed her violently.

"Kate, I'm going to kill you slowly now," he mumbled in a raspy, hate-filled voice. "Very slowly." With his good hand, he reached out for the dress again and held it fast.

With one hand, she reached behind her, fumbling for the buttons, tugging them free, slithering out of the dress like a snake's skin, moving forward now in her cotton chemise, slip and stockings. She heard a soft, regular sobbing and realized it was her own voice. She was crying. *Stop it, Kit,* she chided herself. *No tears now. Only life. Grab life. Run to Daniel. He's alive. Stay alive for him as he stayed alive for you.*

DANIEL WAS ON the deck of the ship, his gun drawn up. Something was happening below. He heard shouts, wrestling, a groan and a thud, and then the noise of someone running... no, not running, but climbing, then weeping. It was Kit's voice, weeping. He leaned forward and peered into the captain's cabin, but could see nothing.

"Kit!" he called out fiercely. "Kit!" Louder now, desperate, frantic.

And she heard him. She heard his voice, and the torn knees, the scraped hands, the bruised face—all those pains disappeared.

Dreamlike, she made her way upward finally, to the next dark deck. A slender shaft of light appeared in the distance, where the other ladder led to the upper deck. Putting her hands out like a blind man's, she rushed forward. The air was getting fresher, the pinprick of moonlight was in the distance, growing larger, and his voice was calling her. Daniel was there, waiting for her. *I'm coming, I'm coming*, she murmured under her breath, working so hard to make it out of the ship that her lungs now screamed for her to stop, to rest. *No rest, no rest, until I see him. If I have to die, let me die with him.*

A shot rang out, echoing in the ship's hold, a flicker of air pushing past her. Josiah had retrieved the gun. She bent down and ran faster, her chest heaving from the effort. The noise of another shot, this one closer, made her ears ring.

At last, at last, the moonlit square of creamy light, Daniel's shadow at the top, the ladder, her feet scrambling up it, another shot, and this time she heard herself utter a gentle "oh!" as she felt a burning flash in her arm, near her wrist.

Up above, Daniel looked near crazy with worry. He helped Kit out, and saw behind her Josiah lunging forward, the gun in his hand, aiming for the spot between her shoulders...

With one swift, calm move, Daniel pushed Kit to the side, raised his gun, pulled the trigger.... It cracked in the air, like a whip smacking the ground.

Josiah groaned and fell back, a red flower, a deadly bloom, blossoming on his chest, spreading to his shoulder, his eyes wide with surprise that he had been stopped.

Kit was now sobbing, but in Daniel's arms. He lifted her up and carried her off the ship, down the gangway, and along the dock. Gently putting her down on a flat stretch of dry grass, he kissed her forehead. Wordlessly, he held her wounded arm out and inspected it.

"Just a flesh wound," he whispered. "There, there, Kit. There, now, darling. Forgive me for leaving...." His voice cracked.

He nestled beside her and put his arms around her, rocking her, whispering to her. "Kit, I thought... " He stopped, unable to speak.

Burying her face in his chest, she cried out her fear. Now that it was over, her body shook with fright, and she collapsed in his arms, wave after wave of tremors convulsing her. He stripped off his shirt and wrapped it around her shoulders, cooing to her, stroking her downy hair. "It's over," he repeated again and again. "You're safe now."

The night was still. Not even gulls cawed in the nocturnal air. In the distance, Daniel heard his horse whinny and snort and thought of Billy. He might have worked himself free by now. Daniel had better check on him.

"We should get back now," he said to her. "To take care of your arm. We'll go to the Quimbys...Rest there." With great reluctance, he helped her to her feet, but when she swooned in his arms again, he scooped her up like a rag doll and carried her. Her head lolled under his chin and she was quiet, her regular breathing a sign that she had lapsed into a trauma-induced sleep. He wanted her to sleep, to forget.

THEY NEVER FOUND Billy. He had disappeared into the night by the time Daniel brought Kit back to where he had left his horse. He hoisted her up into the saddle, then joined her there, letting her lean against him on the ride back into town. Once there, he awakened the Quimbys, who took them in with shock and concern. Willa and Esther were beside themselves with worry, Esther in particular saying how she'd chided Kit for her worry, and now it had come to pass.

Ellen helped him lay Kit on the bed upstairs and watched as the women washed her scratched face, arms, and legs, and bandaged her arm. He explained to them all, including Charles, what had happened. Ellen peeled off Kate's torn undergarments and replaced them with a matronly nightgown. When Ellen turned to tell him Kit was fine for the night, he rushed into the room, pulled a chair to her bed, and took her good hand.

"I'll stand watch the night," he said.

"Oh... no, stop...." She tossed her head back and forth, and he leaned forward, kissing her forehead.

"It's all right now. He can't hurt you...." But Daniel's own heart ached as he looked at his wife's bruised lip and her bandaged arm. *What other wounds are not so visible,* he wondered. And he vowed to himself never to ask.

Kit's eyes opened, took in her surroundings and looked up at him.

Daniel leaned over and enveloped her in a deep embrace, not wanting her to see the tears that came to his eyes. He pulled back, stroking her cheek. "You have to rest now," he said. "We have our whole lives ahead of us."

Epilogue

Early Summer 1852

WILLA BARTON STEPPED into the parlor and went over to where Daniel sat, twisting his hat between his hands.

He looked up at her, pleading in his eyes. He'd never felt so lost before. He'd been out on the range nearly all day. Josephus had suggested they go hunting. Esther had told him to help Rev. Kessler with the church building. But he was drawn back here. How could he work when he knew his Kit was suffering?

"It won't be long now," Willa said. "Why don't you let me make you some coffee?"

He stood. "Don't you need to be in there with her now?"

"Esther's with her." Willa walked past him toward the back of the house to the kitchen. "And she'll want something when it's over."

A groan from Kit in the bedroom down the hallway wrenched his gut. She'd been in labor nigh on a full day, maybe more. He suspected she'd been having pains the afternoon before but hadn't told him about it. She'd only suggested he fetch Willa in the early morning.

"Why don't you get a fire going, Mr. Winchester?" Willa suggested, poking her head around the doorway. "Take the chill off the house."

Numbly, he obeyed, piling wood in the yawning fireplace at the room's far wall. Although it was early summer, there was still a nip in the air in the shade, and the hacienda-style home was sometimes breezy.

True to their word, the Kesslers and Bartons had helped raise this ranch house with its two small bedrooms and open parlor as soon as they'd settled in the foothills of Monterey. Then they'd set to work building the others' homes, finishing most of it with the help of neighbors before the winter rains came. Nothing had stopped Daniel from building up the ranch, though. He'd used his savings to buy cattle and feed, and he'd rented out some pasture land and fields to neighboring farmers and ranchers. It would take awhile to turn a profit, but in the meantime, they'd be able to live off the land if they worked it hard.

And both of them—all of them—had worked hard. Kit had helped move stones from the ground and had sewn and knitted curtains and quilts and shawls. Even big with child, she'd planted a kitchen garden. It took his breath away to see her face kissed by the sun's warmth on a bright morning just a few weeks ago. How blessed they were!

But now—would he lose it all? Was it supposed to take this long and hurt this bad? He'd been away from his home when his first wife had birthed their son. He tried to remember Willa's labor on the trail, but he'd been so consumed with leading them through the desert, he'd paid little heed. Besides, Kit was his woman, and her suffering he more acutely felt.

With his prompting, the fire roared to life. Willa made a racket in the kitchen with pots and the iron cookstove, but he suspected she was trying to cover the sound of Kit's anguish. A long "aaaaoooh" came from beyond. He put his hands to his head, wishing he could make it stop. He strode toward the hall, but Willa stepped out in front of him and stopped him.

"Where do you think you're going now?" she asked. "Women have been having babies for as long as they've been on earth. You shouldn't be lingering here. You'll worry her if she knows you're about."

He swallowed and shook his head, but decided he should do as he was told. He'd head out to the corrals and check... on something. He'd keep busy.

He grabbed his hat from the post by the door and opened the door but stopped dead in his tracks when he heard....

A baby's lusty wail! On and on it cried, sounding as healthy as a newborn calf. He sucked in his lips and took a breath, not wanting to show his tears.

The bedroom door opened, and Esther stepped out.

"Mr. Winchester! You're just in time! Come in and see your new baby daughter!"

A girl—Kit had given him a girl!

He rushed into the room and nearly stumbled toward the bed, so eager was he to see his wife was alive and well.

There she lay, her hair spread about the pillows, her brow moist, her face serene. By her side, in her arms was a gurgling bundle of pink.

"Daniel," Kit said as he knelt by the bed. "Meet Sarah Abigail Winchester." She smiled at him.

He kissed her on the forehead and stroked the baby's head.

"I thought I was the happiest man alive when you married me, Kit," he said, his voice a raspy whisper. "I didn't know such happiness could be compounded so."

She reached out to squeeze his hand. "Nor I, Daniel. Nor I."

ABOUT THE AUTHOR

Libby Sternberg is the author of women's fiction, historical and young adult novels. She received an Edgar nomination for her first young adult mystery and writes humorous women's fiction under the name Libby Malin. All her books have been critically acclaimed. *Kit Austen's Journey* is her first inspirational. She lives in Pennsylvania with her husband and has three children, of whom she is immensely proud. Visit her website at www.LibbySternberg.com.

NOTES FROM THE AUTHOR:

When I first became aware of the "inspirational" genre as a copy editor, I have to admit I'd expected these books to be "preachy" in tone. Instead, I found absorbing stories where faith was not treated as a stranger but rather as an integral part of the characters' lives, no matter how "off stage" it might be in any particular yarn. I also discovered sympathetic characters who struggled with moral issues in a way most people, no matter their religious background, can relate to. This kind of story called out to me as a writer because all of my books involve a transformative journey for the main characters.

This particular story, *Kit Austen's Journey*, came to me early in my writing career, and I had already penned a version. Like many early efforts, it sat on the shelf collecting dust while I honed my writing skills. But it beckoned me back when I decided to write an inspirational of my own because I knew from my research already what a strong role faith played in the western immigrants' lives.

Kit Austen's Journey might seem to be an odd entry into the inspirational market because its central character, Kit Austen, engages in deception for a good part of the story as she flees her abusive—even murderous—husband. Her lie is not without a price, however. Not only does she struggle mightily with her conscience over her deception, but she witnesses how the lie distorts the relationships she has with others on the wagon train. When she finally reveals the truth, she must humble herself to ask forgiveness even from those who'd wronged her.

———————————

Read an excerpt of a sequel to *Kit Austen's Journey*, involving Kit's granddaughter, Ruth, set during the time of the San Francisco Earthquake of 1906. To learn of this book's release – as well as other releases – get on the Istoria Books mailing list at the publisher's website – **www.IstoriaBooks.com**

Mending Ruth's Heart

by Libby Sternberg

Prologue

March 1904

MY MOTHER THINKS my heart has hardened. Every day she looks to soften it, but I must admit her efforts only seem to thicken the callous that grows on that unseen organ. Or at least it feels so to me, with her regular urging to "get out and visit friends" or "take a ride to Grandma's" or "come with me to church this Sunday, won't you, dear?" or, worst of all—"black makes you look jaundiced, you could at least try on that deep blue suit I had made for you. You are still young, Ruth, just over nineteen...."

With every admonition, I feel myself recoiling ever further from the gentle rubbing against humanity that would, perhaps, tenderize my outlook. Was it ever so with mothers and daughters—why do we pull away from the one who cherished and led us before we knew the world?

I have been this way for six months now, ever since my fiancé, Miguel deTorquescero, was lost in a mud slide on the Big Sur, that cruel landscape that dares the Pacific to take it down. Well, the sea conspired with the skies that day, unleashing storms that blended both waters into a massive flood, the two claiming victory over the proud earth, bringing it low, teaching it not to be so boastful.

My beloved, returning to Carmel Valley with six fine ponies for the new small ranch at which I was to be matriarch—assuming God blessed us with children some day—was lost along with the horses. It was by the grace of God, or so says Mother, that Father wasn't lost, as well. He'd witnessed the whole catastrophe.

Shaken by the incident, Mother stayed very close to Father the week after it happened, often talking to him in his language—Spanish—instead of the English that she'd spoken since childhood. Her grammar was good if her accent poor. When she said *"corazon,"* she never enunciated the wispy "z" correctly, pronouncing it with the precision of Mr. Leiden, our Teutonic grocer in town, instead of the fluidity of a Spaniard.

For a week after the tragic event, I was stricken mute and ill, unable even to go to the memorial service, which, since his body had not been found, seemed a betrayal to me. How could they be so sure that Miguel had perished? Perhaps a thump to the head had dazed him and he wandered, lost in direction and mind, searching for a love he felt but could not name.

That comforted me for some time after. That is, until the remains washed on the rocks. A proper burial took place then. And I managed to stay upright at least, if not sociable. But, oh, what a struggle it was to hear the useless words of comfort, especially from the priest. I know the poor fellow was well-meaning, but how could a merciful God take Miguel away from me? Was I so small in His eyes that He deemed I did not deserve love? I ponder this daily.

Never an over-talkative woman, I became even more miserly with my speech after that, finding consoling communion with other mute animate beings—the yarrow that sparkles in the sun on the byways of the valley, the towering redwoods that pierce the sky, the gentle mewing lambs and bellowing cows on my parents' wide spread.

My father seems to understand. He says little to me while I help him work the ranch, just a nod here or a hat tip there, sometimes a tiny smile that only I can read.

I am my father's daughter, with raven hair and honey skin, the blood of the conquistadors running through my veins. My younger brother, Josephus, stole some of my mother's fairer traits. His hair, while curly, glints gold on clear days, and his skin, while not pale, looks sun-touched rather than blood-warmed. He is a rascal, prone to teasing, a year younger than I.

He fits in, while I always feel a bit apart, not quite belonging to either the world of my mother or my father. Miguel had grounded me. Now I am adrift again.

Chapter One

Two years later – 1906

DUSTY AND HOT, I approached the ranch house. Before I pulled off my gloves, I knew something was different. I'd already noticed my grandparents' buckboard horses feeding in the corral closest to the barn. I'd seen their rig nearby. They didn't get out much these days—we go to them to visit—so my surprise turned to dread as my feet clomped up the two steps to the wide porch.

Before entering, I overheard something that made me pause. My mother's voice, clear and direct.

"It's not right to grieve so long. The Bible says—"

"That argument is hardly likely to persuade her," my father said, his warm accent a mere whisper in his perfect English. "She feels abandoned by her faith."

"It's not healthy, though," my mother remonstrated. "She's gotten thinner. Her hair is limp and dull. She wears nothing but black…."

"Throw away those clothes as soon as they wear out," my practical grandfather, Daniel Winchester, remarked. "Buy her new in every color under the sun."

At that, my grandmother, Kit, chuckled softly. "Unfortunately, Sarah is such a clever seamstress that Ruth's clothes are likely to last a dozen years before she'll need more."

"Thank you for the compliment," Mother replied. "But you see what I'm up against. She could go on like this for years."

"She needs a mission, something to do," Grandmother Kit went on. "She needs something to help her get past this. It has become the center of her world."

"She needs a change," my father interjected. "On that we can agree."

"She needs a new love," my mother murmured, "but that is out of our hands."

My face flamed. Of course my mother would seek to replace Miguel in my heart. She never had been fond of him, once even suggesting to me that he needed to be more careful with his money. But he'd used it to buy a spread for us, for me, so that we'd not be dependent on either of our families. He'd borrowed, yes, to stake the claim, but it had been a good investment—had he lived. As it was, it had been sold off at his death, and the money given to his sister, Anita, and her young husband, a bequest of which I'd approved.

I was about to storm away, but a hand on my shoulder startled me. Turning, I saw my smiling brother, a finger to his lips, urging me to shush. Now a conspirator with him, my mood relaxed, and we both continued to eavesdrop.

"Maybe they'll say something about me," Joe whispered.

But they didn't—they kept talking about me, and it was a wonder to behold how they had mapped out my future without my consent. It seemed this meeting had been convened so that I would go back to Grandmother and Grandfather's house with them—they'd contrived a suitable excuse for this necessity.

Being of advanced years, my grandparents needed "someone to help oversee" the running of their household since their housekeeper, Maria, had just left to be married. I guessed that my parents knew I'd see through this ruse without the presence of my grandparents to persuade me. Saying no to them would be far more difficult than putting off my mother had she suggested this scheme alone.

Squaring my shoulders, I prepared for battle, however. I would not let sentiment—or my great affection for my grandparents—rule. After they'd worked out the last detail of this magnificent plan, I entered the parlor, letting the door slam behind me, which caused Joe to shout in protest.

"I'm not going anywhere," I said with conviction. I bent to kiss my grandmother and did the same for Grandfather Daniel. "I can recommend new help for you, if you'd like. But I am quite content here. Now, if you'll excuse me, I have some chores to finish."

I was about to head toward the back of the house and out to my unnamed tasks when my father's voice stopped me, strong and commanding.

"Ruth Consuela Sanchez, you will come back here and show proper respect. Your grandparents traveled to visit with you, and you can at least spare a few moments to show your appreciation. It troubles me that you would not see that retreating to engage in make-work is both insult and offense. That is not the girl I raised."

A man of few words, he stopped me with this heart-slapping speech. I turned, but my expression remained grave.

"I'm sorry, Father…and Grandmother and Grandfather," I said, nodding toward them. "But I could not help but overhear you contriving to think of things for me to do. Surely it is not unreasonable for me to be troubled by such talk and want to smooth my temper before it makes for worse offense than my absence."

At this, Father did not balk. "Then, control your temper. You let it rule you too often. You will stay here and be amiable."

No one else spoke, so his command seemed to have created the exact opposite effect, igniting nervous tension instead of calm. I had to inwardly smile. My father was a strong presence. He had overcome the objections of my grandparents when courting my mother, I was told, by making it clear that, while he wished for their blessing and would work hard to earn it, he'd not tolerate any misperceptions about his heritage. Mother often said I'd inherited my "stubbornness" from him.

"As for our plans, I have but one for you." Now he looked around at the rest of the assembled, even Joe, who'd managed to grab a lemon cookie from a tray near the chair where Grandmother sat.

"Papa, I know you want what's best for me—"

"No. I do not. Or at least, I do not know what is best for you any longer, my *niña*" he said with grim determination. "I do know, however, what is best for me and your mother. We need an agent to negotiate with the Southern Pacific managers in San Francisco who we believe are overcharging us for our feed shipments here and our beef shipments north. I was going to go, but I don't want to leave the ranch during foaling season. You will go in my stead."

My mouth dropped open. Mother's eyes widened. My grandmother and grandfather smiled. Joe frowned and nearly spat out his cookie.

"I could do that, Father!" he said.

"Yes, he could," I said in one of the few moments of agreement with my brother. "Better than I. And it is not yet foaling season." I crossed my arms over my chest, glaring at him.

"No!" my father bellowed. "Josephus's strong hands are needed here. And you, Ruth, are quite capable of arguing with any man. You have a quick tongue when you choose to use it. If you can not let go of the wrath that colors your disposition, then at least use it in the family's service by flinging it upon the agents of the Southern Pacific. I will accept no argument."

My mother, who'd watched this interaction with wide eyes, chimed in. "And it *will* be foaling season by the time we've outfitted you for the trip," she said.

And that was how I ended up, in the year 1906, planning to go to San Francisco, my black wardrobe thrown away, and my grief ripped from my heart as if a scab had been pulled from a festering wound.

This novel will soon be available through Istoria Books

About Istoria Books

Istoria Books is a boutique publisher handling only fiction, selecting books we consider to be "good stories, well told."

All our ebooks are priced below $5.00, and we run many sales and special offers.

Visit the Istoria Books website (www.IstoriaBooks.com) and sign up for the mailing list to learn of special discounts and deals.

Literary, Mystery, Romance, Women's Fiction, Short Stories, Historical and more…

Istoria Books
www.IstoriaBooks.com

www.ingramcontent.com/pod-product-compliance
Lightning Source LLC
Chambersburg PA
CBHW071126170626
46809CB00002B/512